HOLE HOUSE

D.M. SINCLAIR

Also By D.M. Sinclair

A Hundred Billion Ghosts

A Hundred Billion Ghosts Gone

Psychic Simon

Deeper Downs

Hole House

D.M. Sinclair

And if thou gaze long into an abyss, the abyss will also gaze into thee. So, maybe don't do that.

Nietzsche (paraphrased)

1890

Near New Haven, Connecticut

Chapter 1

The screaming went on for what felt like half a minute. But the rain didn't stop at all. That was the annoying part.

It had already rained for two days before he did it, and he'd half-expected that after he did it, the clouds would part, the sun would burst through, and the mud would dry up to make his escape fast and easy. But none of that happened. It was like the weather wasn't even grateful for what he'd done. True, the weather hadn't asked him to do it. But the least it could do was give him a little congratulatory fog, or maybe a warm westerly gust of appreciation. Instead, after he did it, the ungrateful weather got worse. The rain grew more intense and never seemed to let up. It pressed in against the windows until he felt like the house was submerged and sinking, groaning from the pressure and soon to be crushed.

After three days, he got tired of waiting for the rain to stop. Surely the rain had nothing to do with what he'd done. It was the climate and nothing else. He'd completed what was required of him, and now he would be allowed his exit.

He'd never know until he tried. Rain or not, he was going to leave.

Or, at least, he was going to try.

He spent all day gathering what he thought he'd need and packing it into his steamer trunk. A selection of his clothes, of course. It was easy to fit all of them in, now that he had the whole trunk to himself. But what to fill the rest of the space with? He didn't dare take anything hanging on the walls, or anything that was attached to the house. He feared that there would be repercussions for moving those. But he did grab a few personal things—some of his books, his violin in its case, a pillow that he was inexplicably fond of because of the frilly donkey sewn onto it, some grooming products, and his papers and files. All of it fit easily.

The whole time, he listened. He expected to hear some kind of protest. But apart from the incessant drumming of the rain, the house remained silent. Unnaturally so. The floors didn't creak underfoot like they'd done when he moved in, and the doors had lost their squeak. Even his footsteps no longer seemed to echo when he moved from room to room. The air felt dense and heavy, too thick for sound to carry through. It was as though the house had been hushed.

He took that as a good sign.

Under the congested skies, it was hard to tell when evening had fallen. But when the gray light coming through the streaming rain started to turn black, he lit his most watertight lantern and ventured out to the carriage house. The house itself was on the top of a slope and the carriage house was behind it at the bottom of the hill, connected to it by underground stairs that sloped down from the basement. But he didn't go that way, even though it would have kept him dry. That would have meant going through the basement, and he wasn't going to do that. So he went outside into the rain and down the slope behind the house, and he was drenched by the time he got there.

He hitched the Cleveland Bay, Miss Stephanie, to the carriage. She didn't protest but was plainly not happy about being made to work on a night like this. He wondered what he'd do with her when he got on the train. Sell her, he supposed. Perhaps she'd be as happy to get away from the house as he was.

It was pitch dark by the time he loaded his trunk onto the carriage and was ready to leave. And the rain had grown, if anything, even more spiteful. Miss Stephanie waited gloomily at the bottom of the porch steps as he hovered on the threshold of the front door.

Was there some invisible force trying to push him back inside? Or was it his imagination? He couldn't tell.

He turned back to the interior. With the fire mostly out and the candles all snuffed, the inside was blacker than outside. The furniture felt like looming, listening things. A dark audience waiting for him to address them.

"I'm leaving." He said it as loudly as he could. His voice did not echo; the shadows swallowed it.

And there was no response. Nothing cursed him in reply. Nothing tried to stop him.

He was almost disappointed. Almost.

He turned again and took a full step out onto the porch. And still, nothing stood in his way. Nothing tripped him up or tethered him. No lightning came from the heavens and no crack in the Earth opened up to swallow him.

He closed the door behind him and trotted down the porch steps without looking back. Miss Stephanie snorted an acknowledgment as he clambered up onto the carriage and shook the rain off his coat.

He did not look back at the house. He could hear the rain on it like a shadow in the sound, and that was enough to know that it was there, and was watching him go.

The path to the road had turned to muck, and it took the horse a few seconds to get the carriage started. But she managed to get some momentum and drag the wheels through the mire. And, finally, he was on his way and the house was behind him.

He didn't expect to meet anyone on the road. Not in this weather, and certainly not at this time of night. He expected that he'd be able to make good speed into the city. And then it would be over.

So he wasn't paying close attention and didn't see the lanterns until he was almost upon them. There were three, lit and dangling among the trees right where the path met the road. He was so surprised when they loomed up suddenly out of the dark that he hauled back on Miss Stephanie too hard, and she stumbled. The weight of the carriage pushed her and she slid ahead on her hooves in the muck before finally managing to get stopped.

There were three mounted men in the dark, each holding a lantern above his head. He didn't know if they'd been waiting for him or if he'd just happened to meet them as they turned up his path. But now they had stopped, and he found himself nearly surrounded.

He didn't say anything. Didn't know what to say. He blinked the rain from his eyes and tried to see the men in the dark.

"Are you Arthur?" one of them bellowed across at him. The rain tried to pound his voice out of the air and bury it, but Arthur could still make out the words. And despite the splattering hiss of thick raindrops in the mud, he couldn't miss the note of accusation in the man's voice.

In the flickering light of their lanterns, he caught reflections on small circles of gleaming metal fixed to the fronts of their wool coats.

Badges. They were police officers all the way from New Haven.

So this was it then. The house was letting him go, but the law would not.

Or perhaps the house had summoned them to stop him. One last act to confirm that it owned him.

"Yes," he sighed. And then he repeated it in a shout because they could not have heard him say it so quietly and with such resignation.

He briefly considered trying to escape, but the officers' horses would easily overtake his carriage, especially in the mud. In this rain, in the dark, he'd be lucky if he could even stay on the road.

The lead officer urged his horse closer to where Arthur sat, its hooves squelching in the muck. In the scant light from the officer's lantern, he could see the horse's eyes fixed on him as hard as its rider's. Like the horse knew what he'd done.

The horse turned parallel to the carriage and came up alongside Arthur. Water poured off the brim of the officer's hat in a steady stream. "We are told, sir," the officer said, "that your wife missed some appointments over the past several days. I wonder if you could account for her whereabouts."

Arthur hadn't really prepared an answer. There were any number of lies he could tell. But there, in the rain and dark, he decided that he didn't want to run. He was out of the house; anything that came after would be an improvement. Anything. If they threw him in the deepest dungeon where bites from the ugliest rats gave him the foulest-smelling boils on the hardest-to-scratch parts of his body, it would still be better than spending one more night in that house.

The officer waited. The other officers watched him and held their lanterns closer so they could see Arthur's face.

Arthur found, to his surprise, that he was laughing. He didn't know at what. The thing he'd done certainly wasn't funny. Neither was being arrested for it. Even the weather was the exact opposite of hilarious. But he laughed. He laughed until the officers shifted in their saddles, uncomfortable that they might be dealing with a madman. And, Arthur thought, maybe they were. Is that what had happened? Had the house driven him mad? He didn't feel like a madman, but he also didn't know what it felt like to be mad. Maybe this was it. If so, it wasn't all it was hyped up to be. It was certainly wetter.

When he spoke again, he simply told them the truth. Mostly.

"I can tell you, I last saw her three days ago. In the basement," he said through his gasping laughter. He motioned back at the house with one hand. "Though by now, I think you'll have some trouble reaching her."

132 years later...

Chapter 2

Mae had expected the auctioneer to stop on the steps and do his thing right there. Courthouse steps were in the name of this whole process, after all. It was called "buying a house on the courthouse steps." There were only five steps in front of this courthouse—and it wasn't technically a courthouse—but she still hoped he'd use them.

This auctioneer, though, took one look at the sun and abandoned the steps altogether. Instead, he mumbled something about the heat and moved the proceedings over to the shaded gazebo in front of the municipal center. He crammed his gas station slushy cup into his patio chair's cup holder, which was far too small for it. Then he sank himself into the chair with all the commitment of a man who intended that chair to be his home for the foreseeable future and maybe to raise a family in it. And, for now at least, he ignored the small crowd that had gathered in the sun and focused his attention instead on indifferently sorting through his various papers and trying to get his slushy cup to stand up straight.

Mae had always been intimidated by the thought of doing this. But now that she was here, her anxiety had gone into overdrive.

Buying a property through a real estate agent was scary enough. Buying one here, in a ceremony that seemed to have traditions and formalities she wasn't privy to, bordered on terrifying. It felt like skydiving for the first time, except it required more paperwork.

But still, it was too late to turn back. She'd made her decision and now she had to follow through. Not that buying a house to live in with her mother was a bad decision. Her mother would soon need the help, and Mae had unreservedly decided that she would provide it. But still, there were a lot of more sensible home-related choices she could have made. She could have found a nice, move-in-ready, entirely uncomplicated house sold by a real estate agent. There was no shortage of them.

But then she'd seen a picture of the house. She couldn't remember how she'd arrived at it while browsing real estate listings. Most likely it had been a link from a link from a link from maybe a banner ad. But the picture of the house had immediately appeared to have a golden halo around it, and she'd been smitten. 8623 Selby Street was a pink three-bed, two-bath bungalow with planter boxes under the windows and a little porch on the front, and—sheer heaven—a view overlooking a cove on the Connecticut River. Perfection. Her mother would spend her golden years on a porch with Mae, looking at a cove.

She had hesitated momentarily upon finding out that it was an estate sale at auction because she didn't know how those worked. And maybe it was being sold at auction because the house was in a terrible state of repair or wasn't nearly as nice on the inside as it looked in the picture. But she'd always believed that your heart knows what it wants in the first two seconds of thinking about something. She called it the "whammo" moment, though she rarely told anyone that because it sounded dumb. But she knew that anything that came after the whammo moment was her head farting things up. Whammo moments were when she made all her important decisions. They were why she'd taken every job she'd ever had, and lived everywhere she'd ever lived. And they were why she'd never even come close to getting married, though it had been hard to explain "whammo" to a couple of men over the years.

This was definitely one of those moments. She was going to buy that house. No other house. That one. Whatever was wrong with it, she could fix. It would be a project. And even if it was the wrong decision, then at least she'd made it decisively.

So now here she was, the very next day, outside the gazebo at the municipal center in Northern Fairfield County. She had her life savings—diligently put aside every month for all 17 years since her 18th birthday—divided into several cashier's checks of various amounts that could be added up like bills to form any bid she wanted. And she had every intention of using them.

Even before the auction started, Mae was concerned about where she was standing. The auctioneer was 20 feet away, and there were clusters of people around the railing of the gazebo forming a human wall between her and him. And those people were carrying on conversations that meant she might not be able to hear him. Worse still, the street behind where Mae stood was filled with school buses engaged in some kind of honking war with cars trying to get past them. None of this made her confident that the auction would go well for her. What if the house came up for bidding and she didn't hear him announce it? She'd miss her only chance at nabbing the dream house she'd been madly in love with, sight unseen, for 22 hours.

The auctioneer finally launched into a bored introductory speech. All the other bidders had obviously heard it many times before and didn't bother to interrupt their conversations. Even the auctioneer seemed to find it tedious, obviously having rehearsed and repeated it to the point where he no longer needed to be conscious while delivering it. He fiddled with his papers and his drink at the same time as he spoke, the actions of his body completely disconnected from the actions of his mouth. He was like a puppet operated by two different people, one operating the head and entirely focused on the speech, and the other trying to figure out how the arms worked.

Mae strained to hear, but a couple of the buses behind her got into an altercation and she picked up only stray words: "...appointed as foreclosure... terms of sale... cash... percent of sale price... balance is due... without any warranties... subject to the condition..."

She needed to get closer.

But as the auctioneer neared the end of his speech, many of the other gathered people came to this same conclusion. They pushed forward into a tight semicircle around the gazebo, the auctioneer, his chair, and his slushy. Mae tried to move with them but they were faster and more forceful. By the time the auctioneer started, she was still stuck behind the crowd and barely within earshot.

"First up for sale," the auctioneer said. He kept the crowd in suspense by pausing to slurp from his cup. Then, refreshed and blueberry-tongued, he went on. "Crane Trust three-five-seven-oh-oh-six-one. 3242 Emily Drive. This property has an opening bid of $60,000. Does anyone wish to qualify?"

That was not her house, but still, Mae's heart pounded. It was on. She had one chance to get this right. And the pressure of the auction felt like a sporting event, like she was kicking a field goal or stepping up to the plate. Her nervousness was shouldered aside by a rising sense of electric excitement. She cautioned herself not to get too addicted to this or she'd be back buying foreclosed houses every weekend just for the rush.

She watched keenly how the bidding progressed on the first property, just in case she got into a war on hers. The bidders, most of whom seemed intimidatingly practiced at this, bid up a few times just by saying "dollar," forcing the auctioneer to call out absurd bids like "$61,002." When that didn't work, they went up by 100. And when that didn't work, one stocky, poker-faced bidder—clearly a serious real estate investor even though he'd shown up in an *Uncanny X-Men* T-shirt—took over by pushing the bid up to the next thousand. Everybody else backed down, and the auctioneer called it with the semi-traditional "once, twice... okay, we're done!" *Uncanny X-Men* acknowledged his victory with a triumphant slight nod and then showed his paperwork and presumably his cashier's check to the auctioneer.

So that was how it was done. Mae felt ready. Well, not so much ready. But at least not completely ignorant of how to make this happen, which is how she'd felt just a few minutes ago.

The auctioneer called out the next property. It still wasn't hers. She'd printed a list of the properties up for auction and she knew exactly when hers was coming up. It was to be seventh, though Mae still feared losing count and missing it.

She checked the printout, which she'd neatly pressed into the file folder cozied up to her checks. She found the picture of her house, then flipped back to the property that would be auctioned sixth, right before hers. She checked for the listing number or lot number or whatever the number was called. All she had to do was listen for that number, and then she'd know that hers was next.

Mae repeated it in her head several times. Three-five-seven-oh-oh-six-six. Three-five-seven-oh-oh-six-six. As soon as that one sold, she needed to be ready. She wrung her hands and listened.

She listened through three more properties, her muscles coiling tighter and her blood pressure boiling higher with each one. She watched as the level of blue slush in the auctioneer's cup sank lower and lower, an inverted thermometer of Mae's anxiety. She studied the faces of all the other bidders, trying to read their intentions and how serious they were in case she found herself bidding against them. She might be forced to take one or more of them down, and she wanted to know what she was up against.

And yet still she felt completely unprepared when she finally heard the number. Three-five-seven-oh-oh-six-six was announced. The one before hers. Mae held her breath while the auctioneer called out some address she didn't care about and some bidding requirements that didn't matter. She held her breath more while he waited for bids. And she decided that it wasn't healthy to hold her breath that long and finally let it out while he scanned the crowd, looking for anyone interested in three-five-seven-oh-oh-six-six. It must have been a real dumpster because for a long time nobody bid on it. But three-five-seven-oh-oh-six-seven would be next, and she would bid, and she would win it. She was coiled and confident. This was it.

Somebody finally stepped forward for three-five-seven-oh-oh-six-six. It was a gangling, trim-bearded, 30-something guy in a plaid coat. He bid $70,000 and won it unopposed by other bidders, then presented his paperwork and disappeared into the crowd.

It was time. Hers would be next. She braced herself.

An explosion of honking erupted behind her, and Mae looked irritably back. An SUV pulling out of the courthouse parking lot was engaged in a battle of wills with a compact car trying to parallel park in the street. And as she watched, a school bus trying to get past them both joined the showdown. All of them made valid, well-researched points with their honking. But it meant that Mae could hear almost nothing at the auction.

The auctioneer appeared to be calling out another property, but she couldn't hear him.

But this had to be it, didn't it? Right after three-five-seven-oh-oh-six-six. It had to be the one. The drivers in the street went on deliberating with their honks, and Mae still couldn't hear a word. She hurled herself into the crowd, ignoring the angry protests of the other buyers, until she got to the front and could pick up the auctioneer's words.

"...opening bid of $70,000. Does anyone wish to qualify?" He sounded considerably less interested than he had at the beginning when he'd already sounded completely disinterested.

But Mae was fired up. She dove forward and hurled her file folder at him. "Me! Mae Potts!" This wasn't even bidding yet; it was just qualifying. But she was still determined to be first. Maybe he'd be impressed with her take-charge attitude and just grant her the property out of respect, foregoing the auction part altogether.

"Anybody else?" the auctioneer said. He joined Mae in scanning the faces of the crowd.

Mae's heart leaped. Nobody else wanted her house. It really was going to be that easy.

Except that no it wasn't. Because the gangling bearded guy reappeared out of the crowd and came forward. She stared at him, mortally offended at his very existence, while he handed his paperwork to the auctioneer. He glanced at her briefly. But after that, he kept his eyes low as if he was doing this just to annoy her and was slightly embarrassed about it.

She thought about begging him just to let her have it. Maybe if she asked nicely. Maybe if she told him about her mother.

To her surprise, he spoke first. "Are you sure you want this?" he asked.

"I have wanted this," she growled, "since yesterday." It didn't sound like as passionate an argument as it felt.

But they didn't get to carry on their debate because the auctioneer tilted the top of his pen toward Mae, prompting her for a bid. "$70,000?"

Mae felt like her mind had left her body. This was otherworldly. It was happening, and she was in it, and she needed it to go her way. She nodded, but it felt like her head stayed still and the whole rest of the world wobbled up and down.

The auctioneer turned his pen to the gangling guy, who glanced at Mae and said, "Dollar."

"$70,001," the auctioneer said. His pen swung back to Mae like a compass needle that refused to commit.

Mae thought about playing the game and saying "dollar" right back. She could play chicken with this guy, pushing dollars or hundreds until he backed down like she'd seen so many others do today.

But she didn't want to. Her heart was beating too fast. The stress was squeezing her too hard. She wanted the house very badly, but she also wanted this to be done.

"$80,000," she said.

It was the most she could bid. The sum total of all the checks she had brought. She knew it was a breach of protocol to jump the bid that much. Or at least she thought it was. The sharp look she got from the bearded guy seemed to confirm it. He'd expected another dollar bid, or maybe 100. She'd added $10,000, and it had altered his perception of reality.

She stared at him hard. She could see his jaw muscles trying to force his teeth through each other. He glanced at her again and she caught a hint of rage in his eyes.

And then he shook his head at the auctioneer. He wouldn't fight her.

Her heart skipped a beat, and then another one.

"Sold," the auctioneer said. She wanted him to drag it out long, like she'd scored the winning goal at an Italian soccer game. Instead, he said it like she'd just bought a hamburger. And then he took a slurp from his cup before waggling his fingers at her to give her paperwork back to him.

She handed over the folder again. And while he fiddled with that, she couldn't help herself. She jumped with glee just a little. Enough to be embarrassing, but not *too* embarrassing.

The gangling guy looked ashen. If there was an exact opposite of jumping for joy, that's what he was doing. She wondered why it meant so much to him. He couldn't possibly have wanted it as much as she had. He'd just bought another property before this one; wasn't that enough?

He leaned toward her. "Can I talk to you when this is done?"

"There's nothing to say," she said. "I'm sorry. I guess I just wanted it more."

"Yeah, but why?" he asked. "What are you going to do with half a house?"

What game was he playing? Half a house? She wanted him to leave her alone. "It's a whole house," she said. "I've seen the picture." She pointed at her printout in the auctioneer's lap.

He looked at it only for a second. And then smirked a little. "Lady," he said. "I don't think you bought what you think you bought."

Her heart sank into her shoes.

"Excuse me," she said to the auctioneer.

He was busy copying information from her folder onto a form in his lap and projecting an unmistakable attitude of not wanting to be bothered. "Unh huh?" he mumbled without pausing his scribbles.

"This might be a stupid question, but can you tell me the address of the property I just bought?"

He stopped scribbling. His eyes swiveled up to her. But he kept his face aimed downward because he intended to go back to writing after giving her the absolute minimum amount of attention. "You don't know?"

She wrung her hands. "I just need to verify. For my own verification." That sounded dumb and she knew it.

His eyes swung down to the paperwork and back up to her. "9140 Whitemarsh Road," he said.

She felt the blood drain from her face. She felt her heart seize. That was not it. That was the wrong one.

She had to stop this. Surely it wasn't too late. She snatched her clipboard back from him. "No," she squeaked, her heart pounding too hard for her to get her usual voice out. She could only make wild rodent noises. "No, no, no, no." She fumbled frantically with the papers on the clipboard, found the printout of all the properties listed in this auction. She aimed the clipboard at him and jabbed at the listing with her finger. "9140 Whitemarsh Road is three-five-seven-oh-oh-six-six. You sold that one already. I heard. You sold it to that guy." She pointed at the bearded guy, who had taken a few steps back to stay out of the line of fire.

The auctioneer didn't look at what she was showing him. Didn't even bother looking at *her* again. He made a point of emphasizing how much he was not looking at her and how much he was committed to the task of writing her information on his sheet. "9140 Whitemarsh Road," he said, "is split into two units. That guy bought the first unit. You bought the second one."

"The dumpster that nobody else wanted? I don't want that! It's a dumpster! I assume!" She knew nothing at all about what she'd just bought other than that nobody else but Mr. Beard had bid on it. That could not be a good sign.

The auctioneer loudly finished writing on his sheet and then loudly finished his slushy. "You probably shouldn't have bought it, then," he said. And he tore the sheet off his clipboard and handed it to her. Thus, apparently, sealing the deal.

Mae took the sheet in a daze. She didn't look at it because she wouldn't understand anything written on it anyway, but she assumed that it said something like, "Congratulations, you just torched $80,000." Except it would be in legal-ese, with little splatters of slushy syrup spreading in blue circles across the top edge.

But there was still hope. Wasn't there? Her beautiful house-on-a-cove hadn't been sold yet. If she could get her money back, she could still bid on it. But the auctioneer had made it pretty clear that nothing would be given back. So she strode to Mr. Beard, who had assumed an unmistakable air of "I-told-you-so."

"You want it?" she said. "I'll sell it to you. Right now. *Right now.*" She emphasized the last words with a finger-jab at the ground, as if they were standing on the exact moment in time when this had to happen.

"Fair enough," the guy said, stroking his beard. "$60,000."

Mae had never wanted so badly to punch someone. "$60,000?" she raged. "I paid 80!"

"Yeah," he said coolly. "Because you bid it up to that."

"But it started at 70! Give me that much!"

He shook his stupid head. "Sixty."

"Can you two move aside please," the auctioneer said irritably, waving them aside with little flicks of his slushy cup. But he didn't wait for them to move. "Next up," he announced, "three-five-seven-oh-oh-six-seven! 8623 Selby Street."

That was it. Her cove house. All her future sunsets with her mother. She needed her money back. But the starting bid was $70,000, and she didn't have that anymore. She spun to the auctioneer. "Will you take $60,000? Please? This guy will give me $60,000." She thrust her finger at the beard guy.

"The opening bid is $70,000," the auctioneer said icily.

"$70,000!" somebody called from the crowd. Mae couldn't see who it was, but she instantly hated him.

"Hundred!" somebody else called out, and she hated him more.

"Hundred!" somebody else yelled from the back of the crowd, and for the first time in her life, she considered murder.

The realization sunk in. She'd lost it. Even if beard guy gave her the $70,000 she was asking for, it would no longer be enough.

As the bidding went higher and higher out of her reach, she looked at Beard Guy's face, trying to figure out what part of it she'd most like her fist to make contact with. The beard was a strong contender, and she wondered if she could punch it off. For a moment, she thought she detected a flash of guilt and shame in his eyes. Just for a moment. But it didn't matter. She made up her mind in an instant. Whammo.

She wouldn't sell him her half of the house. It was hers now.

"Okay then," she said to him, as calmly as she could force her voice to sound. "I'm keeping it. What did I buy?"

Chapter 3

T he house was further from town than Guy had anticipated. On a map, it looked like a quick jaunt, maybe 20 minutes from Bethel, 45 from New Haven. But Whitemarsh Road, once he got onto it, refused to take him straight to the house. Instead, it insisted repeatedly that he wanted to take a more scenic route in literally every other direction, while at the same time offering him nothing at all to look at. There was nothing around but shallow, grassy hills and groves of half-hearted trees. He was pretty sure that he hadn't seen a single house or marked property since turning onto Whitemarsh from Route 6. And that had been 15 minutes ago.

Guy's heart beat faster as a house finally came into view, and it had to be the one because it was the only house for miles. It stood on a hilltop at the end of a swooping, sloped arc of dirt driveway. And at first, as Guy strained to see it through the branches of the decrepit trees that insisted upon blocking his view, he was thrilled. From far out at the end of the drive, the house in all its "high style" Queen Anne Victorian glory appeared to be everything he'd hoped it would be.

But still, he drummed on the steering wheel of his pickup as he drove and couldn't keep his left foot from dancing erratically on the floor. He'd bought the house sight unseen and still didn't know what he might find when he got inside. For all he knew, the interior was a vast colony of murder hornets.

It was not wise to buy a house without viewing it first. Guy knew that. The banks and trust companies auctioning these houses were not usually forthcoming about details, so buying a house at auction was often like opening Al Capone's vault. But he was not stupid. With every other house he'd bought at auction, he'd done exhaustive research in advance, often with inside sources who provided valuable information. And he'd made some good purchases that he'd been able to flip for profit.

But not *much* profit. Usually enough to get by, sometimes a little less than that. He was tired of it. It was exhausting living on nickels and dimes, and always racing to get the next property just to keep himself alive. He needed a big score. He needed a profit that would keep him comfortable for a while, not that would pay only for his next flip.

More than anything, he needed a rest.

And then this place had popped up. It had been inserted into the auction the day before, so he hadn't had time to do the research. But it was a split Queen Anne Victorian in the middle of nowhere—candy for a certain kind of buyer. And even when you combined the starting bids for its two units, it was cheap. Not cheap in the sense of pocket change. It was still a ton of money, and he'd have to sell his own house and leverage everything he had to pick it up. But for a house that size, it was ridiculously cheap. And if it was in reasonable shape and he could make it good-as-new, then he'd finally bring in decent money and stop dangling by his fingertips.

But if the house was a catastrophe...

He put that out of his mind and strained to see through the trees. The house was huge. Three stories, with a 50-foot conical-roofed corner tower prominently looming over the corbelled wrap-around porch below. Expansive bay windows dominated the front, and several tall chimneys hinted at multiple working fireplaces within. It was difficult to tell from this distance if any of its original shiplap siding had survived the 20th century, but if it hadn't, he could deal with it. Paint was cheap as long as the structure of the house was good. And from here, it looked that way. He could see all the bays, porches, and rooflines that he'd imagined. It looked like a dream. Or at least, it looked that way from a great distance through the branches of dead trees with the sun behind it while he was driving with smudged sunglasses on. Getting half of it for the price he'd paid seemed like a miracle. He just wished he'd been able to get both halves.

But surely the woman—Mae, was it?—would sell. She hadn't wanted it in the first place, and she was transparently new at the whole property thing. Not an experienced house-flipper like him, with a plan and a crew. She seemed, to put it bluntly, like a fruitcake. He hadn't yet said so to her face but he could imagine it happening sometime in the future. It had been obvious at the auction, and he'd quickly decided not to bid against her. He'd been able to tell that if he got into a war with her, she'd push the bids into the stratosphere just because she didn't know any better. So he'd decided to let her win it, counting on her freaking out and selling it back to him at a comfortable discount. He didn't particularly enjoy exploiting the poor woman's inexperience, but the opportunity was *right there*. And he was still confident that, once she saw the place, she'd realize it was too much for her to handle, and sell it to him immediately. Maybe he could even talk her down to $55,000. Then the whole place would be his, and this massive undertaking could begin.

But as he drove closer to the house, his heart began to sink. And then it continued to begin to sink. And then it sank. And when he finally cleared the dead trees, and the harsh sun went behind a cloud, the house came into full, unobstructed view. And he started to sweat. It got so bad so quickly that he worried he was having a cardiac episode. And soon he decided that he undeniably was, but also that if it killed him, it would be a mercy.

The roof, which had looked so impressively grandiose from the road, now revealed itself to be a shattered honeycomb of gaps and holes, many of its patterned shingles scattered on the ground in front of the house. The tower, his favorite part of the whole house in the old pictures he'd seen, leaned slightly outward like it was drunk and on the verge of passing out. Some of the windows, including the once-gorgeous curved bay set into the tower, were boarded over or smashed. The porch had turned into less of a porch and more of a loosely-associated rabble of rotten planks, and all of its turned balusters were rotted or broken. Vines—not the decorative kind, but rather the invasive kind—had overtaken the walls in spots, and crept all the way up the full three stories on one side. And the Camperdown elm tree—a tree so important that it was protected by various historical preservation societies—hadn't been protected nearly well enough because it had uprooted and toppled through the side of the house. Now the rotting remains of it were propped up at a steep angle against the floor of the second story, providing a convenient ramp for wildlife to walk into the luxury mansion of their dreams.

The house was not good. It was, in a word, bad. This would not be a renovation. It would be a teardown and rebuild. One that he couldn't come close to affording. The house, if he looked at it a certain way, looked exactly the way he felt—the arrangement of windows and doors resembled a horrified face that was seeing death.

He didn't dare park too close for fear that the whole front wall would be dislodged by vibrations from his arrival and collapse onto his truck. He sat in the driver's seat, breathing hard and sweating harder, and looking at the house. Looking for any reason for optimism. Looking for any sign that every plan he had for his future hadn't been crushed by that historic Camperdown elm.

He didn't know how long he'd been sitting there stewing in his demolished hopes when he noticed a green Toyota hybrid crunching up the dirt drive behind him. He hadn't expected his co-owner to arrive so early, but that had to be her. He wondered how she'd react when she saw the house. For the first time, he was grateful that she'd swooped in and stolen half the house from him. She'd saved him a $70,000 loss. He'd already lost everything; that would have been *more* than everything.

She pulled in behind him and climbed out of her car, gazing at the house with a kind of awestruck wonder as she stepped up alongside Guy's window. He noted that she'd come dressed in overalls and work boots as if she expected to start renovating the house immediately. Her hair was tied up and she even wore a painter's cap with pink and purple splatters across the brim. All she lacked was a paint roller, but he expected she probably had that in the back of her car. In a small way, he admired her naive initiative.

"Wow," she said.

"You get what you pay for," Guy said. And as soon as he'd said it, he realized he couldn't tell what her "wow" had meant. Was it "wow, this place is amazing" or more like "wow, what's that gross smell?" And even now, looking at her face, he still didn't know.

She continued past his car and up to the porch steps, and despite how much Guy dreaded seeing the inside of this place, he decided that it wouldn't be fair to send her in alone. One wrong step and that tower could fall on her, or she could be eaten by a swarm of ravenous groundhogs. So, with a reluctant sigh, he threw open his truck door and followed her.

The closer he got, the more his crushing disappointment grew. The front of the house was crumbling. Broken bricks lay scattered on the porch and the dirt beneath it. One of the biggest bay window frames had broken completely free of the wall and one corner swayed visibly in the breeze. And as more details became clear, he could see that none of them were good. Even if they discovered that the inside was a pristine full-scale replica of the Hanging Gardens of Babylon, the damage he'd already seen was too extensive to be fixed at anything other than a monumental loss. He was officially doomed.

The woman's foot went through the bottom porch step the moment she put weight on it. She recovered quickly and put the same foot through the next step up. The third step, anticipating her stepping on it, collapsed on its own to avoid the indignity.

The woman looked suspiciously at the pile of what had formerly been steps. "Is it safe?" she asked, briefly forgetting her disdain for him.

"Definitely not," Guy said. And he decided that if she was going to survive this, it would only be because he went first. He jumped onto the porch, avoiding the steps altogether, then turned back and held out a hand to help her up. She pointedly ignored it and hopped up on her own.

It took him several tries just to get the door unlocked. Both the key and the lock were badly corroded, and the first time he tried to get the key in, he had to rock it side to side just to clear all the flakes of rust out, along with a startled-looking spider. Finally, he managed to plunge the key all the way in, but even then it took considerable effort to actually move the deadbolt. When it finally opened, it did so with a dusty grinding noise like a medieval torture machine.

And at last, they stepped inside. Where it got worse.

Chapter 4

M ae still hadn't mentally processed that she had spent $80,000 on a decrepit ruin. But that's what she'd done.

The outside of the house was bad. But the inside looked like the second half of a disaster movie after the aliens had finished blowing up the world's monuments, the earthquakes had subsided, and all the tsunamis had receded into the sea. It had nothing that could accurately be called a "wall" or a "floor" or a "ceiling." It had things that might once have been walls, floors, and ceilings, but those things had long since lost track of their function. The ceilings lay crumbled against the walls, which lay crumbled on the parts of the floor that didn't lie crumbled in the basement.

There was a heavy smell of decay like something had died and then been left to rot in the sun on top of something that had died the day before. Yet not everything was dead. There were things moving in the rubble. They were small things, mostly, scurrying around in the shadows, but every now and then one of them would dart out into the light, and they would see it more clearly. Most of them were rodents of various descriptions, but Mae feared that a few of them were snakes. And she wondered how the two mortal enemies managed to live together so harmoniously. Maybe the house was an unending battle royale for them until only one species was left standing. Or maybe they had put aside their differences in order to survive in what was surely an unforgiving environment for anything with a heartbeat.

Before she took a single step inside, she had changed her mind. She wouldn't hold onto the house. She would sell to this guy. Her buying half of this place had done him a favor. If she wanted revenge for how he'd made her lose her cove house, then sticking him with this nightmare seemed like the way to do it.

But slow down, she told herself. Don't seem too eager to sell, or he'll bid down. He's slimy that way. Make him think you want it.

She squeezed past him. "Whoa," she said, trying to sound thrilled.

She leaned in and looked to one side and the other, taking in as much as she could without doing anything dangerous like walking on the floors. The entryway had a fireplace of its own, which was impressive even if most of it had collapsed. Beyond the entry was a hall that went off to her left past the stairwell and some doors. And straight ahead of her was an archway into a wide living room. None of it looked good, or safe. But if she was going to make a show of it, she'd have to explore a little.

She prodded the floor with her toe and, finding that it narrowly passed the toe test, shuffled along it like she was crossing an Everest crevasse. The floorboards groaned and snapped under her weight, and the walls shifted and creaked like they might topple in from both sides. The moaning protest of a house that wanted to be left alone to die.

The living room was in even worse shape than the entryway. It lay in ruins. The previous owners had left behind pieces of antique furniture that hadn't fared any better than the structure of the house. If anything, they had fared worse. There was a rust-colored settee with one leg snapped off and two faded couch cushions, and a sagging armchair missing one arm. Boxes and boxes of various sizes and contents lay strewn about the room. Piles of furniture and carpet lay in different states of decay. The floorboards were gone in most places, exposing the sub-floor and insulation. The windows were missing panes of glass, some broken by a storm maybe, others broken by vandals or wandering teenagers. The walls were bare and cracked, the wood paneling peeling off in sheets. It smelled like cat urine, mold, and old fabric.

She didn't say anything, mostly because she didn't want to breathe in any more of this air than was absolutely necessary. And the guy—she had to keep reminding herself that his name was, generically, Guy—didn't say anything either. She glanced over and caught him having a stricken look that he quickly covered up when he saw her looking at him.

Guy cleared his throat. Maybe to indicate that he was about to say something knowledgeable and important, or maybe to clear the dust and mold out of his airways. "Mae," he said. "That's your name, right? Mae?"

She nodded without looking at him. Instead, she ran her hand along an intact part of the fireplace and looked up at what remained of the ceiling. She could see two different rooms up there, divided by the debris of a wall. Bedrooms, probably. And one of the bedrooms also had a fireplace. She could imagine how it looked before it had turned to ruin. Ornate, but in a warm and inviting way. Ooh, she thought, that's actually pretty nice.

"Mae, we need to discuss—"

She didn't hear the rest of his sentence. She was looking at the living room again, this time ignoring all the debris and detritus. It was a great size, and the fireplace was one of those giant Citizen Kane deals that you could practically walk into. She could imagine sitting on that settee at a time when it didn't have mice in it, and gazing into that fire. It was a mansion but she could imagine that it had once felt homey.

She interrupted whatever Guy was saying. "Where's the kitchen?" And she trotted past him into the hall.

He followed her from the entryway down the hall past the shattered remains of a dining room—with yet another fireplace, amazing!—and finally into the kitchen. She hadn't expected that it could surprise her, but it did. Because in addition to the same kind of decay she'd already seen in the rest of the house, the kitchen appeared to have burned. That was a new standard. Light leaked through the half-burnt curtains, and through the crack in a door to outside that hung open and swayed in the breeze. In the center of the kitchen was an island with a stove on it, half-smashed and also burnt. Pans hung from the wall next to the few intact cupboards that were stained with grease. The walls were disgusting, coated with a thin film of filth and grime. Thick cobwebs hang between the sink, cupboards, and countertops. The ceiling squelched and hung, the plaster having cracked long ago under water damage. And the air was thick with the smell of old grease, dust, and smoke; the stench of burnt wood and ashes. As Mae stepped in, there was the sound of a walnut-sized insect crunching under her shoe. It was the only sound in the room, apart from the buzzing of flies, but it was enough to make her stomach lurch.

And yet... cooking in here would once have been like Thanksgiving every day. She could see floral curtains and hand-carved cabinet doors. Which way did the windows face? East? That meant breakfast sun. Yes, the kitchen was burnt and wrecked and infested. But after dancing around it for just a few seconds, she could only see it the way it had been 100 years ago, the stench of grease and ash replaced with wafts of pumpkin spice carried on warm air from the open stove. And it was wondrous.

She rounded the corner at the far side of the island.

And suddenly her foot caught on something and sent her tumbling headlong into the darkness.

Guy reacted quickly, lunging forward and grabbing her by the arm just before she disappeared completely into a wide gap in the kitchen floor that had been totally obscured from their view on the way in. He held her dangling above the gap for a few seconds, then finally yanked her back to safety.

"That'll have to be fixed," she said, hardly troubled at all by having almost plunged into the basement. Yes, it was a big hole in the floor. But how hard could that be to repair?

"Have you seen enough?" he asked impatiently.

"No," she said. "What's upstairs?"

She trotted back out into the hall and found the stairwell. It was mostly intact but badly scuffed. Easy to repair, she thought.

The first bedroom she looked at had seemingly never been finished even when the house was lived in. But its state now went far beyond simply being unfinished. The floor was pitted with small sinkholes and raised in other places. Water stains trailed down the walls and warped the wooden panels into a pattern of shapes that suggested trees or clouds. The ceiling, a patchwork of boards of varying shades of gray, was deeply dented in places. Piles of trash made of black, peeling paper lay in chaotic heaps behind the door. A pile of sticks and twisted metal sheets blocked one corner and spilled into another pile that looked like it might have been the beginnings of a decrepit bookshelf. A single shard of glass from a broken window glittered on the floor.

And yet, it was *perfect*. She could imagine a four-poster bed, maybe a wardrobe. The walls could have that Victorian-style wallpaper if she found the right one. She guessed there would be a good breeze in here if the window was opened in the summer.

She didn't stop the tour until she'd seen everything. There were eight bedrooms in total—eight!—divided between the second and third floors. Only one bathroom on each floor, but that was workable. The third floor bathroom had a big cast-iron tub, which was better than workable. And also on the third floor there was a cozy little corner study with sloping ceilings, and a kitchenette with a counter and a sink. Best of all, part of the counter was attached to a hinged section of the wall—a concealed door, for no reason other than that every old mansion needed a concealed door—that led outside onto a round balcony with a wood-paneled balustrade wall. She worked out that it was the top of the tower she'd seen from outside. It was certainly too dangerous to step out there, but she could see it being amazing once it wasn't so lethal.

The house was gorgeous, she decided. Or it *could* be. A house like this didn't deserve to die. A house like this needed to be saved.

"Whammo," she said softly.

"Sorry?" Guy said from behind her.

She glanced back at him. "Nothing," she said. "I'm not selling you my half."

"You... er... you what?" he said.

"I'm keeping it," she said.

"Okay," he said cautiously. "Do you want to buy my half too? I can give it to you for $80,000."

"No," she said. "I can't afford that. But I want to renovate it with you. We merge the two units back into one big house and we renovate it together. Partners." She couldn't believe she was saying it. But the words just came out of her in another whammo moment, and she let them.

He tried to say something but couldn't make it into a sentence, or even words. His first attempt sounded like, "W...?" His second attempt sounded like a hiccup. And his third attempt was, "Huh?"

"Look at it!" she said, spinning in the middle of the room. "It's beautiful!"

"No," he said. "It isn't."

"You can't look at it like it is. You have to look at it like it *can* be!"

"It *can* be torn down," he said. "Can I look at it like that?"

She stopped spinning, anxious now. She couldn't let him do that. "No," she said. "No, no, no, you can't. You have to fix it. You have to make it what it used to be. One big gorgeous mansion." The plan formed rapidly in her head. So rapidly that she could barely keep track of it. "You were planning to spend $140,000 to buy both halves, right? $70,000 per half?"

He nodded, but it was zombie-like.

"So I saved you that much," she went on. "That's my invest-ment. You can put that into the renovation. You're ahead of the game. When the house is done and you sell it, all I want is my $80,000 back so I can buy another house for my mother. You can keep the rest of the proceeds. As long as you sell it to someone who will love it."

She could see him doing mental math. Or trying to figure out what planet she was from. "I still can't do it for that," he said. "Not without cutting a lot of corners."

She put up a hand like a traffic cop. "No," she said. "No, no, no. You have to do it right. This house is a work of art. And it can be beautiful again. If you take this deal, it's on the condition that I'm your partner. You're in charge of structure and construction and everything that keeps the house from falling apart, but I'm in charge of aesthetics. All I want is for this gorgeous old house not to be ruined. Do we have a deal?"

10 months after that...

Chapter 5

The floors were finally done. Actual hardwood floors. Well, not actual hardwood. But actual floors.

Guy was thrilled. When he walked around the inside of the house now, his feet no longer thumped hollowly on exposed plywood or crunched on century-old tiles that had crumbled to a kind of sharp-edged gravel. And unlike just a few months ago, there was little fear of crashing through some rotted section of subfloor and plunging onto the compacted dirt of the basement. Instead, he could walk around the whole interior and make satisfying shoes-on-hardwood noises. He'd specifically chosen this laminate floor because of how much it sounded like hardwood when you walked on it, and now he got to enjoy that sound while he was also enjoying the 33% he'd saved by not using actual wood. He could even skip if he wanted to. The floors could handle that. Or dance, which is what he most felt like doing.

Because the last of the floors were done. That meant that the whole job was nearly done. And that meant that his time in the house was nearly done. He wouldn't have to sleep on an air mattress in the corner of the smallest bedroom on the second floor anymore. He'd be able to go places and do things that had nothing to do with fixing this house. And that was good. That was the beginning of a bright future he'd been anticipating for nearly a year.

He trotted through the dining room with its two-toned wainscoting (done) and working acrylic chandelier that looked like real crystal in an ornate antique-looking ceiling medallion (done). He swept past the staircase, now with factory hand-carved banister and railings (done) and an imitation leaded glass window bay (now, also, done) that cost a fraction of what an actual leaded glass window would cost. And he slid on the smooth floor into the front entry with its carved oak fireplace (done, though not actually carved) and door with beveled glass (done, though not actually beveled glass). And then he was out in the sun on the wrap-around porch, which was not done. But it didn't dampen his spirits at all because it would be painted later today so it was also, in a way, sort of done. Almost everything was done, done, done and everything was going to be great. Or at least okay. Or at the very least, done.

It was cool outside, even by March standards, but the sun was out and all the snow was finally gone, dissolved into deep, chunky puddles that dotted the muddy property and had bits of construction debris floating in them. The puddles fed into a slushy, sawdust-filled stream that flowed down the slope behind the house and past the carriage house at the bottom of the hill. It was not an appealing look for a front yard, especially with so much splintered timber and ripped-up drywall still lying around. But despite all that, the sun lifted his spirits even further because the winter had felt endless. The trees—birches and maples clustered into groves on either side of the drive—would be skeletal and gray for another month at least. Most of them were dead and would stay that way, but a few might still sprout. Yet Guy hoped he wouldn't be here to see them turn green. The house was nearly done. He would sell it and be gone. He had the buyer—some Wall Street goon named Cameron Something—dangling from a hook and ready to be reeled in. In two days, Cameron Something would come and see the renovation for the first time, and would almost certainly hand Guy a check on the spot. Then he'd be out of this tortuous nightmare and reaping the benefits. Everything was going to be great.

After a few minutes of taking in the crisp air, he checked for a car coming up the drive. Mae was due to get back any minute with paint, and he didn't want to see her right now. He wanted to enjoy this feeling of accomplishment, of completion, of an assured future. Just for a while. Mae showing up had the potential to make all of those feelings go away.

But he didn't see her car. Just the few remaining vehicles from the crew, mostly belonging to painters and flooring people now. The painters were working on the windows from a scaffold at the back of the house where he couldn't see them, so he could easily pretend they were already gone. All the big trucks full of lumber and tools had left for good, and the dumpsters piled high with materials torn out of the old walls had finally been hauled away, never to return. The only really big piece of debris still lying around was the six-foot hunk of ugly, misshapen rock sunk into the dirt next to the driveway. They had dug it out of the back yard during the brief period when Guy had flirted with the idea of putting in a pool. The promise of many such rocks hidden beneath the mud had discouraged him from that plan. Now he just needed someone to finally haul this one away, which he'd been assured a month ago would happen within a few days. It had been there so long that he thought he might actually miss it now. He'd even given it a name: Big Ugly Rock. Because it was all three of those things.

He turned to go back inside, planning to jump up and down on the new oak-looking floors in the second floor hallway and listen to how little they had cost.

"Mr. Gillis? A word?"

It was Luther, coming around the side of the house toward him, his big work boots making sucking noises in the mud.

Guy had known Luther Corcoran for fifteen years. Luther had been his construction foreman on a dozen renovations, every one that Guy had done since he'd decided that flipping houses was his true calling. He'd known Luther pretty much as long as he'd known anybody. And yet Luther still insisted on calling him Mr. Gillis. He seemed to like the formality and how it kept Guy at a distance.

Luther was a large man in every direction except vertically. His shoulders were wide enough that he had to turn slightly sideways to get through a standard-size door. But his gut stuck out far enough that turning sideways didn't actually solve the problem. And yet the top of his head couldn't have touched Guy's chin if he tried. He had a jowly face under a Yankees cap that never left his head, which was under a hard hat that also never left his head. He kept his tape measure—which he affectionately called "Pearl"—hooked to the brim of his cap. It seemed like enough weight that it would constantly be pulling his gaze downward, but somehow Luther made it work.

There had been times during this renovation when Guy had dreaded talking to Luther. Guy had once calculated that, on average, every word Luther spoke to him cost him $173 in extra expenses. A full sentence could run into five digits. But the house was looking so good now that he had stopped worrying about Luther's "words."

So Guy turned around and smiled. "Luther! Good morning!"

Luther's work boots thumped up the porch steps. Which were, Guy noted again with glee, almost completely done. When he'd bought the house every one of those steps was broken. Now all of them were freshly repaired and enthusiastically doing their job as steps.

"Indeed it is a good morning, Mr. Gillis," Luther said. Luther never, ever betrayed any emotion, either positive or negative. His voice was eternally as flat as the laminate floors he installed. And today was no exception. Despite agreeing with Guy's assessment of the goodness of the morning, the corners of his mouth didn't creep upward even a millimeter, and no more than the minimum tooth exposure took place. "Now do you think you could accompany me to the basement? I have some new information I wish to impart."

Guy had never stopped being surprised at how Luther, despite looking like a manatee wrapped in plaid and sawdust, always talked like a Harvard philosophy professor. Or what Guy imagined a Harvard philosophy professor talked like. "What kind of information?" Guy asked. He hoped that Luther was going to show him something else that had recently been completed—the breaker box, maybe, or something to do with the HVAC. Yet in the back of his mind, a little nugget of dread had already formed. This could be something bad. It probably wasn't. But it could be.

"It's easier if I show you," Luther said.

Guy studied his face for any hint of anything. But whether Luther was going to say that the house was on fire or that he had brought cupcakes, his face gave no hint of either. The little nugget of dread lodged deeper into Guy's brain. Luther had never brought cupcakes before and it would be pretty surprising if he started now.

Guy took one more look up the driveway and was relieved to see that Mae's car was still nowhere in sight. If Luther was going to expose a new problem, it would be better if Mae was nowhere near. Much better.

Despite being just a big, empty, unfinished space that the house sat on, the basement was possible to get lost in. It had more corners and alcoves than it needed, some of them almost completely unlit. And it had a scary oak door hidden in the back, beyond which were scary stone stairs going even deeper, down to the carriage house. It felt more subterranean than a normal basement, darker and damper like a cave complex where you might find hibernating bears or a colony of bats. And the renovations had done nothing to change it. Guy had claimed that he wanted to retain the basement's original damp-and-rough scariness as a kind of historical preservation. But it was more accurate to say that he just hadn't wanted to explode the budget by doing anything down there. He hadn't even attempted to pour concrete over the floor, which was nothing but exposed, hard-packed clay. The basement had never been on his priority list. It was a place for the breaker box, the furnace, and, probably, pill bugs. And that was it.

Luther's face and voice remained in total agreement that they weren't going to make this easier for Guy by giving him hints. Guy would have to sit through words to figure out what kind of news this was. "Remember last May," Luther said, "when we began this project and I said that step one should be engaging a structural engineer to make sure there weren't any serious foundational issues?"

Guy's dread expanded further. It now occupied most of the available space in his skull. "Yeah, but we agreed that it was probably fine. I definitely remember us agreeing."

Luther shifted his cap and hard hat, maybe to loosen up the memories. "My recollection is that you agreed a structural inspection would be too expensive, a notion with which I disagreed vehemently. So that was more of a one-way agreeing, opposed by a disagreeing in the opposite direction."

Guy's mind ran through the list of justifications it had come up with at the time. They still seemed convincing to him. "Yeah, but where would we even find a structural engineer at such short notice?"

"I'm a structural engineer."

Now that was a surprise. It wasn't cupcakes, but still surprising. "Really? You're a structural engineer too? How did you never tell me that before?"

"There are many things about me that you don't know. I also have a black belt in Brazilian jiu jitsu and an extensive collection of Battlestar Galactica memorabilia. But those seem less relevant presently."

Was Luther proud of those hobbies? If he was, he certainly hadn't notified his voice about it. Guy reluctantly went back to the subject of his now-intense dread. "So what are we talking about here?"

"What we're talking about here is, my guys discovered something this morning. In summary: your sleeper walls are sinking."

Already that didn't sound good. And if Luther's brief initial summary was bad, the details would be terrifying. But Guy had to ask for them. He closed his eyes and squeezed them with his thumb and finger, hoping the extra pressure would wring the dread out of his mind. "How bad?" he asked.

"You can see it if you look." He pointed at the outside wall of the basement as if it should be obvious. "This building is 135 years old. In those days, in this area, they just built the sleeper walls resting on the surface soil. And the surface soil is soft and muddy. Consequently, the weight of the ground floor has compacted the soil."

Guy felt the weight of his dread also compacting the soil. He didn't want to have this conversation. He wanted to skip and/or dance on all the new floors he hadn't skipped and/or danced on yet. "Which means..."

"Which means that the ground floor has been sinking for 135 years."

"The house is sinking?"

"You misunderstand me. The *sleeper walls* are sinking. The outer wall foundations are sat on a layer of firmer soil deeper into the ground. They are not sinking."

That didn't sound so bad. Even in Luther's Kansas-flat tone, that sounded like a spark of hope. "So that's good?"

"In a sense."

"In what sense?"

"In the sense that the inevitable collapse is not necessarily imminent. Which, granted, could be considered a positive. But on the negative side, with the sleeper walls sinking, the roof is no longer receiving enough structural support from the ground floor. And, consequently, the trusses are bending."

The spark of hope extinguished itself with a little *pff* noise and a curl of smoke. "So because the basement is bad, the roof is collapsing?"

"Not presently. Again, a positive. But give it a few years."

On one level, Guy knew that this was a disaster. Serious structural issues meant more work, more investment, more time. It meant that he couldn't bring his already-impatient Wall Street buyer in until it was fixed. It meant that he would have to find more money somewhere when he knew very well that there wasn't any more to find. This was more than just a disaster. This was a death blow to the promising future that only moments ago had seemed very close.

On another level, Luther had said that the inevitable roof collapse was a few years off, so...

"How many years are we talking about?" Guy asked, allowing the tiniest note of conspiracy into his voice. He hoped that Luther would pick up on it.

Luther did. In a display of the most extensive transformation Guy had ever seen Luther's face go through, one of his eyebrows shifted slightly upward. "Five. Ten maybe."

So Luther hadn't immediately questioned where Guy was going with this. That seemed like an encouragement to press on. "And this is something that wouldn't necessarily be obvious today? Say, to a home inspector?"

Luther's eyebrow stayed where it was. "*We* have been here for 10 months, and did not discern the problem until today," he said. As usual, there was absolutely no expression in his voice. And yet Guy couldn't help taking from it that maybe Luther would be okay with this.

But was Guy okay with it? He was certainly okay with not making the extra investment and not staying longer at the house.

But was it something that could come back to bite him? Could someone get hurt? Could he get sued? All seemed possible.

But at the same time, finding more money to fix this seemed pretty impossible. So...

A sudden *clomp clomp clomp* on the floor above them announced that Mae had arrived and was loudly coming over to the stairs in her clogs. Guy had known Mae less than a year but he'd become very familiar with the sound of her shoes. And he'd hoped not to hear them during this conversation with Luther. But there they were. He hoped that maybe she wouldn't realize anyone was in the basement and wouldn't come down, but that hope also proved futile. He heard her clogs hit the basement stairs without missing a beat.

Guy lowered his eyebrows and shook his head slightly at Luther, trying to silently say, "Don't mention any of this to her." Luther betrayed no hint of having received the message, but his one eyebrow did slide back down those few millimeters to its usual semi-permanent resting spot. Guy didn't know what that meant.

Mae appeared at the bottom of the stairs and squinted into the shadows, hunting for them. She had her standard renovation outfit on—overalls and an old T-shirt splattered with dried, multi-colored splotches. And of course her hair was tied up under her white painter's cap, which she wore even on days when she wasn't painting. She spotted them across the basement under the one bare, swinging light bulb. "What's happening?" She must have seen the look on Guy's face because she instantly seemed to glean that something was seriously wrong.

"The floors are done!" Guy said, as cheerily as he could force his voice to sound. It was utterly unconvincing. And, to boost its positive feeling a bit, he added, "Yay!" But, much like the house's sleeper walls, it didn't hold up very much.

"I saw," she said, evidently not as thrilled with the floors as Guy was. "They're laminate. You probably thought I wouldn't notice.

But what's this about?" She waggled her finger between Guy and Luther.

Luther glanced at Guy, and Guy tried again to non-verbally convey, "Please please please don't say anything."

Luther didn't get it. "Sleeper walls are sinking," he said, flat as always. But from how quickly he blurted it out, Guy realized that Luther might actually be a little scared of Mae.

Mae swept her eyes around the basement. Guy knew that she had no idea what sleeper walls were, but she looked for them anyway. "Which means?"

"Roof collapse is inevitable," Luther said.

Guy winced. There it was. She was now aware of their doom.

She closed her eyes for a second as the full gravity of it hit her. But she pushed through, ever pragmatic. "What do we have to do?"

Luther didn't hesitate. "Concrete foundations to replace the sleeper walls."

Guy interjected himself into the conversation, trying to make her aware of the real issue. "And tell us, Luther, how much will that cost?"

Mae shook her head. "Doesn't matter. Do it."

Guy stammered, flustered to the point of near-panic. "Does... does... doesn't matter? It—"

Mae ignored him and kept her gaze locked on Luther. "If we don't do it, the roof comes down?"

Luther nodded. "Inevitably."

"Okay," Mae said. "So do it." She shifted her gaze to Guy. "I'll be painting the study."

And then she *clomp-clomp-clomped* back up the stairs. Guy heard her clogs cross the new (and done) floors above them and then start up the staircase to the second floor.

He was confident she was out of earshot now, but he took a step toward Luther and lowered his voice anyway. "Be straight with me. What am I looking at for this?"

"I'll have to work it up," Luther said. "I can't exactly bring an excavator down here. We'll need to dig them by hand. That means a pretty substantial crew—"

"Skip it," Guy said. "What's the real estimate?"

Guy had learned years ago that Luther consistently had two estimates for every task. The first would be the amount of time and money that it would take to do it properly. It would be up to code, using the best materials and done with utmost care. But all Guy had to do was wait, and eventually Luther would come back with the better plan that was cheaper, faster, and further out toward the fringes of legality.

Luther's expression didn't change. He knew the dual-estimates routine as well as Guy did. "You could dig them yourself by hand. Which is essentially free."

"Great," Guy said without hesitation. "I'll do that."

"We're talking about trenches eight feet deep," Luther pointed out. "A lot of them. Are you sure you want to?"

"No. But how much will it be if I get you to do it?"

Luther's eyes shifted upward as he started an enormous calculation in his head. "Well for starters, I'll need to bring in a few extra guys—"

"Forget it," Guy said. "I'll do it myself. Can I borrow a shovel?"

Shaking his head with the closest approximation of a disapproving look that his face had ever managed, Luther went off to find a shovel. And Guy stood in the middle of the basement, surveying the job he was about to tackle and trying to convince himself that it wasn't at all impossible. It was free. That was what mattered.

As he kicked at the clay, looking for soft spots to start digging, he felt a sudden burst of air against his right ear.

It was a faint brush that was there one second and gone the next, like someone had squeezed a turkey baster next to his cheek and then run off to hide. And though he knew he was alone in the basement, he whirled around twice looking for who had done it.

The air against his head had been cool, but not cool enough to make him shiver. And yet, for some reason, he shivered.

Chapter 6

Luther showed Guy where to dig the trenches for the new foundation support, and Guy drove some steel tent pegs into the earthen floor and tied blue vinyl rope between them to outline the boundaries. It was many more trenches than he'd hoped to dig. Because until now, he'd hoped to dig *zero* trenches.

He couldn't predict how long it would take, so he planned to use the rest of the day as a test to gauge the scale of the job. If it went very well, maybe he'd finish in a single day. If it went okay, maybe he'd finish by the weekend. If it went poorly, he might be doing it into the next week. And if it went *very* poorly, he'd be in the hospital with a muscular back injury by sundown.

The biggest challenge, though, could be Mae. She was painting the study on the third floor, and the chances that she'd stop that and come down to the basement again today were remote. But if the job took days, then she'd undoubtedly start to wonder what he was doing and come to check. And lately, very few encounters with Mae went well.

After some heated disagreements with her at the beginning of the reno, Guy now mostly tried to keep his distance. It was occasionally challenging because some of the time, like him, she stayed in the house. She'd claimed one of the small bedrooms on the third floor, along with the kitchenette and the bathroom with the cast-iron tub. And she used the space sometimes to avoid the hour-long commute to her mother's condo in Hartford. But even when she was staying in the house, she and Guy rarely interacted after hours. And she had some kind of tech job or something that mostly kept her away during the day. So he was fortunately left to his own devices much of the time, and he used those opportunities to sneak things in that she wouldn't like, such as laminate floors. But then there were days like this, when she was working in the house and would probably not leave. It just made things harder.

He thought about spitting on his hands before he gripped the shovel because that's what people always did in movies before a big digging job. But that seemed unhelpfully gross. Plus it wasn't his shovel, and Luther might not want spit on it. So he just picked it up and started to dig.

The shovel edge pierced three inches into the clay and stopped hard, jolting his arms all the way back to his spine.

It took him a solid minute to recover from the shock. He spent that minute hopping in a circle and loosely shaking his arms while the shovel vibrated like a tuning fork, its edge deep enough in the muck to keep it vertical.

When his skeleton had finally stopped quivering, he leaned on the shovel handle and rocked it backward, scooping out the three inches of soil he'd managed to penetrate. Even breaking that little bit of the floor free required his entire body weight, but it finally broke off and lifted out. He scooped it aside, scraped at the gap with the edge of the shovel, and crouched to look at what he'd hit.

It was a patch of smooth, gray rock, slick from the earth he'd removed. But he hadn't removed very much—just a shovel-width, three inches deep. So he couldn't yet tell if the obstruction was just a large-ish rock crammed into the dirt or a mile-deep tectonic plate that wouldn't move until a continent collided with it. That kind of geologic event seemed unlikely to happen today.

So he poked the shovel into the ground a few more times around the gap he'd created, careful this time not to jolt himself to his core, and cleared away more of the clay.

Already it was looking more and more likely that it was a very large rock. Even if he found its edges, it was obvious that it would be too big for him to pry loose using only a shovel that was already bent a little at the end.

It was too early to let himself get frustrated, so he didn't. If there was a big rock in the dirt here, that was fine. He could get a couple of Luther's guys to help remove it. As long as he dug the rest of the trenches himself, that wouldn't be a big expense.

So he carried the shovel across to the other end of the basement where he'd outlined another trench in rope. It was furthest away from where he'd hit that rock, and therefore the least likely to contain another rock. The logic seemed solid.

Once again he resisted the urge to spit on his hands, then drove the shovel hard into the earth.

And again, the shovel sank a few inches into the soil and stopped hard, sending a spike of pain through his entire body like a shock wave.

Furious now, he kicked at the ground with his toe where the shovel had dug in, and exposed another slick, smooth patch of sheer rock.

Worry started to mix with the frustration. Could it be that the whole basement only had a few inches of soil in it with solid rock underneath? If so, then what were the sleeper walls sinking into?

Soon, his total ignorance of structural engineering combined with his desperate need for good news, and together they led him down a meandering path to optimism. Maybe this was good. Maybe the sleeper walls only had a few inches to sink. Once they did that, the house would be propped up by this vast sheet of compressed rock that had twice now nearly shaken his teeth out of his head. He'd do one more test somewhere in the middle to confirm, and then he'd go to Luther with what he was now fairly convinced was positive, financially encouraging news.

He dragged the shovel to what he guessed was the center of the house. If the slab of rock stretched across the entire basement, then he was certain he'd run into it here just as he'd done at both ends. He pushed the shovel into the earth gently this time instead of jamming it like a pickax.

It sank into the soil. Past three inches. Past six inches. He kept pushing, stunned and beginning to feel like he was slowly stabbing an enormous, sleeping behemoth to death. The shovel kept going until the blade was all the way underground.

Guy cursed silently. It didn't help, so he cursed out loud.

This was apparently not a huge, unbroken sheet of rock that could support the house. It was likely a lot of separate rocks. He was losing hope. Digging was one of the most straightforward parts of the entire construction process, expertly practiced worldwide even by preschool children in sandboxes, and it was proving to be too difficult for him. It was time to give up.

He jammed the shovel into the dirt next to him. He intended to leave it there for Luther to find when he came down here with his expensive crew of diggers, all much better at digging than Guy.

The shovel *clanged* into hard rock again, just a couple of feet to the side of where he'd just dug. Curious, he yanked it out and jammed it into the ground a few feet on the other side of where he'd hit soft earth. Once again, it stopped a few inches into the ground. So there was a rock on either side, with a gap between them maybe five or six feet across.

Desperately needing to feel at least some sense of accomplishment from all this, Guy dug into the soft spot in the middle where there was no rock. At least he could clear that patch and go back to Luther having accomplished a small part of his task. Maybe Luther would discount him $5.00 or so for the section he'd cleared on his own. Better than nothing.

So he dug, first downward to get things started, then expanding to either side, hunting for where the gap ended and the rock began.

He soon forgot all about the $5.00 discount.

The perimeter of the gap was not jagged rock like he'd expected. It was a smooth cut edge of gray stone, like the corner of a step or a patio. It wasn't natural—it was carved, and deliberate. It had a gentle curve to it, like he'd uncovered a small section of a circle a few inches under the clay.

With the edge of the shovel, he started cutting through the soil to either side, tossing dirt across the basement with increasing fervor, ignoring how much he had started to sweat. The curve of stone continued, smooth and unbroken, until he'd traced out an entire circle about six feet wide. Outside the circle, as far as he could tell, everything was stone. Inside the circle, there was only soft dirt. It was like somebody had bored a perfectly smooth, round shaft into a stone basement floor and then, for some reason, filled the shaft with dirt and clay. And filled the rest of the basement with it as well. Maybe to bury the hole?

Guy, already sweating, started to sweat in a more serious way. Partly from the exertion of all the digging, but mostly because it was becoming increasingly clear that this was a problem. It was a structural irregularity in the basement with no discernible purpose. If it was exposed, it could freak out any potential buyer who came down here. An unfinished dirt basement was already a liability. An unfinished dirt basement with an inexplicable hole in the middle of it was legitimately freaky.

So it couldn't be exposed. He'd cover it up again and nobody would be the wiser. Maybe one day the house's new owners would decide to finish the basement and would uncover the hole in the process. But that was their problem. His problem was ensuring that he was long gone by the time that happened.

Despite the sweat and his exhaustion, he started frantically shifting all the earth he'd moved, urging it all back where he'd found it.

He wanted his nice, unbroken, hideously irregular compacted clay floor back.

He'd only just started doing that when Mae showed up at the bottom of the stairs. "What is that?" she asked right away.

Guy didn't know what expression was on his own face, but he was sure it was different from Mae's. His felt like sweaty, dirt-streaked confusion. Hers was a kind of mesmerized awe like she was witnessing the birth of a fawn. She came down the last few stairs and he saw that she was barefoot. Which meant that she had deliberately tried not to be heard. Or else her feet were hot. But he chose to believe the first thing.

"It's..." Guy struggled to find the right word. But not for long, because there was only one word for it. "...a hole."

Which was, indeed, what it was.

Mae sidestepped around the edge of the hole, probing the lip of it with her foot as she went, testing to see if the edge might collapse under her if she stepped too close. "Yeah, but what for? Why is there a hole?"

"No idea."

"Is it a well?"

"I don't think they dig wells in basements. Even 100 years ago they mostly did that outside."

Her face lit up with a theory. "Ooh, do you think somebody kept a prisoner in there? Like that lotion guy in *Silence of the Lambs*?"

She sounded a little too excited about that possibility for his liking. "That would be... bad. Right?" he asked. He was, alarmingly, not entirely sure how she'd answer.

But she didn't answer. She had already moved on. "Is it decorative? Like, a feature?"

"Holes are not high on the dream feature list for most people."

She poked at the dirt with her toe. "How deep is it?"

"There's no way to know."

She shot him an annoyed look. "There are lots of ways to know. You're holding one of them in your hand."

He propped the shovel against the nearest wall. "It doesn't matter. It's just another thing. Like the rotten timber and the blocked chimney. No different. I fixed those, and I'll fix this. Leave it to me."

She peered at the hole for a long time. He could see her eyes tracing around its perimeter as she considered, and before she said it, he could already tell that this would not be left to him.

"Give me the shovel," she said. She stretched out a hand toward it.

"Why?"

"Because I want to find out how deep it is."

"It doesn't matter. I can get Luther to cover it up."

"I want to know what it is first."

"It doesn't matter what it is."

"Aren't you curious?"

"No. Aren't you curious what it will do to the resale value?" It wasn't a great retort, and he wished that in the heat of the moment he'd come up with something wittier.

But it did seem to have had an effect. He could see her reconsidering, weighing options that he'd already weighed himself. And he watched her, hoping and expecting that she'd come to the same conclusion he had.

Which she didn't. "I want to see what it is," she said. And she walked past him, grabbed the shovel off the wall, and carried it back to the center of the hole.

He watched her labor over a few shovelfuls of dirt and clay while he hunted for the most diplomatic way to say what he absolutely needed to say. What he finally settled on was: "Okay. Fine. Do what you want." Which was diplomatic enough, but said nothing at all.

He stormed upstairs, leaving her to her digging. By the time he got to the top of the stairs, he had already planned to ask Luther to bring in a cement mixer with a chute long enough to reach through the basement window. They would cover the entire floor with cement and bury the hole for good.

He didn't tell Mae, though. Because, as with everything else, it was better if Mae didn't know.

Chapter 7

M ae was three feet into the ground before she decided that she wouldn't be able to do this herself. She'd already made a pile of muck next to the hole and hadn't really considered that it might need to go somewhere. And the deeper she got, the more difficult it would be to get the dirt up and out of the hole.

But Luther had a crew doing clean-up outside, so she went out and enlisted three of them who didn't seem busy. Two of them—Rodrigo and Marcel, she found out—shoveled like coal-stoking demons while the other—they called him The Major—used a wheelbarrow to move the muck out. She was afraid that he'd have to carry it all up the stairs. But instead, he propped open the big, heavy oak door in the recessed area behind the furnace, and bounced the wheelbarrows full of muck down the long, gradual stone steps to the carriage house. He made a pile just outside the carriage house door, out of sight from the main house, that she assumed would be hauled or bulldozed away later.

After two hours they were eight feet underground and needed to use a ladder. They had scraped the sides of the hole clean and revealed it to be a smooth, perfectly circular, unbroken wall of rock all the way down. It had no bumps or irregularities at all, no edge of bricks. Just smooth stone that didn't change color with the depth, and seemed too perfectly round to be natural. It was absolutely, inexplicably flawless. Mae admired it as much as she was intrigued by it.

The work got harder, with the diggers having to hoist buckets of dirt up to the edge so it could be hauled away, and their progress slowed to a crawl. By mid-afternoon, they'd only gone another foot. And then Luther came and made the diggers go back to doing whatever their other jobs were. Mae hoped that she hadn't gotten them in trouble, and had to beg Luther to let her keep the ladder so she could continue digging on her own.

As the afternoon wore on and Mae's muscles turned to jelly, she got so desperate that she actually considered asking Guy for help. But she quickly decided against it because of how terrible an idea it was. She'd discovered early in the renovation that Guy didn't like how she did literally anything. Probably it was because she did things *right*, whereas he seemed to have an almost allergic aversion to that. And she'd taken to watching him like a renovating hawk just to make sure he didn't sneak in corner-cutting, cost-reducing, heritage-destroying modifications to the house. She'd let her guard down as the house neared completion, and then just this morning she'd discovered that he'd attempted to pass off laminate floors as genuine hardwood. They weren't even close to realistic, and yet somehow he'd thought she wouldn't notice. Now it was too late to change them. That was her fault for leaving him alone for a couple of days while she stayed with her mother and actually put in some decent hours at work. Especially now, with the house so close to finished, she'd have to stick closer to Guy. So she'd already booked two weeks off work—social media would have to manage itself—and brought enough of her stuff to hole up in the little bedroom on the third floor and make sure the finishing touches to the house weren't done with a sledgehammer.

And Guy obviously wanted nothing to do with this bizarre hole. He didn't share her intrigue, or her determination to keep it as part of the house's mysterious history. If she tried to involve him in digging it out, they'd most likely end up coming to blows, maybe smacking each other with shovels. So she was on her own.

Judging by how much she needed to extend the ladder, she was at least ten feet deep. It was after 6:00 in the evening and there was little light coming in the small basement windows anymore. She was getting tired of the wet, earthy stink and the constant squish of mud under her feet. On top of which, her muscles were almost entirely drained and her clothes were so drenched in sweat and mud that she felt like she could lie down on the bottom of the hole and blend in like a chameleon. It was time to quit. She'd get back at it tomorrow and keep going until she needed a longer ladder. Then she'd get a longer ladder and keep going some more until she found the bottom or Guy poured concrete on top of her.

But when she jabbed the shovel into the bottom of the hole, intending to leave it there overnight, it hit something.

It wasn't the sharp, solid *crack* she would expect when hitting stone. It was a dull and hollow *thud*. And for a moment she had the ridiculous thought that she'd hit a pirate treasure chest. Or, worse, a coffin.

She jabbed the shovel down again and got the same sound. *Thud*.

Pirate-treasure-filled coffin or not, she'd found the bottom.

She stopped trying to dig and started scraping instead, dragging the shovel blade sideways across the dirt. It resisted mightily, but she peeled strips of clay and soil away and rolled them up like sod until she had cleared a patch several feet across and made a pile of dirt rolls against the wall of the hole.

It was not a treasure chest. So at least she was clear on what it wasn't. She just wasn't at all clear on what it *was*. The little bulb dangling overhead barely managed to drop any of its light to the bottom of the hole, so all she could see was a dark, flat floor that

was a different color from the smooth stone sides of the hole.
And she wasn't sure what it was made of. It wasn't stone and
wasn't quite wood. It was something else.

But it was the bottom. She could at least be satisfied with
having reached it, even if it was mightily disappointing that the
bottom hadn't explained anything about the hole at all. She
hadn't solved the mystery, but at least the mystery no longer
had so much dirt in it. If anything had ever been buried in the
hole, then it had been buried deep, and it was gone now, and
the hole had been filled again. All of which seemed like a lot of
inexplicable effort.

She was unsatisfied, but that was overridden by how tired
and muddy she was. She leaned the shovel against the smooth
wall and stepped onto the ladder.

And stopped.

Because a breath of air, cool and damp, had brushed against
her ear.

She stayed frozen, one foot on the ladder and one on the soft
bottom of the hole.

It was the basement of a century-old house. Drafts were not
surprising. The way Guy had restored this place, he'd probably
used cotton swabs and gum to seal up gaps, so air getting
through was expected.

But this hadn't felt like a draft. It was too focused. She'd felt
it on her ear but not on her cheek.

It was a breath.

And with it came an inescapable feeling—her imagination,
but inescapable anyway—that she wasn't alone in the bottom
of the hole.

She stood still, trying to convince herself that the breath had
been random airflow, and that the feeling was just her mind mis-
taking that airflow for something it wasn't. Minds did that, didn't
they? They could see faces in clouds and religious figures in the
burn marks on tortillas. Could they not also conjure up from a

minor draft somebody intentionally blowing in her ear? It was the bottom-of-a-basement-hole equivalent of a Virgin Mary taco.

But she stood still anyway, trying not to breathe. She wanted to see if it would happen again. She was afraid that it would and worried that it wouldn't. So she tried not to move any air herself, and to keep her head in the exact same spot. Maybe, if it happened again, she'd be able to tell where it was coming from. Maybe she'd be able to spot the exact gap that Guy had failed to fill.

And then it happened again.

She couldn't tell where it was coming from, because it wasn't coming from anywhere.

She was certain now. Something had breathed on her.

The feeling of not being alone intensified. It didn't seem like a trick of her mind anymore. It was a certainty. And not only was she not alone, but something was in her space. Close to her. Far *too* close.

She had to wrestle with her instinct to run, to get out of there, to get far away from whatever it was. Her primal instincts told her that it could only want to hurt her and that she shouldn't be here. Fight or flight, her instincts told her. Those were the only choices.

But she won the battle against her survival instinct. She lifted her hands and foot off the cold aluminum of the ladder and turned around.

She could see nothing. The hole was as empty as before.

But it didn't *feel* empty. She felt crowded. She could feel the presence like electricity and musk in the air.

Her voice trembling, she said the dumbest, most obvious thing. "Hello?"

There was no response. For ten seconds. Twenty.

And then there was.

Chapter 8

Guy woke before sunrise and got ready as quietly as he could. His bedroom was at the opposite end of the house from where Mae was sleeping upstairs, so it was unlikely she'd hear him. But he didn't want to deal with her so early, so he moved silently, grateful that Luther's new floors didn't creak even a little.

By the time he got downstairs, the sky was lightening and Luther had just arrived in his truck, along with a few of his crew. Guy shushed him, pointing upstairs as an explanation, and they both descended to the basement.

He was immediately annoyed.

True to her word, Mae had emptied the hole all the way down to its bottom. She'd successfully turned a small problem into a much bigger one, and they had nothing to show for it other than a deeper hole. She didn't seem to have found buried treasure or bones, so what had been the point of all that digging? Now he was left with the problem—and the expense—of filling it in again and making sure it would not be detected by his Wall Street buyer when he showed up to look at the house. Which would be, Guy reminded himself, tomorrow. He thanked Mae sarcastically in his mind and made a mental note to do it out loud the next time he saw her.

Luther unspooled Pearl, his tape measure, and hurled the end of it across the hole like an expert fly fisherman casting a lure. Guy marveled as Luther measured the hole in every direction, dancing around its edge, crouching at its lip, even jumping fearlessly across it with his tape measure thrashing around him like a bullwhip. Somehow, whenever Luther was measuring or planning construction, he turned into the world's shortest, roundest, plaid-est circus acrobat.

Finally, he straightened and his tape measure snapped back into its spool, which he snapped back onto the brim of his cap. The whole process had taken 15 or 20 seconds, and yet Guy felt as if Luther already had a topographic 3D rendering of the hole in his mind, accurate down to the cubic millimeter.

"What you've got here," Luther said, "is a hole."

Good. So they agreed on that. "Have you ever seen anything like it before?"

Luther tapped his bottom lip with one finger. "I have seen many holes. The hole itself is not the vexing part. What's confounding is the location. A hole like this in the basement... I can detect neither purpose nor function. It's just a hole." He crouched and ran his hand along the edge. "Impressive craftsmanship, though, I have to say. Somebody put a lot of care into this. It's actually rather beautiful in its way. Observe the sharpness of that edge. Like the blade of a knife. Look at the smoothness of the sides. Whoever dug this hole... it mattered to them. They cared to do it right. A craftsman dedicated weeks to this and made sure to leave not a single flaw. You have to admire it."

"So how do we cover it?"

"Dump some concrete over it."

"Great." Guy liked how easy that sounded. "When?"

"I can have my brother-in-law's truck here this afternoon."

Concrete was relatively cheap, and although Guy had planned not to do a pour in the basement, it was infinitely preferable to the alternative, which was his buyer being scared off by the hole. But a worry drifted into his mind, and he reluctantly brought it up. "If we do that, then we don't need to fix the sleeper walls, right?"

Luther shook his head. "Wrong. But I don't recall having a conversation about sleeper walls, do you?"

Guy liked how easy that sounded too. "I sure don't." He suddenly had an optimistic feeling, like problems that had seemed huge yesterday suddenly weren't so bad anymore.

Then Mae's clogs came down the stairs, and the feeling evaporated

Mae hadn't even fully stepped off the bottom stair before she was confronting them. "What are you doing?"

"We're going to cover the hole," Guy said like it was obvious. He didn't want to mislead her or give her hope that it wasn't going to happen. He wanted to be direct and forceful.

"You can't do that," she said with just as much force. "We don't even know what it is yet."

"Yes we do. It's a hole."

"But what's it for? What if it's important?"

Guy couldn't think of a better response than the one he'd already given. So he repeated it. "It's a hole."

Mae stormed past him and over to the hole. Luther, sensing that she was not to be interfered with, took a couple of steps back. He waited with his hands behind his back, looking a little sheepish.

She gave them both a fiery look. "Leave it. Until we know for sure what it is and why it's here, leave it open."

Luther looked at her, then at Guy. Then shuffled toward the stairs. "I'll wait outside," he said. He disappeared up the stairs like a rabbit into its hole, except upward.

Guy rubbed his eyes. He'd had enough of these discussions with Mae to know exactly how this would go. They'd had a similar fight over the leaded glass window bay in the stairwell. She'd insisted on restoring the original leaded glass, which he'd costed out at about $23,500. He'd countered with a proposal to use imitation leaded glass made with stick on Insta-Lead strips which looked just as good, and cost $17.99 for a pack of 72. He had let her win the argument, agreeing that it was infinitely preferable to retain the original hand-crafted old-world authenticity of the house. They'd parted on good terms. And then he'd gone to a craft store and bought a pack of the stick-on strips. She still hadn't noticed, even when one of the strips had peeled off and sat on the stairs for a whole day.

He fully expected that this discussion about the hole would go similarly. He prepared himself mentally for the ego bruising of letting her win, comforting himself with the knowledge that he wasn't actually letting her win at all. He would cover the hole with concrete no matter how the discussion went.

Still, he was curious. "Why? What's the point of keeping it open?"

The flicker in her face betrayed that she didn't know. She floundered for a reason. "Because it might be important."

"Okay. Name one purpose it could possibly have that would be important. What purpose would mean we should keep it open?"

He watched her mind working. Every turn of her mental gears was reflected in her face, the muscles around her eyes and her cheeks driven by a complex internal mechanism programmed to find an answer.

Guy tried to prompt her without it sounding sarcastic. "Trash hole? Torture hole? Water hole? Really deep hot tub? Maybe all of the above? Some kind of hot trash torturing water tub?" He hadn't meant to turn sarcastic, but it was hard not to be. He felt a little bad. "Is any of those a good reason to keep it open?"

Eventually, her mental mechanism ground to a halt. "I don't know," she said. "That's the point. We just don't know."

Guy decided to hit her with his best, most fully-formed logic. "Whoever buried that hole, they buried it for a reason. And I bet that reason is: because they didn't need it anymore. What- ever purpose this hole served—and I'm like you; I have no idea what that was. But whatever purpose it was, the hole did it already. It's done doing it. Maybe it used to have a point, but it doesn't anymore."

Her head was lowered like she didn't want to look at him. But she shifted her eyes toward him and looked like she didn't want to say what she was about to say. He found himself surprisingly curious. What could this be? "I heard something," she said.

He hunted for the relevance in that. It eluded him like a little butterfly that didn't want to be caught. "Something?" he said.

"When I was at the bottom of the hole yesterday. I heard something."

She was being deliberately vague, and it annoyed him. He had no time for this. "Heard what?" he said, trying not to sound impatient but coming off as exasperated instead. He felt bad again. But less bad.

She re-lowered her eyes. "A voice," she said.

Guy didn't feel bad anymore. She obviously wanted him to ask what it had said. But she just-as-obviously had imagined it, so it didn't matter what it had said. He felt he was cunningly undercutting her entire plan for this conversation by not asking for details.

"It said, 'Stop!'" she said, undercutting his clever undercut.

Guy was even less impressed than he'd expected to be. "That's it?"

"Or, 'Don't stop!' I'm not completely sure."

He tried to keep from guffawing. But he wanted to. "That seems like an important difference."

"Or it might have been, 'Doorstop!' At first I thought it said, 'Dustmop!' But now I'm pretty sure about the 'stop' part."

"So it was either 'stop' or 'don't stop'?"

"Or, 'Bookshop!'"

He paused for just long enough that he was pretty sure his silence said more than his words ever could. Then he followed it up with: "Okay, I think we're done here."

He tried to go upstairs after Luther, but she grabbed his elbow and held him back. "I know it sounds stupid," she pleaded. "And meaningless and crazy. All of that. But I heard it. And I just need some time to find out what it means. Just a little time, that's all. And if I don't find out anything, then you can do whatever you're doing and cover it up."

He didn't want to be persuaded. But something in her tone dug at him, and when he looked into her eyes, they didn't look crazed. They looked pleading. And sad. He couldn't bring himself to shut her down. Not completely.

He sighed. "The buyer is coming tomorrow. That means I need no hole in the basement floor by the end of the day. Plus the rental furniture is arriving this afternoon, and you need to arrange it. It was *your* idea."

"So I've got the rest of today." She seemed at least partially satisfied with that, even if she was pointedly ignoring the responsibility he'd just reminded her of.

"No," he said. "Concrete needs time to dry. We're pouring it *this afternoon.*"

She looked like she wanted to punch him. Her fists balled so hard that he could see her nails cutting into her palms. "So I've got a few hours?!" she raged.

He silently admitted that he'd been a little misleading. But out loud, he said: "It's more like two or three. Luther's probably already on his way to get the truck. And there's the rental furniture—"

"Fine," she said through gritted teeth. She made a sweeping motion at him with her fingers. "Get out. Go."

He figured out that she was trying to sweep him toward the stairs. "Go? Why?"

"Because I have things to do, and only three hours to do them."

"What are you going to do?"

She didn't answer.

And he quickly figured out what that meant. "You're going to listen for the voice? What do you think it's going to tell you?"

She waggled her fingers at the stairs again. "Go."

He obliged and backed toward the stairs. "'Gumdrop'?" he said, sensing that he was descending into outright mockery but feeling like she deserved it. "'Carrot Top'? 'Soda pop'? If it says 'belly flop', let me know." He let her scowl chase him up the stairs.

Chapter 9

Mae climbed down the ladder and sat cross-legged at the bottom of the hole. She closed her eyes, did some meditative breathing, and listened.

She wished for silence from everywhere outside the hole but never seemed to get it. Always there were work boots stomping across the floor overhead, or shouts from construction guys and painters outside, or vehicles arriving. Most of the sounds were distant and muffled by the walls and windows, but it was enough noise that she never really got the quiet she wanted.

After a while, she started to feel cold. She hadn't noticed the day before how chilly it was at the bottom of the hole. Had it actually been that cold before? Or was that new today? She wasn't sure. Maybe cold air just settled at the bottom of the hole because it was so low. But she didn't want to take the time to go find a jacket. So she hugged herself, tolerated the chill, and tried to listen.

Nothing. No sounds but the annoying ones from outside and above, and her own breathing. Not a whisper of stopping or not stopping.

It wasn't working. She kept her eyes closed, but she could feel the curved wall of the hole all around her, cold and looming. Surrounding her. Trapping her.

She shivered.

Besides the cold, an oppressive claustrophobia set in. And it rose steadily as if the hole was being pressurized.

As if the wall of the hole was tightening slowly around her, constricting. Not to squeeze her, but to force her downward.

A peristalsis forcing her deeper, deeper into the Earth—

Her eyes snapped open, and in spite of herself, she jumped to the ladder and scrambled back up to the basement floor. She dashed across to the wall where she stood with her back pressed against it, breathing fast, heart pounding.

She couldn't look down into the hole again. She knew it would appear the same. But it had *felt* different. Strange. Frightening. Whatever had spoken to her the night before had not felt like that.

Her legs trembled. She needed to sit down. She shifted over to a collection of junk in the corner: bits of broken furniture, half of a wardrobe filled with mouse droppings, even an old TV from maybe the very first generation of consumer TVs. Guy had complained about her keeping all this stuff and junking up the basement, but she was convinced she could restore, re-finish, and/or re-purpose some of it. She could absolutely do something that started with "re" to it. She sat on the corner of the old TV and tried to catch her breath.

Her leg dislodged another piece of junk and slid it off the TV onto the floor, and she bent to retrieve it. She'd forgotten this thing existed. A few months ago she'd seen one of the construction guys throwing it into a dumpster along with other trash from around the house, but she'd climbed up the side of the dumpster to recover it. She'd thought it might make a historic wall decoration for a rec room or something, but had never found a place for it.

She brushed dust and webs off it. It was a "for sale" sign, mostly intact despite being decades old. It had the agent's name at the top: "Honest Bob Kinson," and his phone number. And at the bottom in letters that were meant to look elegant: "This could be your forever home." It was apparently meant to be positive, but she could see other ways of taking it.

So at some point before the house fell into ruin, somebody had attempted to sell it with the help of somebody very honest named Bob. Whether they had succeeded or not was unclear, but for some reason, Honest Bob had never taken his sign back. He'd left it near the house, still with bits of a bird's nest stuck to the top.

The agent's phone number couldn't still belong to him. Could it? Did people keep their phone numbers that long?

She carried the sign upstairs and dug her phone out of her bag. She snapped a picture of the sign just in case and dialed the number so excitedly that it took her three tries to get it right.

"The number you have dialed is not in service..."

So people *didn't* keep their phone numbers that long. Or at least Honest Bob Kinson didn't.

It was time to get creative with Google.

She dug up three "B. Kinsons" in the county. None of the listings specified whether their particular B. Kinson was honest or not. That was something she'd have to discover for herself.

She thought about telling Guy where she was going so that maybe he'd give her more time. But it didn't seem likely. She'd be amazed if he even gave her the time he'd promised her. So she drove off on her Kinson quest and didn't say a word to Guy.

———

The first two Kinsons were not Honest Bob Kinson. She had no judgment on whether they were honest or not. They just weren't the particular honest one she was looking for, because both were women. One was on the phone and not a fan of door-answering, and the other loudly protested that she didn't want to join whatever religion Mae was canvassing for. She'd already joined several and wasn't interested in any other points of view.

The third "B. Kinson" she visited lived in a small, square home somewhere in the nebulous region between Bethel and Danbury. A long driveway barely wide enough for a car led up the front. A single chimney poked out the side. A lawn, almost as small as the house, lay in front. She thought this couldn't possibly be the right one because a real estate agent, even a former one, would surely live in a place with curb appeal. This place was small, bland, and utterly dwarfed in both size and style by every other house in the neighborhood. Even the plastic toddler playhouse on the lawn across the street made a stronger impression.

Still, to leave no stone unturned, she rang the doorbell.

It took a long time for B. Kinson to answer. And when he opened the door, he seemed surprised to see someone standing there, as if he'd hoped waiting that long would mean she'd have left already.

This B. Kinson was a squatty man of at least 80 who looked like he'd been asleep, though he wore a wrinkled and dusty suit as if he'd just gotten home from work. His slicked-back white hair was matted in places and standing on end in others. His face was pitted and cracked like a leather jacket worn long after it should have been thrown out, and even with the breeze outside he smelled slightly charred and acrid, like wet dog and halitosis.

Mae got straight to the point. "Hi, sorry. Are you Bob Kinson?"

He half-closed the door and peered at her suspiciously through the crack. "Is this a legal thing? Are you serving something?"

"No, I'm not. I'm looking for Honest Bob Kinson."

He seemed to brighten at the name like he enjoyed being called that and hadn't been for a long time. He smoothed his hair and opened the door the rest of the way. "I used to be. Well, I mean, I still *am* honest. Just haven't been Honest Bob for a while. Just a Bob who is honest. Sorry, that's complicated. And you are?"

She held out a hand. His handshake was soft and his grip weak. His hand was cold and dry, like stale bread kept in the fridge. She fought to ignore it. "Mae," she said. Now that she was here, she didn't know the simplest way to lay out why she'd come. "I'm sorry to disturb you. This is awkward. I live in a house that I think you sold some time ago, and I wanted to ask you about it."

"I don't do that anymore," Bob said. "I'm retired. You can find lots of active agents on the Internet thing if you look."

"No, I'm not looking for an agent. I wanted to ask you about my house on Whitemarsh Road."

When he'd opened the door, Bob had already been white. He turned suddenly whiter, like a chameleon trying to blend into a snowbank. She saw him shiver so hard his knees almost gave out. "Whitemarsh Road?" he whispered.

Mae felt bad for saying it. She worried that she was killing an old man right here on his doorstep. But she pressed on gently. "Um... 9140 Whitemarsh Road?"

Bob shivered again so hard that it shook loose some of his white hair despite the volume of gel slicking it back. His face turned grave and he backed away from the door again and pushed it almost closed ahead of him, a slow and deliberate slam. "I don't know what you're talking about," he said.

But he stopped with the door still open just a sliver. "Aw fudge," he said heavily. "Yes I do. I do know what you're talking about. I know the place."

Apparently the "honest" part of "Honest Bob" had kicked in. Mae went with it. "Can I ask you some questions about it?"

He blinked a few times through the tiny crack of the door. "I can't right now. I'm very busy. Just in the middle of a lot of things. Don't have the time." And he pushed the door closed.

Two seconds later he pulled it open again. "That's not true. I'm not doing anything. I fell asleep watching *The Price is Right*. What day is it?"

"Um..."

He swung the door open wide. "We can talk on the porch. I think I have some French macaroons if you'd enjoy those. Maybe some Scottish shortbread." He winced and slapped his forehead with the heel of his hand, like the internal pressure to stay honest was causing him actual pain. "No, no, none of that is true. I have birthday cake Oreos."

"You, um, also don't have a porch," Mae pointed out.

Chapter 10

B ob unfolded some lawn chairs with barely enough fabric left to take the weight of a human, and deposited a plate of colorful Oreos on a little table between them. All despite Mae's insistence that she didn't want to sit, or eat Oreos. But she sat and ate an Oreo because she wanted to make him comfortable and ensure that he'd be forthcoming.

It seemed to work because it was Bob who brought up the subject again. "So, how long have you lived there?" he asked. He barely looked at her, but rather stared across the street at the toddler playhouse, maybe wondering how much he could list it for.

"I don't really. I mean, I do. I've been staying there."

He frowned. "You own it?"

"Well, half of it. It's complicated."

He nodded as if she'd just confirmed something for him. He looked over at her and gave her a half-smile that seemed almost sympathetic. "Everybody looks for their forever home. You found yours. You just don't know it yet."

Mae didn't know what that meant. But she decided that what he thought about her living arrangement didn't matter. "Who was your client? Who did you sell it for?"

"Me. Bought it myself from a trust figuring I could get way more than they were asking. That didn't work out. Never did sell it."

"Couldn't find a buyer?"

"No surprise there." He paused. "You know what I mean. That place has a *history*." He lowered his voice for dark emphasis on the last word.

Mae made a guess. "What, like, somebody died in it?"

"Several people," Bob clarified. "Many. Lots. I don't know the exact number." He helped himself to another Oreo, adding more black crumbs to the ones already gathering above his upper lip.

Mae sat back in her lawn chair, pondering, and then decided sitting back wasn't a good idea because the lawn chair felt like it might snap closed with her in it. She sat forward again. "Why so many? What did they die of?"

"Murder. Suicide. Some of them just up and disappeared. Never found." He looked over at her again, harder this time. "But I bet you can guess where they disappeared to."

Mae's heart skipped. Had he really just said that? Did it mean what she thought it meant? The way he was looking at her now chilled her. A knowing look, like they were both members of a very exclusive club.

She said nothing and hoped the look on her face would encourage him to clarify.

He likewise kept his eyes on her, waiting for her to say it. But it was Bob who broke first. "You've been to the basement, right?"

There it was. Bob knew about the hole. But how much did he know? Mae leaned forward in her chair and then decided that wasn't a good idea either because the chair almost buckled and spilled her onto the lawn. "The hole?" she said.

"Of course the hole," Bob said.

Mae's *Silence of the Lambs* scenario snapped into focus. "Somebody kept people in there as prisoners? Until they died?"

Bob looked flustered, like what she was saying made no sense to him. He picked up another Oreo and twisted one side of it off and on. "I don't think so. How would that work?"

Mae became less certain that she'd figured this all out. "So they just fell in and nobody came to rescue them?"

Bob's perplexed expression deepened. He used the detached side of the Oreo like a spatula to scrape the frosting off. "How would anybody rescue them? I'm not sure that's even possible."

"I don't know. With a ladder?"

"Miss, I don't think they make ladders that tall."

Mae started to wonder if they were talking about the same hole.

Bob sighed resignedly like he was the unlucky one forced to tell her a relative had died, or she was getting fired. He put the mutilated Oreo back on the plate. "I suppose somebody needs to tell you. You'll find out eventually, but things will go a lot quicker if I just tell you."

Mae gripped the arms of her chair. And quickly decided that this, too, was a bad idea because there were sharp, rust-laden bolts sticking out of the plastic on the bottom. "Tell me what?"

Bob cleared his throat and unsuccessfully smoothed his hair. He hopped his chair a few times until he was almost facing directly at her, and he leaned forward. He paused for a long time, searching for words.

Mae waited. Somewhere down the street, a dog barked.

Bob finally found his words. He spoke slowly. "You own the house now," he said. "So you own the hole."

So far, not very illuminating. Obvious, even. "Uh huh," she said.

"That means you have to do it," Bob said gravely. "You won't like it. But you have no choice."

"No choice for what?"

Bob seemed to ignore her question or to think she'd figure out the answer for herself. He leaned forward even more so she could smell the birthday cake frosting on his breath. "You need to throw someone down the hole," he said.

Mae felt her jaw drop. She didn't believe him, of course, but she'd never heard anybody say anything so dark and so absurd with such sincere gravity. "W…" she stammered. "W… why would I do that?"

"Because the house won't let you leave. Not until you give it what it wants. So you have two choices: either you throw someone down the hole, or you throw yourself down it." He sat back in his chair, picked up the rearranged Oreo, and ate the whole thing. "That's it," he said around the cookie.

Mae wasn't sure how you're supposed to respond when somebody said something on that level of crazy. She didn't say anything for a long time while she thought about it. Finally, she chose not to humor him and to remain rational. "I'm not going to do either of those," she said.

"Yes you are," he said frankly.

"I won't."

"You will. Or you can stay in the house forever. But you won't want that either. When people try to do that, that's when they start to lose their minds. And then the murders and suicides start, and it gets unpleasant. I guarantee, the other two choices are preferable."

Mae felt like she was missing whole chunks of this story and wasn't entirely sure he'd be able to fill them in. But she tried anyway. "So, let's say I do put someone in the hole. What happens to them?"

Bob pointed at her as if she'd just made an excellent argument and he wanted to congratulate her for it. "Now that, I can't help you with. I've never been thrown down the hole, by me or by anyone else. So I don't know. But, I mean, I can guess."

"Please."

"Okay. One possibility is: they fall for a long while and then they hit the bottom. Not so bad. It's over quick. The other possibility is: their bodies are consumed and their souls are enslaved for eternity.

Not as quick. Kind of goes on forever. Still... not so bad when you think about it. But I try not to."

Mae marveled at how this story had started in a very dark place and yet somehow found even darker corners to slink into. But even if she accepted it based on his logic, there was still something that didn't make sense. Several somethings, in fact. There were whole big reams of somethings that weren't consistent and even made her start to think they were talking about a different house altogether. But whether it was the right house or not, she felt strongly that she needed to get away from Honest Bob Kinson. He was perhaps a little *too* honest.

"We could move out," she said.

He shook his head. "It won't let you."

"We can sell it."

"You can try. It won't let you. It will do everything in its power to make sure the house stays yours until you do one of those two things."

"We could just walk away."

"Can you afford to just walk away? How much money do you have tied up in that place?"

All of it, she thought. And for Guy, even more than that.

"Hold on," Mae said, still somehow optimistic that all of this would make sense in the end. "You owned the house. So... you had the same choice we do?"

The physical response was immediate and alarming. Bob lowered his eyes and sank back into his chair. His hands shivered on his knees like he knew where this line of questioning was going, and he didn't want it to go there.

Mae found that she was tense. She could hear the pounding of her heart in her whisper. "What did you do?"

Bob smoothed the wrinkles on his knees, then fidgeted with his fingers, twisting them around each other like there were globs of frosting on them that he couldn't get off. He said nothing for five or six breaths.

Finally, he let his hands come to rest on his knees and looked straight at her. "I just want to be clear: I never lied to those people. Honest Bob never lies. It's on the sign."

Mae shivered. The same dark chill she'd felt at the bottom of the hole. "Bob... you pushed someone into the hole?"

"I didn't lie to them. Never once." It seemed to be the only way he could cope with the memory. But the fact that remembering it caused him pain didn't earn him any sympathy with her. Had he shoved someone into the hole and left them there? Was he the *Silence of the Lambs* lotion guy?

Mae felt thrown off balance. The world tilted 40 degrees and tried to dump her off her chair, but she clung on. She'd never talked to a murderer before. Now she might be sitting across from one, eating his birthday cake Oreos. "Who was it?" she asked when what she really wanted to do was get up and run. She wasn't afraid that he'd push her down a hole too; she just didn't want to be in his presence anymore. Now that she knew about it, murder radiated off of him like a pungent stink that invaded her other senses. Maybe it was why he served such sweet-smelling cookies.

"I didn't get their names," he said. He'd already given up trying to look apologetic. He was just stating facts now. "Their car is probably still in the gulch in front of the house."

Mae shook her head. "We never found any car on the property."

"Well unless somebody else found it after me, it's there."

She shook her head again. She was beginning to think he was making all of this up, and that she'd be greatly relieved if he was.

"Never mind," he said. "You're missing the important part. I never lied to them. Honest Bob doesn't lie. It's right there on the sign."

"So... you *told* them you were going to push them into the hole?"

"No, see, now you're getting hung up on details. Put all that aside. Did I ever once say anything to them about the house that was false? No. I told them about the voices, I told them about the blood stains. I told them about everything, as required by state regulations and by the nickname on my sign."

So he'd heard voices too. But blood stains? The house had been in such a state of ruin when they bought it, it might have been impossible to spot things like that. But that was not foremost in her mind. "And then you pushed them into the hole and left them there?"

"Well, I wouldn't say I left them there."

"So you went back for them?"

"Why? I couldn't exactly go down after them, could I?"

"If you felt bad, you could have helped them get out again."

He blinked at her. "How?"

Exasperation crept into her voice. "Ladder? Rope?"

He blinked at her again like she had switched to another language and failed to inform him. "You keep saying that. I still don't think they make ladders that long. Or ropes, come to think of it."

"Twelve feet?!"

This time, his brow furrowed so deeply that she thought the skin of his forehead might rip open and slingshot off his skull. "Twelve feet?" He shuffled forward in his chair toward her, and she instinctively pushed her chair back. She didn't want him closer to her. "It only goes twelve feet?"

"How deep was it for you?"

He was no longer listening to her. His eyes flicked back and forth. "Do you know what that means?" He was suddenly animated. Excited. It took years off of his face. "Somebody closed it. Must have been somebody who owned it after me. They found a way and they closed it! I didn't think it was possible, but somebody did it! That's fantastic!"

Mae's mind raced back to when she'd arrived at the bottom of the hole. Had she imagined the floor sounding hollow? Or had it actually sounded hollow? She couldn't convince herself either way. "So... that's not the bottom?"

Bob chuckled. "Twelve feet? Not even close." He smiled and grabbed her hand. "That's good news. You may be better off than I thought. You can get out of the house and have a normal life without murdering anyone. That's good." He squeezed her hand like he was a doctor telling her she'd just beaten a disease.

But there was more. He leaned closer and spoke urgently. "From this point on, the only thing that matters is: do *not* open that hole."

Chapter 11

G uy wondered where Mae was and if she'd found out anything interesting. But more than that, he wondered why he'd been forced to set up the rental furniture instead of her. When the truck arrived with it, she was nowhere in sight. So while the guys from the shop were happy to bring it inside for him, he had to arrange it himself. He knew nothing about feng shui or any other guiding principle of furniture arranging, but he did his best. And, luckily, he'd only been able to afford enough to stage the entryway and living room. If he'd had to arrange the upstairs as well, he might have lost his mind. And he had other things to lose his mind about—like concrete.

They weren't going to fill the hole with concrete after all. Luther had estimated that the hole would require about an extra eleven cubic yards of the stuff. That was somewhere around $1300 just to fill the hole, which was on top of what it was already costing to cover the rest of the basement floor. But of course, Luther had a second estimate. In this case, he pointed out that if they covered the hole with plywood and reinforced it a little, then poured the concrete over that, it would save the $1600. There was literally no reason not to do it.

Once they'd agreed on the plan, Luther hinted that if Guy had anything he wanted to hide, now would be a good time to put it in the hole because, after today, it would be permanently entombed beneath the basement floor. Guy got the strong impression that Luther was talking about corpses, and that he had done that kind of thing before. He had once told Guy that he'd built a sun deck for a low-ranking member of the Providence Mafia, and now Guy wondered if the relationship went somewhere beyond deck-making.

While Luther went to get his brother-in-law's cement mixer truck, Guy went down to the basement with some fresh sheets of three-quarter inch plywood sheathing and some iron rods for support. The plywood seemed like more than enough to cover the hole, and Luther had loaned him his tape measure, Pearl, and a rotary saw which did not possess a given name, so that Guy could trim the wood to the right size.

Guy stood at the edge of the hole and looked into it. It remained as resolutely empty and pointless as it had always been. He wondered again: why? What possible purpose could it have served? Had somebody planned to do exactly what Luther had suggested and cram a corpse down there, then cover it with dirt? If that's what it was, then where was the corpse? And why was the hole so smooth and perfectly round? Who dug a corpse-hole like that, and put so much effort into finishing the edges? Corpse-holes, he imagined, needed to be dug in a hurry with shovels, and should really be rectangular to accommodate the lying-down shape of the corpse. And why was he thinking about this? He had work to do.

He crouched and slid one of the sheets of plywood over one side of the hole to see how much it would cover.

While he was doing that, Luther's tape measure came unhooked from his belt.

And it tumbled into the hole.

It hit the bottom with a dull *thump,* and various pebbles and clumps of soil resting around it bounced and settled.

Guy cursed silently, then out loud. He couldn't leave it there. It was Luther's tape measure. Guy knew that Luther had children, but Guy didn't know what their names were because Luther never talked about them. He talked about his tape measure every day, and Guy knew its name well. It had Luther's initials engraved on it. Guy had always suspected they might be Luther's father's initials, and his grandfather's as well. It might have been passed down through generations, an heirloom for a dynasty of construction contractors. It would explain why Luther kissed it sometimes.

Guy knew he would have to go get it. Leaving it buried under concrete was not an option. And asking Luther to go rescue it—and Guy thereby admitting that he had been careless with it—was only slightly better. He would have to get it himself, and before Luther got back with the cement mixer.

Mae had considerately lifted the ladder and left it next to the hole. Or maybe she had done that to discourage Guy from going into the hole. The ladder was splattered with thick globs of paint, plaster, spackle, and mud from years of construction work, and Guy wasn't sure which globs were dry and which his hands might stick to. He handled it gingerly, holding only onto clear spots, and maneuvered its feet over the lip of the hole, lifted the top end, and started to lower it.

When the ladder was just a couple of inches down, a gust of cool air brushed against his right ear. It was like a whisper from someone an inch away.

Guy was so startled that, without meaning to, he let go of the ladder. And it fell.

In the frozen time while it dropped, he waited for the expected sharp *thud* of it hitting the bottom. But that wasn't the sound it made. Instead, it made a hollow *thump,* accompanied by an inexplicable *crack.* Then it settled against the side of the hole and Guy was able to grab the top and keep it stable.

He glanced around for the source of the cold air. Was there a crack around one of the windows that he hadn't sealed? He'd have to check.

Right now, though, he was more concerned about the sounds the ladder had made when it hit bottom. Those sounds were strange. They weren't right. There wasn't anything in the hole that should have sounded like that. And it made him uneasy, especially after just having something invisible blow on his ear.

Going down the ladder was now the very last thing he wanted to do, right down the list below a dental colonoscopy. But Luther would be back any minute with liquid rock on wheels. Guy had to hurry.

He pivoted himself around the top of the ladder and planted one foot onto a rung. He bounced on it, pressing the ladder into the bottom to test its stability.

Was it his imagination, or had the bottom of the hole moved beneath his weight? He could have sworn that it had sunk half an inch or more, and then bounced up again when he pulled his weight off.

Now he was alarmed. The bottom of a hole shouldn't move like that. Especially not right before he was about to step on it. But it had to be his imagination. Didn't it?

He planted the other foot on the rung and tested his weight once more with a little bounce. If the bottom was going to move in a serious way, he wanted it to happen now, while he could still hold onto the edge.

And he was halfway convinced that the bottom *had* moved again. What was it made of? Had somebody lined it with something soft?

He started down the ladder. Going slow seemed like the best idea so as not to cause any undue stress on the bottom. But going fast also seemed like the best idea, to keep from straining the bottom for too long. He didn't know which was the *best* best idea. So he went slow for the first few rungs, then hurried the rest of the steps.

He stepped off the bottom with excessive caution and tested his weight on the floor of the hole. He unmistakably felt some bounce to it, and he couldn't work out why that might be. He grabbed Luther's tape measure and clipped it to his belt. And he knew he should just climb out with it, his mission accomplished. But curiosity tugged at him.

And something more than curiosity as well. Because maybe the hollowness beneath his feet meant that somebody had buried something under there. And if they had, then that thing was either incriminating or valuable. Or both. And it was the "valuable" option that intrigued him. He didn't expect pirate treasure, really, but he also didn't completely *not* expect it.

His phone vibrated in his jacket pocket, and he snatched it out sharply, trying to let it know how much it had annoyed him. The call display told him it was Luther, probably letting Guy know that his brother-in-law had given him grief for borrowing the cement mixer. Guy had never met Luther's brother-in-law, but he seemed to have an endless supply of construction equipment and an even more endless supply of complaints when Luther borrowed it.

"Luther," Guy said, aware of the impatience in his voice and hoping Luther was aware of it too.

"The cement mixer is en route," Luther said. Guy could hear the growl of the truck's engine in the background. "Estimated time…"

"No rush," Guy said. "I need more time. There's something weird down here."

"Could you be slightly more specific with regards to 'weird?'"

"No," Guy said, and disconnected. He didn't want to say what he hoped for and have it be wrong.

He would do a quick dig, find out what was under there, and still have time to climb up and put the plywood cover on. Maybe, if he was very lucky, with pirate treasure in-hand.

He climbed back up and found Luther's shovel, still propped against the wall from Guy's attempted trench-digging and Mae's successful hole-digging. Then he took off his jacket and left it on the basement floor, because this could be strenuous work. He carried the shovel down the ladder and started poking the bottom of the hole with it, hunting for a weakness. It all seemed equally solid, but he started to wonder if it might be a kind of lid that he could pry off. So he poked around the perimeter with the edge of the shovel, hunting for a gap that he could fit it under and start to pry.

He found one on the side nearest the outside wall of the house. Not really a gap, but a spot where he could see the edge of whatever he was standing on. So it truly wasn't the bottom of the hole. It was a kind of false floor.

A false floor meant somebody was hiding something. His heart beat faster. He stopped prying and cocked his head sideways to listen for any sign of Luther's cement truck arriving. He could hear nothing but crows having an argument outside. And, he now noticed, his phone vibrating in his jacket, up where he couldn't hope to reach it. He hoped it was Luther calling to say he'd gotten into an accident and the cement truck would be delayed.

But he couldn't count on that, so he picked up the pace. He jammed the shovel hard into the hairline gap he'd created on the edge of the false floor and leaned on the shovel with all his weight. The floor resisted. It was enough to make him fear that he'd break the end of the shovel off. Which was a significant fear, because if the tape measure was Luther's child, the shovel was its brother.

The gap widened, a quarter inch at most. It was enough to let him jam the shovel in deeper and lean again. This time, he sat on the handle and bounced. He could feel the false floor giving way under his weight, slowly prying out of place.

And a tiny inkling of worry crept into his mind. He wondered: should he have considered that maybe there might be a significant drop under the false floor? What would happen if the floor broke under him?

As soon as he thought about it, it happened.

A crumbling. Pebbles breaking away, dust coming loose and hissing as it sifted through a gap, wood and plaster snapping. A *twanging* like bed springs breaking under strain.

Then he felt it. The false floor sagged under his weight, and for a sickening moment he thought it would collapse completely and he'd find out the hard way exactly how much space was under it. But some merciful component of its structure refused to give way.

As the surface crumbled, holes appeared. And, inexplicably, cold air blasted up through them under pressure, jets so cold that they made geysers of condensation in the air. The cold stung his hands and face and he couldn't escape it as more and more holes broke open around him.

That wasn't right. That wasn't right at all.

He could see now as the surface broke apart that there was nothing but chicken wire supporting the whole thing, and the wire was taking his weight. But everything else was coming apart in chunks like old plaster. He was left suspended on all fours in the middle, watching the rest of the false floor crumble around him and fall away. The chicken wire cut into his hands and swayed beneath him like the world's deadliest hammock.

For the first time, he dared to look down through the wire at what was beneath him. And he saw only darkness. An unfathomable, impossible depth. His stomach lurched, and vertigo spun his vision around him.

And then even the wire started to break off. He could see that the wire was held to the sides of the hole with what looked like drywall screws. Some ends of the chicken wire were coiled around the screws as if that would be enough to hold any weight you might throw at it. But it wasn't enough, because the ends of the wire started to break free from screw after screw, making coiled *pinging* noise as each end popped off.

He clung to the chicken wire, frozen, following with his eyes as the ends *twanged* free along the circumference all around him. As his weight transferred onto fewer and fewer strands, the wires that didn't break loose started yanking the screws out of the wall instead. He didn't dare move for fear of speeding up the process, hoping desperately that if he stayed still, some portion of the chicken wire would stay bolted to the wall and he could at least hang here until someone came and found him.

He looked down through the wire again, a tiny fraction of curiosity cutting through the panic. He still could see nothing. The hole appeared bottomless. He wondered if he fell, what country would he pop out in? What nationality were the people who would marvel at the man who came hurtling out of a hole in the ground?

He couldn't stay here. His entire body weight was supported by two, maybe three thin strands of wire and some screws that were already visibly sliding out of their holes. He had to get back to the ladder. It was miraculously still standing, its bottom rung balanced across two thin strands of wire. He could try to reach it, or try the comparatively easier plan of falling.

He crawled, trying to ignore how the chicken wire swayed under him and how he could feel himself sinking lower even as he tried to move higher. He paid attention to nothing other than the crawling, but he couldn't escape the awareness of how cold he was. The air coming up from below was frigid. Not just cool, like you would expect in a cave. And not just a layer of cooler air. An actual cold wind. Like he was dangling above an active air conditioning vent.

He filed that away to consider later because right now all he could actively consider was dying. He considered that he didn't want to do it.

The chicken wire hammock rocked under him and the wire dug hard into his hands, hurting more with every inch he crawled. Yet somehow he made it to the ladder. He had a moment of relief.

But he realized quickly that if he lifted a hand to grab it, he'd lose his balance.

He wasn't going to make it.

Chapter 12

Mae navigated the snaking path of Whitemarsh Road back to the house. The road here was narrow, with trees pressing in close on both sides, so she drove with extra caution for fear of taking some of them out. She'd never forgive herself if a tree died because of her reckless driving.

From this point on, the only thing that matters is: do not *open that hole.*

She was still chilled from her visit with Honest Bob. She didn't believe any of it, of course. But he had. He'd believed so hard that he'd murdered people. Thrown them down the hole as a sacrifice to let himself escape. It was insanity.

But she didn't believe the hole had the kind of power he'd described. Or that it demanded sacrifice.

Of course she didn't.

Of course.

She rounded a corner and a dark shape suddenly loomed in the road ahead of her. A truck, much too big for this narrow road, lumbering along like a growling, overfed bear. On this road it could be miles before she had a chance to get around it, and she wasn't sure she could be that patient. Guy might have jumped the schedule and started covering the hole by now.

But that would be... good? Wouldn't it? That would mean the hole was sealed up even better than before. None of the bad stuff Bob had told her about would need to happen. Not that any of it was true. Because it wasn't.

She forced herself to relax, not speed, and wait for a safe opportunity to get around the truck.

She was so focused on relaxing that, for a mile or so, she didn't even notice what kind of truck it was. A cement mixer. Their house was the only construction out here, so could it be Luther?

A clear stretch of straight road appeared. Instead of going around the truck, she pulled up alongside the cab and rolled her passenger side window down.

Luther took a few seconds to notice her, then opened his window and stuck his elbow out to lean toward her. His round, bearded face under his baseball cap leaning out the window looked exactly how everybody would think a man driving a cement mixer should look.

"What's the cement mixer for?" she called across to him.

"Basement," Luther called back.

Mae tensed. The hole had been filled with dirt before, and it had held that weight. Would the weight of concrete be too much? Could it break through and re-open the hole?

She needed to caution Guy. Maybe they could check before they poured.

"Where's Guy?" she called.

"Basement," Luther repeated.

"What's he doing?"

"I think he's digging!"

Alarm shot through Mae's nerves. She almost veered off into the ditch.

The road curved into the trees ahead. There was no telling what was coming at them around the bend. She'd have to pass the truck or fall back. What Luther said next would decide which.

"Why is he digging?!"

Luther shrugged and shook his head. "As I recall, he said he found something unusual at the bottom of—"

Mae jammed her foot down, shot ahead of the truck, and drove faster than she'd ever driven before.

———

She was just a mile away from the house when it started to rain. She hoped it would remain a light drizzle, but it quickly and belligerently became a torrential downpour of huge drops that attacked the roof of the car like an army of woodpeckers. She had to concentrate to keep the car on the road. And the rain only seemed to get heavier as she drove.

This is crazy, she kept telling herself. So what if Guy digs at the bottom of the hole? Nothing Bob had said could be true.

But the distant, disembodied voice still rolled around in her head.

Stop.

Or, maybe, *don't stop.*

Which was it? Had she heard the "don't," muffled and indistinct? Or had it been only a sigh, an inhalation before the "stop?"

She didn't slow down all the way to the house and then fishtailed around the corner into the driveway.

She quickly discovered that the driveway was not made for driving fast. It was barely made for driving slow. It seemed to have been specifically designed to discourage driving up it at all. But she hurtled up it at Formula One speeds, kicking up great plumes of mud in her wake. She weaved through the trees that lined the drive, their branches slapping against the windshield, and struggled to keep the car from skidding right off the driveway and into one of the ditches.

A hundred feet shy of the house, she finally lost control. The driveway went out from under her wheels and the car skidded sideways. She wrenched the wheel hard to the side and stood on the brake, and for a minute she feared that the car would flip over. But somehow it stayed on its wheels. But just as she started to regain control, it plunged into a depression in the ground, pitching down a steep slope through the trees. The brakes and steering wheel no longer obeyed her and she cursed in frustration, feeling like she was plummeting off a cliff. But a tree loomed up suddenly and caught the corner of her front bumper, spinning the car through a quarter turn and finally stopping it halfway down the slope.

She sat and caught her breath, dazed and wondering if she'd hurt anything. She didn't have any pain, but there was always a chance that she'd severed her spine. She was about to reach behind her back and feel for the break when she spotted something through the rain on the windshield.

There was another car further down the hill.

It was deep in the ditch and overgrown, impossible to see from the house or from the drive. It looked like it had been there for decades, and the wild plants in the ditch had slowly overtaken it, transforming it into part of the landscape. But it was a car. She could see the shape of it outlined in weeds and vines. She could even see one of the tires fully exposed like a perfectly round stone protruding from the ground.

Their car is probably still in the gulch in front of the house.

Living up to his name, Honest Bob hadn't lied about that.

Had he been honest about everything else as well?

Then what if Guy had already opened the hole?

She threw open her door, toppled out into the rain and mud, and scrambled up the slope, back toward the driveway, and the house.

Cold air flooded out of the basement door, carrying the heavy stink of wet earth. Something was seriously wrong. And she was certain that she knew what.

Guy had opened the hole.

But she refused to give up hope. Even if Guy had opened it, maybe they could close it again. Somebody else had covered it once, so they could too.

She plunged down the stairs, fighting against the wind to reach the bottom.

"Guy?!" she yelled as she erupted out of the stairs and onto the basement floor.

She couldn't see him. Just his jacket on the floor. He'd been here, but where was he?

The frigid air, as she'd predicted, was blasting out of the hole. It made a sound like a blizzard heard through holes in a garage door. A circle of frost had formed on the ceiling directly above the hole, and it was spreading outward as more icy air blasted up.

"Guy?!" she called again, at the top of her lungs this time so he'd hear her over the roar of the wind.

And this time, he responded.

"Mae?!"

He sounded surprised. Whether he was surprised to hear anyone, or just surprised that it was her, she couldn't tell.

His voice had come from the hole.

She scrambled to the edge, but the cold and the sheer force of the wind forced her to drop to her knees and crawl the rest of the way.

Guy was about ten feet down, right where the bottom of the hole had previously been. But the bottom was almost completely gone. He was clinging instead to what looked like a narrow bridge of twisted wires, so precarious that it swung violently in the wind. She couldn't imagine how he kept his balance, but it seemed to take all his strength because he was on his hands and knees and he looked exhausted, half-frozen, and terrified.

He spotted her and she saw a flash of relief and desperation on his face. "Grab the ladder!" he yelled up at her.

She hadn't even noticed that the ladder was still there, impossibly balanced on the end of the wire bridge. It teetered with every sway of the wire, and she was amazed that it hadn't fallen already.

She drew back from the edge to get the brunt of the cold blast out of her face, and crawled around the hole until she found the top of the ladder scraping across the edge as the bottom of it swayed side to side. She grabbed the top rung and gripped it hard, steadying the ladder, and lay down flat on her stomach so she could pull back and hold it there with the most resistance.

"Got it!" she yelled.

From her spot away from the edge she couldn't look down to see him coming up. But she could feel vibrations coming up the ladder and she sensed his weight. She gripped with all her strength, but the cold blast quickly numbed her fingers and she didn't think she could hold on for long. She thought about yelling "hurry!" but decided that he probably knew to do that.

Finally, his head rose above the lip of the hole. And he immediately spotted the distress she was in trying to hold the ladder. He climbed up one more rung and then sprang off the ladder and landed at the edge of the hole. He immediately collapsed onto his back.

She released her grip on the ladder and it toppled. She heard it grind and clang against the side of the hole as it bounced once somewhere beneath them. Just once. And then nothing. It was gone. She never heard it hit a bottom.

Guy took her elbow and helped her to her feet. "Let's go," he said. He sounded calmer than she expected him to. Certainly much calmer than she felt.

She turned and followed him up the stairs two, even three at a time. The stairs trembled beneath her feet and the drywall next to her cracked beneath her hand, but she sprinted upward and wished Guy would go faster or get out of her way.

They sprinted down the hall with the cold wind pushing at their backs. Then through the entryway, onto the porch, and out into the rain. They ran across the yard in the mud, all the way to the big hunk of rock by the side of the driveway. Both of them stopped and leaned back against it.

And then, like someone had flipped a great cosmic switch, everything stopped. The roar of wind from the basement cut off. The vibrations in the ground settled and went still. And even the rain, torrential only seconds ago, died out like a faucet had been shut off.

For a moment, it felt like nothing had happened.

Mae and Guy breathed fast and stood frozen with their hands on the rock.

The quiet was suffocating. Maybe it only felt that way because they'd just come out of the roaring gale downstairs, or maybe it actually was unnaturally quiet. It pressed against them. But the silence was only from the front, where the house was. Mae could still hear birds, and the wind in the trees, and distant traffic—all of it behind them, none of it in front. In a bubble around the house, there was nothing. It was as if the house existed separate from the world around it, and all vibrations in the air passed through it unimpeded.

Except for one thing. Mae became aware of a high-pitched *trilling*, muffled. A rhythmic pulse, buried enough that at first she couldn't tell where it was coming from. Was it from the house, or from nearer to them? Was it a shriek? An alarm? A wild animal caught in a trap? Was it the screams of souls escaped from the underworld?

As it grew louder, she figured out that, like all the other sounds, it was behind them. She spun to look around the rock and down the driveway.

It was the reversing alarm on Luther's cement mixer truck, backing up toward the house.

Mae and Guy watched as it pulled up right behind them. Its air brakes squealed and its engine finally shut off. The giant concrete drum kept revolving ponderously like an elephant turning over and over in its sleep.

Luther climbed down from the cab and squelched over to them. Neither Mae nor Guy attempted to explain anything to him. They all stood and looked at the house and let their feet sink into the mud.

The house lurked in front of them, resolutely silent.

After a while, Luther said, "Are we still doing this?"

Guy shook his head. Mae could still see hints of raw terror in his eyes. "I don't think so," he said.

Luther nodded. He didn't question why. Maybe he could guess from the looks on their faces and from the unnatural way the house lurked in silence.

"You're still paying for the truck," he said.

Chapter 13

They stood outside for a long time, both of them afraid to go back in. 5:00 came and went, and Luther took the truck away with all the concrete that Guy was paying for. It barely registered with Guy. It felt like a small problem compared to what had just happened in the house.

But he didn't understand what had happened in the house, or how big a problem it was. Because he was still afraid to go in.

The house, which he'd worked so hard to bring to life, appeared dead. He couldn't see anything different about the structure. Nothing was broken, nothing had collapsed. All his renovations and repairs were still there. But it looked different. Drained of color. Soulless. And it terrified him, both on the level of primal dread and because it was a serious impediment to selling the house. Nobody shopped for a house that had "essence of mausoleum."

Guy's mind was threatening to break. Up until now, it had always had a firm mental footing in the real world, and had never been forced to consider anything supernatural, paranormal, supernormal, or paranatural. He didn't believe in ghosts, bigfoots, or Nessies. He'd never been to a psychic, never had his palm read, never had his aura photographed. The world was a bunch of shaved monkeys living on a rock and that was pretty much it. Everything else was wackos making up stories.

But with what they'd just witnessed, his mind was losing all that solid footing and threatened to retreat into a dark corner. He desperately wanted to find a nail somewhere and hammer it just to reassure himself that some part of the world still made sense.

It was closing in on 6:00 and the sun had just slunk away below the horizon when Mae finally broke their silence. "We can't just not go in," she said.

Guy scoffed. He didn't mean to, but the scoff just scoffed out. "You want to go in there?"

"It looks like it's calmed down," she said. "It's been quiet for a while."

Guy resisted the urge to say "too quiet" in a dramatic voice. But it was. It was too quiet.

She was right, though; they couldn't just stay out here. He'd have to go back in eventually. He still had the buyer coming tomorrow. He needed to survey whatever damage the opening of the hole had caused, and come up with a plan to fix it fast. He had no experience with this kind of property damage. Flooding, yes. Fire, a few times. Infestation, mold, rot—all of that he knew. This was the unleashing of what seemed to be supernatural forces from deep within the Earth. He had no idea what that kind of thing could do to drywall.

Guy led the way up onto the porch. He still didn't hear anything from the house. Just the opposite. The silence pressed in harder around them the closer to the house they got. The familiar creaking of the porch steps was still there, but sounded crushed and stifled, like the sound wanted to hide.

The doorknob felt cold. Not from the outside, but from the inside. It gave him pause. Even more pause than the pause he already had, which was plenty. All he wanted to do was pause.

He glanced over at Mae, whose face looked like she was at the very top peak of a roller coaster, about to plunge over. Terrified and thrilled with anticipation all at once. "Ready?" he asked.

"Just open it," she said. "How bad can it be?"

Pretty bad, Guy thought. He imagined a live re-enactment of every scene from *Poltergeist*. Chairs stacked, roaming spirits, the floors breaking apart as decayed corpses emerged impossibly from desecrated burial places. Nightmarish supernatural horrors matched only by the horror of the property damage.

He pushed the door open.

The house felt colder than before, and darker. Deadened. It had always been quiet, but now it was so quiet that it was almost loud. If a house could be silent but not silent, that's what this was.

And it *felt* different. Everything was exactly where it had been before, but he felt like he was looking at it through a gray filter. All the color was muted. All the dust hung perfectly still in the heavy air. He could have sworn it smelled like someone had been there. Not the familiar smell of someone he knew. A stranger.

As Guy crossed the threshold, a shiver went through him that felt like it didn't come from his own muscles and nervous system. Rather, it felt like a quivering hand had taken hold of his spine on the inside and squeezed, transmitting its ancient tremors in waves through his musculature. He couldn't suppress it. It was in his steps and his breaths and he had to ignore it or be paralyzed.

But on the positive side, all the re-decorating and construction they had done looked the same—nothing they'd fixed had been destroyed; everything was intact. Nothing was levitating, no dimensional portals were waving tentacles and strobing light at them, and no coffins were punching up from underground and spilling their corpses onto the new floors. Whatever invisible entity had taken over the house had at least respected their design decisions.

"It's..." Guy said. He wasn't sure how to finish his sentence because he hadn't made his mind up yet about whether he was optimistic or fatalistic. He went with something in between. "It could be worse. The floors are still fine. Look at that finish." The muted light somehow accentuated the shine on the laminate. He was doubly impressed with Luther's work, especially given how cheap it had been.

"We have to check the basement," Mae said. She seemed to be going for a matter-of-fact tone, but he could hear a tremor in it. She didn't want to go down there any more than he did.

But they did have to go down there. It was ground zero, the nexus of everything that was happening in the house. If they were to have any chance of understanding it, they'd have to go down and check it out. At least he didn't have to worry much about damage down there, because the basement had already been awful. Unless the hole had exposed human skulls embedded in the walls, it couldn't be worse than before.

Guy led the way to the basement door. They'd left it open in their haste to flee, so even before he reached it, he was able to sniff the air wafting up from below. There wasn't any kind of smell that alarmed him, and the blast of wind had subsided. But the air was chilled. Not just the usual cold and damp of basement air, but cold like air forced over dry ice. Like air from an open meat freezer. He suddenly worried that there *would* be human skulls embedded in the walls.

Mae was watching him expectantly, but she didn't question his hesitation. She probably felt the cold air too.

Guy took a deep breath. He wanted to hold it as long as he could, to avoid breathing the air down there as much as possible. He wished Luther was here with some masks or air quality testing gadgets. There could be some mix of brimstone and human souls hanging in the air. That was marginally worse than asbestos.

He started down the stairs. Mae hesitated briefly on the edge, then followed close behind him, using him as a bulwark against whatever might come surging at them.

After a few steps, he realized that he was running his hand along the smooth curve of the wall as he went. He always did that because there wasn't a railing, and his natural instinct was to hold onto something. But he pulled his hand away this time because the wall was wet with condensation where the warm air from above met the colder air coming up the stairs. And it didn't just feel wet. It was sticky, too, like the water didn't want to come off of his fingers. Like it was mixed with petroleum jelly. He had to wipe his hand on his pant leg to get rid of it.

That was bad. That would need a scrub. And if it kept doing that, the drywall wouldn't hold up for long. His mental calculator spat out a few more inches of receipt paper.

As they neared the bottom of the stairs, he could see that the light was still on. That was a good sign. At least it wouldn't be total devastation down there. But the temperature seemed to drop another degree for every step he went down, and that was less encouraging. And there was a sound now. The first sound he'd heard anywhere near the house.

A moan, low and sorrowful, filled the basement and drifted up the stairs to where they crept.

And while he knew it had to be just moving air, he couldn't quite convince himself it wasn't coming from something alive. It carried with it the desperate, pleading cry of something that had spent centuries miserably alone.

He didn't want to keep going down. But he did.

One step, and pause.

Another step, and pause.

The moan carried on, a drawn-out, unceasing lament. But he couldn't tell if it was warning him away or calling him down.

Another step. Another pause.

"Go," Mae whispered, and poked the back of his shoulder.

She was right. He steeled himself and took the last few steps fast, stopping at the last one as soon as he could see.

The basement, like everywhere in the house, looked different. The jumbled arrangement of walls felt closer, pressing in. He was fairly certain that if he measured, they'd be right where they'd always been. But they *felt* closer, as if photographed through a long lens that crushed depth. And the shadows felt deeper. All the corners seemed pitch black, and the spaces between the joists in the ceiling looked like inverted canals of shadow that rippled as the naked bulb swung, pushed by an invisible hand.

Guy stopped at the bottom of the stairs. He didn't want to step off until he'd seen the hole.

And there it was. It appeared bigger than it had been before. It was a presence, a living thing lying in wait on the floor. A staring eye and a gaping mouth all at once, both staring straight at him and threatening to consume him. The cold air flowed from it like a constant exhale. He could see it in dust particles being pushed to the ceiling and spreading out between the beams. It wasn't a gale like before, but it was enough to make the moan they'd heard on the way down. It sounded like the doleful breathing of the Earth.

Mae again nudged his shoulder from behind. She wanted him to move on. The last thing Guy wanted to do was set foot in that place again. But he did it. One foot. As soon as it touched the dirt floor he felt a vibration transfer into him. A slow tremble like an engine running roughly, deep underground. The floor felt changed too; it seemed to have a slope to it that hadn't been there before, like a sink with its bottom angled to ensure that everything in it would flow into the drain. He felt for a second like the dirt under his foot might give way in a landslide and gravity would take him irresistibly into the hole.

But the ground held, and he put his other foot down. He sidestepped to give Mae room, and they circled sideways across the basement floor together, keeping close to the walls and far from the hole.

Guy wanted to look down into it. But he couldn't tear himself away from the relative safety of the walls. He didn't trust the floor around the hole, and didn't trust the hole not to suddenly reverse its flow of air and inhale him.

But Mae got impatient. Before he even knew she was moving, she had taken several quick steps forward and then shuffled sideways the last few feet to the edge of the hole.

"Mae..." He tried to caution her, but she ignored him. But she was so close to the edge now that it made him nervous for her. So he was forced to move forward with her, ready to grab her arm if anything should happen.

What happened was that she leaned out over the hole, much too far for his liking. He gripped her elbow, and instead of taking that as the precautionary move he'd intended it to be, she used it as a stabilizing force that allowed her to lean out even further and let him take some of her weight. He held her arm with both hands.

She peered straight into the hole for ten seconds or more while he held her back from falling. He was supporting so much of her weight, he knew that if he let go right then, she would certainly fall in. He wished she would stop looking and step back.

She looked down while the hole breathed cold at them and its heartbeat vibrated pebbles on the floor.

"I don't see anything," Mae finally said. "It's just... dark. Like it goes on forever."

"I know. I've seen it."

He tried to pull her back. And he desperately wanted to get out of here. Out of the basement and out of the house. As far from the hole as he could. "Can you just get back, please?"

She finally complied, and they both backed away from the edge.

The hole breathed at them.

Besides his primal dread at the horror he was witnessing, Guy now had an even more primal dread at how terrible this was for his business. The house was legitimately unsellable now. He tried to imagine anyone ever making an offer on a house with a hole in the basement that breathed cold, dead air. It only worked when his imagined buyers were idiots, so he started to think about where he could find people like that.

But Mae, as usual, seemed to not be thinking about that at all. "I met someone today," she said, not looking at him. "A man. He used to be a real estate agent 30 or 40 years ago. He once had to sell this house."

So that was the mission she'd been on today while he'd been dangling from chicken wire.

"He told me..." She hesitated like she wasn't sure how to tell this part. Or even if she wanted to. "He told me things about the house. And about the hole."

"What things?"

"You're not going to like them."

"I already don't. Just tell me." Whatever they were, he wanted to hear them. Being told things meant that his broken mind wouldn't have to figure them out for itself.

She told him. And his broken mind broke some more.

Chapter 14

G uy had kindly hauled Mae's bruised and beaten car out of the gully with his winch, and now she lay across the back seat with the windows open a crack, listening to the crickets in the dark. The sounds were far away off behind her, probably on the other side of Whitemarsh Road. No crickets dared come near the house. They seemed to have all had a big, national cricket conference and agreed to zone the house as off-limits. Perhaps they'd strung cricket police tape across the front edge of the property to warn other bugs away. Or maybe they were simply too scared to come near it. She'd always imagined crickets as fearless. Yet this house scared them.

She could see the house looming outside the windshield. She'd seen it at night many times before, and it had never scared her. But it scared her now. It seemed to exist inside its own shadow. There was no moon, so the darkness outside was absolute. But the darkness around the house was somehow even *more* absolute. It absorbed whatever scant light managed to reach it. It was a square mountain against the night sky, a wide, black gap in the stars. It was vastly, impossibly dark.

Mae felt like she was taking all of this pretty well. She had never really considered how she'd react to finding out that supernatural forces were real, and malevolent, and existing literally in her own basement. She'd always believed that there were things beyond human comprehension, but until now they'd felt like things that you believed in without proof, and she was comfortable with that. It allowed for scary mysteries to be kept at a distance. But now that she'd witnessed them without ambiguity, she thought she was adapting to it pretty quickly. It hadn't shaken her faith in the workings of the universe to its core the way it might do to some people. At the moment, she was just kind of annoyed that her car was too small to fully stretch out in.

She stared at the black mass that was the house, and she thought.

Either you throw someone down the hole, or you throw yourself down it.

When she'd left Honest Bob's house, she'd mostly believed he was a nutbar. She couldn't even think about what he'd done, and she knew she would eventually have to go tell the police about it. But when he'd told her about it, while she had believed that he'd done it, she hadn't really believed that the hole had demanded that he do it. It was crazy. It was impossible. It was all in his head.

And then she'd arrived back at the house, the hole had been opened, and all hell had broken loose. Maybe literally. Now she didn't know what to believe. Could it be true that they were stuck with the house until somebody was thrown down the hole? No, it couldn't. But yes, maybe it could.

But Guy had a buyer coming tomorrow. He'd seemed pretty certain that this guy was going to buy it. He'd called it a virtual lock. The hole couldn't prevent them from selling it if somebody just showed up and bought it. Mae had a moment of relief going down that mental road. It was a pleasant, sunshine-filled road with flowers along the side and probably butterflies.

It was also a very short road that dipped suddenly into a swamp, because another thought immediately occurred to her.

"Whammo," she whispered aloud.

They couldn't sell the house. It would be unconscionable. Either they'd be subjecting the new owner to the same psychological torture that she was now going through, or they'd be setting him up to murder somebody, thinking he was saving himself.

She couldn't sell it. She knew she couldn't. The house would be hers forever.

Or rather, half of it would be. Guy would have to decide what to do with his half. Or they'd have to come to an agreement.

She sat up a little and looked over at Guy's truck. Even he had refused to stay in the house tonight. So he was sleeping in his truck the same way she was doing. Or rather, he was *not* sleeping in it, because she could see him lit by the pale glow of his dashboard LCD screen, sitting up behind the wheel, scratching his beard, and staring at the house.

She opened the car door with her foot and squirmed out into the driveway.

It was colder out than she'd thought. Spring had well and truly sprung now so she expected it to be a little more comfortable. Maybe it was the cold from the hole spreading across the ground outside the house like a pipe leaking cold dread.

Guy let out a sharp, startled "waah!" when she hauled the passenger door of his truck open and climbed into the seat next to him.

"Sorry," he said after he'd figured out it was her. "Still a little jumpy. I almost died today."

"I know. I saw."

"Thanks for making that not happen, by the way."

She shrugged. "All I did was grab a ladder."

"Yeah, but you did it well." He looked out the windshield at the front door and drummed his thumbs on the steering wheel, deep in thought.

"What are you doing?" she asked.

"Thinking."

She thought she knew the answer, but asked anyway. "About what?"

He let out a long, tired sigh, and didn't pull his eyes away from the house, looming nearly invisibly in the dark ahead. Mae wondered what part of the situation was foremost in his mind. Maybe he, like her, had already realized they couldn't sell the house anymore. Obviously, that would be a blow to his plans, so he had a right to be a little gloomy right now. She gave him some time to get it out.

He followed up his long sigh with a shorter one. "You know..." he started. He seemed to reconsider his words, and started again. "You know those little Swiss roll cakes with the chocolate on the outside?"

She blinked at him. What was he talking about? Swiss rolls? What? "Uh huh," she said.

"There's a whole box of them in the cabinet in there and I'm trying to figure out if I want them bad enough to go back in."

She stared at him while her mind tried to shift gears radically enough to process that. It couldn't quite get there, and stalled out instead, finally resorting to laughter. She couldn't help it. And she worried that he'd be offended and think she was mocking him, so she put an apologetic hand on his forearm to let him know it was fine if he wanted Swiss roll cakes but it was also funny.

Fortunately, he laughed too. "What?" he said through a laugh. "They're good. Well, now I'm definitely not giving you any."

They both seemed to remember at once that they had bigger things to worry about. They stifled their laughter and looked up at the black, lurking shadow of the house. For ten seconds they just looked. And the house loomed in the dark, indifferent and silent.

"I wish we left a light on in there," Mae said.

"I think I did," Guy said.

Great, Mae thought. So either the house's pool of shadow was too deep, or something had shut the light off. Both were bad options. "Have you ever had a house like this before?" she asked. Of course he hadn't, but she was curious.

He shook his head. "I found a whole herd of feral cats in one once."

"That's not similar."

"I don't know, some of them were pretty scary. Oh, and I found a dead guy in a house in Bridgeport."

"No way."

"About seven or eight years ago," he said. "Bought it at auction; the previous owner had been evicted. That's what they told me. But when I got there, the guy was still inside. And he wouldn't leave."

"Because he was dead?"

He shook his head. "Not yet. I had to get a real estate attorney, send a demand letter, and file a complaint with the court. The lawyer told me it could take a month to get to trial. Maybe two. And the guy could stay in the house that whole time. I could *not* make him leave."

"Did you ask him why he wouldn't leave? He must have had a reason. Maybe he was desperate."

"No idea. I just know he was evicted."

"Poor guy."

"I guess. Anyway, after a week or two, he stopped answering his phone. Turns out, he had some kind of heart episode. He'd been dead for days by the time I broke in. Then there was all this extra clean-up to do. I spent more on Febreze than I did on drywall."

Mae shivered. "Okay, we're done with that story. And, by the way, it's still not similar."

"No," he agreed. "I've never had anything like this. I'm not sure anybody has."

They both looked out at the house. They had to lean forward to see the whole thing. Seeing the stars above it was relief from the dark.

"We can't sell it," Mae said.

"I know," Guy replied. He rubbed his chin with his thumb and index finger. The rough scratching sound on his beard was also the sound of his mental machine turning over.

She breathed a sigh of relief. Maybe Guy wasn't so bad after all. She found herself warming up to him in a minuscule way.

"Wait," he said, stopping his beard scratch and looking sharply over at her. "Did you say 'can't?'"

"Obviously."

"No no no, that's wrong. We *have* to sell it. Even more than before."

The surprising little spark of warming-up-to-him chilled instantly.

"You're not going through with the showing tomorrow?" she said incredulously.

"Yes I am. Of course I am. Luther's coming in the morning and we're going to cover the hole. It'll be fine. This guy will see how great the house is, he'll buy it, and then it will be his problem. Not my problem or your problem. *His* problem."

"Guy, you know that's not right."

"I do?" He pretended to think about it. She could tell that all he was really thinking about was how long he should pause for maximum sarcasm. "No. No, I don't know that. It seems pretty right."

"You would actually sell them this house knowing..." She couldn't figure out how to describe exactly what she meant. And, in her defense, it was pretty indescribable. "Knowing what's *in* it?"

"If we don't sell the house, I lose everything. Everything I have. I'm broke. Ruined. You get that, right?"

"I don't like it any better than you do."

His voice rose, just below a shout. "Are you sure? I don't like it at all, but you seem to like it a little bit."

She raised her voice too, and suddenly they were yelling at each other. "You can't sell this house!"

"I'm selling it! And I need you to be on board. I can't do it without you!"

"Well I'm not doing it!" She directed her very best fiery glare at him, but it seemed to have no effect. She'd have to work on that.

"Then I'll do it without you!"

"You literally just said you couldn't do that!"

"It was a figure of speech! I totally can!"

"You can't! I own half the house. I'm not selling!"

That seemed to be an incontrovertible point, so she decided not to give him the chance to controvert it. She hurled the door open and stormed out into the mud. And she couldn't decide fast enough what expressed her anger better: slamming the door or leaving it for him to close. So she just pushed it halfway closed, kicked it in the hopes of leaving a dent, and then sloshed through the mud back to her car, where it took her nearly an hour to fall asleep angry.

Chapter 15

G uy woke up with the sun. Not on purpose, but because
there wasn't any shade in the cab of his truck.

For his first few waking moments, he blissfully forgot everything that had happened yesterday, and everything that was due
to happen today. He didn't know why he was in his truck, but
he didn't question it. It seemed like a nice day and there was
no good reason to get up. He could close his eyes for just a few
more minutes and listen to the birds.

But there were no birds. Not close by. There was only silence,
and a towering black monolith filling his windshield, demanding to be thought about.

It all fell on him at once.

The hole was open. It was scary. The buyer was coming.
Today. There was no coffee.

All of those things were problems. And the weight of them
almost made him roll over and give up.

But he snapped out of it, forcing himself to jump out of the
truck and jog in place to wake himself up.

The house loomed over him as he did it. Despite the brilliant morning sun, it seemed to exist in a shadow, as if less light hit it than anything else in the world. Its windows and door had never looked so much like a mocking face.

Stop thinking about it, he told himself. There's only one thing you need to think about. Today is your chance to sell this house and get away from it. You need a plan.

Luther hadn't shown up yet, so he had time to think. He made the drive to Southbury and picked up two coffees, one for him and one for Luther, and expressly none for Mae. He didn't feel like being generous with her right now. He was still stewing from their shouting match the night before. But he was more than happy to get coffee for Luther because Luther was going to help him. Luther would earn a coffee.

Guy drank both coffees on the way back, and by the time he arrived at the house just after 8:00, he'd come up with something that felt sort of plan-like. Luther was on the porch and Mae seemed to still be sound asleep in her car. Guy wanted her to stay that way, at least for now.

As Guy walked up the porch steps, Luther stood outside the front door, looking warily at it. "Something is different," he said. "The house feels..." He paused to think. Guy waited for him to come up with the most Luther-ish word for it. Probably something with six syllables that was normally used by art historians to describe late Gothic church facades. "Weird," Luther finally said. "It feels weird."

"Luther, you have no idea," Guy said. And before they went inside, he told Luther everything. The freshly opened hole, the human sacrifice curse, everything. It sounded even more bizarre spoken out loud than it had while he thought about it all night.

But Luther didn't even blink. When Guy was done, his only response was to nod and say, "Interesting." It was the exact same response he would have had if Guy had explained penguin migration.

"So yes," Guy said. "The house feels weird. And we need to de-weird it before my buyer gets here. We've got two hours. Come on." And he led the way inside, forcing himself not to hesitate on the threshold.

Nothing had changed since the night before. And he didn't feel any more at ease in the house. If anything, he wanted even more badly to get out. The pressurized closeness of the air, the heavy silence like hands pressed over his ears, the hard, cold smell of an unwelcome stranger just passed by and still lurking around the corner. All of it made him want to run back out the door. He'd heard many times that a buyer knows in the first ten seconds if they can live in a house. In this place, any buyer would need only one or two to know that nobody could live here. Nobody.

Guy's plan had three steps. And he wasn't confident in any of them.

"Okay," he said, "step one. Air fresheners. We need plug-in air fresheners in every room. And not just those little ones that smell like clean linen. I'm talking industrial strength. I want this place to smell like fresh-baked cookie flowers."

"Acknowledged," Luther said. He could have just said "okay," Guy thought, but that was Luther.

"Step two," Guy continued. "We need to kill this silence. We need Bluetooth speakers, all synced up and playing 'Sunshine, Lollipops and Rainbows' on a loop."

"Wise," Luther said, nodding. "But thus far, none of these measures seem to require my particular skills. I'm curious as to why you summoned me at all."

"That's the most important part," Guy said. "We need to cover the hole."

Luther shook his head. "I can not get the truck again today. My brother-in-law—"

Guy waved off his concern. "I know there's no time to do concrete again. But we need to do *something*. And I know you're the man to figure out how. You can do anything." No harm in a little subtle flattery, Guy thought.

Luther nodded sagely and pulled his hammer from his tool belt. He checked it over, as if examining it for any imperfections that might cause air resistance when he swung it. "Lead on," he said.

man to figure out how. You can do anything." No harm in a little

Luther peered down the hole while Guy stayed against the wall. Was it his imagination, or had gravity shifted direction? Was everything being pulled toward the hole, like a singularity in space. He had the urge to grab onto something just in case.

"I have never seen anything like it," Luther said. His flat tone was, for the first time, comforting.

"Great," Guy said, impatient and desperately wanting to get out of the basement. "Can we cover it, please?"

Guy held one end of a plywood sheet and Luther held the other, and they maneuvered it into position over the edge of the hole. Luther had rejected the three-quarter inch sheathing that Guy had planned on using before, instead suggesting a pressure-treated hardwood. It was heavier, less flexible, and maybe more likely to block any demonic monsters that tried to climb out of the hole. Maybe.

The hole continued to exhale a steady stream of cold, earthy-smelling air at them. It hadn't changed at all from the night before. And both Guy and Luther instinctively tried to avoid breathing it directly. They leaned back from the edge as they moved around it, and Guy fought the urge to cover his face behind his elbow.

They slid the plywood until it covered as much of the hole as possible without toppling in. Covering part of the hole raised the pitch of the low moan by a note or two, so it sounded like the hole was protesting. It didn't want to be covered. Guy tried to ignore it. It was just moving air. That's all.

"This will require several of these," Luther said as he kicked the edge of the wood with the heel of his boot to shift it a few inches. "Possibly as many as ten to maintain stability. And it will obviously not be permanent."

"We can't just have a bunch of plywood in the middle of the floor," Guy said. "It'll look cheap."

"The whole basement is crude," Luther pointed out. "But I do have a suggestion to distract, if it's helpful."

"Hit me," Guy said.

"A ping pong table."

Guy's immediate thought was that it was dumb. But the more he thought about it, the more he thought it would work. It was a classic misdirect. Instead of being confused by the random plywood in the middle of the basement floor, the buyer would be all like, "Hey, ping pong!"

"Where do we get one of those in a hurry?" he asked.

"My brother-in-law has one in good condition," Luther said as they grabbed another sheet of plywood together and positioned it up against the other, extending out over the hole.

The moan of protest rose higher, getting closer to a wail. Forced through a smaller space, the air flowed out stronger, and became harder to avoid.

The job grew more challenging as they tried to cover the middle of the hole while still keeping the plywood stable, but Luther expertly knew how to overlap them just enough to support each other. Guy was, as usual, amazed. For all his questionable practices and skirting of the fringes of code compliance, Luther did truly have a talent for building.

As more and more of the hole was covered, the sound it made grew angrier, no longer a lament, but angry now. Furious that they were trying to block it. Almost as if it sensed they were trying to murder it, and it was raging in protest.

Guy fought to ignore it. Just air. Nothing but air.

After fifteen minutes, they dropped the last plank into place, and the hole was completely covered.

The sound of the air cut off suddenly. Gagged. Muzzled. Dead.

Guy couldn't help a sense of relief. The constant wail of protest had been pushing him to the edge, making him want to scream back at it.

In addition to the silence, the temperature in the basement rose immediately by several degrees. That was good too. Things were looking up. Guy's dread was gradually shushed by a cautious optimism.

"It could be more stable," Luther said when they were done. He stepped around the circle of the hole, scanning their construction. "I'll nail the planks together and see if I can peg the edges into the clay so it doesn't slide. Then—"

With a noise like a blue whale ejecting a kayak paddle from its blowhole, a great eruption of air blasted the planks apart from below.

In the nearly frozen time of the moment, Guy saw the planks spinning in the air, careening off the ceiling, digging hard into the walls, and bouncing. One hit the overhead light bulb but somehow didn't break it, instead kicking it into a chaotic swing that whirled shadows into the chaos.

One of the boards struck Luther with its corner, smacking his cap and hard hat clean off. He went down hard and the plank landed on top of him. He disappeared beneath it like it was a rigid, splintering blanket trying to smother him.

Another came tumbling at Guy, and he barely had time to get his arms in front of his face before that plank hit him so hard it nearly knocked him down as well. But he held his footing and the plank delivered a hard, full-body slap, then bounced backward off him, landed flat on the edge of the hole, and finally toppled in.

It took a few seconds for the boards to settle completely and the clatter to fall silent. Guy stood in dazed disbelief, waiting for something else to come at him.

But nothing did, and finally the basement went quiet.
Except for the low, steady, tragic moan of the hole.

Chapter 16

B ack at the house, Guy and Luther were doing something to get ready for the buyer to view the house. Mae didn't want to know what.

But there were things she did want to know. And she thought she knew where to find them.

The Town Clerk's Office was in the same municipal center where the house auction had happened all those months ago, so Mae paused to look at the gazebo before she went inside. That was where all of this horror had started. That was where she'd made the decision that may very well have doomed her forever. Her life had irreversibly changed right there, and not for the better.

It was a nice gazebo, though. It had evergreen bushes around it with little flags planted between them. She couldn't hate it. She'd happily read a book there.

Once she got inside the municipal center, the Town Clerk's Office was not hard to find. It was also not big, not tidy, not well-lit, and not currently staffed by anyone. There wasn't a bell to ring for service, and even if there had been one, nobody was there to hear it. So Mae sat in one of the two provided chairs and looked at the painting of a seagull on the wall. The seagull was walking on some rocks instead of flying, maybe because this office wasn't big enough for it to really stretch its wings.

She sat and simmered about her disagreement with Guy the night before. She still found it offensive that he was showing the house at all. For a flicker of an instant in the truck last night she'd felt like he might actually be a decent human. Then he'd gone and proven that he had no conscience to speak of, and now she was glad to be nowhere near him. It didn't matter how the showing was going, because she refused to sell. Even if those people wanted to double the asking price, move in tomorrow, and gift her a fruit bouquet, she'd be ready with a polite "no." They would have no idea that she was saving lives, and saving them the cost of a fruit bouquet.

The house was hers (and Guy's), not to be sold until she figured out how to close the hole again, or at least how to appease it with minimal human sacrifices. And the place to start doing that was here at the Town Clerk's Office. So far, the seagull had not been helpful.

It was more than fifteen minutes before somebody finally showed up: a freckled, bespectacled girl who couldn't have yet finished high school and who immediately appeared terrified that someone was sitting in one of the chairs. She froze in place, staring at Mae with her mouth open.

"Hi," Mae said brightly.

The girl didn't appear to know what the word meant. She didn't respond, but at least managed to close her mouth.

Mae stood up from the chair. "Sorry, I was hoping to do, like, a land registry search or something. I don't know how this works. But I'm trying to find the history of a property, like who owned it before. Is that information public, by any chance?"

The girl circled behind the desk and squeezed her hands together. "Can I be honest with you?" she said.

Mae was thrown. She hadn't expected visiting the Town Clerk's Office to turn into some kind of confessional. At least not with her on the receiving end. "Um... sure," she said.

"I don't really work here," the girl said.

Mae was thrown even further. "Oh. I'm sorry, I thought—"

"My sister works here," the girl interrupted. "But she's sick today, and I told her I'd watch the desk. I didn't really expect anybody to come in. And if anybody came in, I was just supposed to tell them to submit a request and wait for the results to be mailed to them. Do you want to submit a request and wait for the results to be mailed to you?"

Mae grasped the edge of the desk and tried to look pleading. "I don't really have the time. Do you think you could look it up for me right now?"

The girl considered for a few seconds and then finally shuffled sideways and sat at a huge slab of a PC that had time-traveled in from the ancient world. "Oh, I guess. Since I'm here. I've always wanted to look up something but I've never had a reason to. What are you looking for?" She started up the PC, and its fans made a noise like a taxiing fighter jet.

"Records on a property. Is that information public?"

"I don't know. Is it?"

"I... don't know. that's why I'm asking you."

The girl tapped her chin thoughtfully. "It might not be. But if it's just between you and me, then it's not really 'public,' is it?"

Mae silently wondered if she was getting this girl in trouble. But surely a non-employee of this place wouldn't have access to anything sensitive. Would they?

"What's the address?" the girl asked.

"9140 Whitemarsh Road."

From the other side of the massive PC, Mae heard the slow click of hunting-and-pecking accompanied by the girl's soft, tuneless humming. It took Mae a few seconds to realize that it wasn't actually tuneless; it was the jingle from a DQ commercial.

Finally, the typing stopped, and the sister of the town clerk let out a delighted "Got it!"

"What did you find?" Mae asked.

"That's the Hole House!"

Mae nearly fell over. Was the hole famous? Did everyone know about it?

"It says something about the hole?" she asked, anxious about the response.

The girl pluralized it. Emphatically, and enthusiastically. "Hole-*sss*!"

Mae's tension intensified. There was more than one hole? How many people were being thrown into holes in this community? "Hole-sss?"

"Yeah!" the girl said brightly. "Arthur, Desmond, and Gretchen."

So, there were *three* holes? And they had names? Mae wished that this girl's sister would come back from lunch. She was a civic official, paid a nominal salary by a small city government, and maybe she could help all of this make sense.

"The holes have names?" Mae asked, because she felt like that was the key point of clarification.

"Why wouldn't they?" The girl sounded puzzled.

Mae needed a rewind-and-reset. She leaned across the desk. "Sorry, can we start again? What was your name?"

"Uh huh!"

"Great. Can you just tell me what it says about the property? Like, maybe read it to me?"

The girl cleared her throat as though readying to deliver a third-grade book report. "The house was built by Arthur Desmond Hole," she read. "For his wife, Gretchen."

Comprehension smacked Mae in the face. "Hole is his *name*!" she said out loud without meaning to.

But the understanding quickly gave way to more confusion. Why did a man named Hole own a house with a hole in the basement? Had he decided at a young age, upon learning his surname, that his destiny in life was to have a house with the deepest hole in the world under its basement floor? It didn't seem like much of a calling. But he'd certainly achieved it.

"I've heard of him," the girl said. "He invented doughnuts."

That also didn't seem like much of a calling, and just made things even more confusing. "Doughnuts?"

"Uh huh. They're like cakes with a hole in the middle." She shaped one out in the air with her index finger. "They're everywhere."

"His name was Hole and he invented doughnuts?" And he owned a house with a hole in it, she didn't say.

"I have a list of all the other owners here," the girl said, swirling her finger at the monitor. "Do you want me to print it?"

"Are you allowed to do that?"

"I don't know. Maybe. There's a button for it."

—————

Armed with the three-page possibly-illegal printout and her phone's data connection, Mae sat in the gazebo outside the municipal center, which actually was the lovely spot for reading that she'd expected it to be.

The printout, which she'd been most excited about, turned out to be little help. The last registered owner of the house was Crane Trust, the trust that Mae and Guy had bought the house from. Honest Bob Kinson, listed as Robert Kinson, was named as trustee in 1982 and then removed as trustee in 1986. And it seemed that after that, the house had just sat there, slowly disintegrating, until the trust decided to divide it into two units and sell it at auction. To Mae and Guy.

Before 1982, there were 41 owners listed. Mae did the math in her head. The house was built in 1889, and Bob Kinson abandoned it in 1986. That meant it had changed hands, on average, about every two years. She was not a real estate expert, but that seemed like a lot. She made a note to look into every single one of the owners later. But for now, she wanted to know about the man who had first built the house.

She went into her full-bore research mode. She was prepared to scour the Web, the Dark Web, the Even Darker Web (if that was a thing), ancestry records, immigration records, archival newspapers... she would find out who Arthur Desmond Hole was. She was committed, determined, ready to spend days if that's what it took.

In 20 seconds, she found out that he had a Wikipedia entry.

> Arthur Desmond Hole (May 23, 1845 - Feb 3, 1891) was an English-American inventor, industrialist, and entrepreneur who falsely claimed to have invented the doughnut. He was arrested in 1890 and confessed to killing his wife, though her body was never found. He was hanged for her murder in 1891.

Mae paused to take that in. It was a rip-roaring start. A legacy of doughnut fraud and murder. Add that to his penchant for living in a house with a supernatural hole in the basement, and this Arthur Hole was fascinating. She considered scanning the article for any mention of a house but decided to absorb it in sequence.

Background
A descendant of Earl Fitzwilliam, Arthur Desmond Hole was born in Lincolnshire in 1845. The son of industrialist Peter Xavier Hole,

young Arthur showed little of his
father's aptitude for business.
After failing with five bankrupted
factories, he finally emigrated
to America in 1870, probably to
evade his considerable debts. He
promptly founded a baked goods
business in New Haven, Connecticut, and claimed to have invented
the doughnut, despite doughnuts
having existed in their modern
ring-shaped form since at least
1845. Many failed legal battles
later, Hole was forced to close
his failing business and start up
another, this one producing industrial rubber products. According
to Hole, the rubber products used
a similar recipe to his doughnuts
but were both less chewy and more
successful. It finally allowed him
to live comfortably in America
and, if not pay off his debts, at
least pay large henchmen to murder
those who tried to collect them.

Mae was mildly surprised to find that last part included. Apparently nobody cared to edit Arthur Desmond Hole's Wikipedia
entry for objectivity.

Personal Life
Hole married Gretchen Voigt in
1872 and murdered her at their
home outside New Haven in 1890.

```
They had no children for him to
murder.
```

Well, Mae thought, that was short and to-the-point. And the first mention of the house. There was no mention, though, of how he'd murdered her, or why. Maybe it was unknown.

The next section title made her heart jump. This was it. This was what she needed.

Occult Connections
```
Hole was widely reputed to have a
lifelong fascination with the oc-
cult, taking part in practices as-
sociated with occultism, spiritu-
alism, Hermeticism, and primeval-
ism.
```

That was it. No detail. No mention of the house, or of the hole. Mae was at once thrilled and frustrated. And also puzzled—what was primevalism? The other three she had heard of, and all of them were highlighted with links to other Wikipedia entries. But primevalism had no link, no further information. Like she was supposed to just know what it was.

There was only one more short section.

Death
```
Hole was hanged at Connecticut
State Prison in 1891 for the mur-
der of his wife, Gretchen. He
confessed to killing her in 1890,
but investigators were unable to
recover her body, saying he had
hidden it "too far down."
```

Mae shivered. "Too far down."

It was frustratingly short on detail, but she knew exactly what it meant. Arthur Desmond Hole was the first to throw someone down the hole in his basement. And Bob Kinson was the last.

But how many had there been in between?

She balanced the list of previous owners on her lap, started a new browser tab on her phone, and began, seriously, to Google.

Chapter 17

G uy stood at the bay window in the dining room. His pulse did a pitched drum solo in his ears and his stomach clenched like it expected to be punched by a prize fighter. He noted again that the air fresheners were doing their job—the house smelled like a florist on top of a bakery. And the silence was effectively beaten down by "Sunshine, Lollipops, and Rainbows." It was now playing for the ninth time since he'd been standing there. That was a whole lot of sunshine, a big bucket of lollipops, and at least a dump truck full of rainbows. Yet still, Guy was tense.

A car gleamed in the daylight out on Whitemarsh Road. And cars on Whitemarsh were rare because it led to nowhere from nowhere. It had to be him.

His sure-thing Wall Street buyer had arrived.

This was it. Everything was riding on this. He'd had this guy on the hook, drooling over the house for months. He'd practically already bought it. Guy would need to get Mae to sell her half, sure, but he was sure he could convince her once this Cameron guy had signed on the dotted line. On the other hand, if Cameron was (understandably) freaked out by a supernatural hole in the basement, then there was little hope of selling to anyone, ever. Guy thought for the first time that if this showing went badly, he might actually throw himself down the hole. That would both put him out of his misery and relieve Mae of the need to murder anyone, which she seemed not to be a fan of.

But of course there was no need for murders anyway. All that stuff about throwing someone down the hole was nuts. If he wanted to sell the house, then a hole in the ground couldn't do anything to stop him. The only way it could impede this showing at all was by simply existing and being weird. It was already doing both of those things, but he'd try to sugarcoat that.

The car out on Whitemarsh passed the end of the driveway and kept going. And Guy was simultaneously annoyed and relieved. He had a little more time for his palms to sweat and his stomach to bunch up before the buyer got here.

But no, he didn't. Because the car slowed and pulled off onto the shoulder, then did a U-turn and came back toward the driveway. The driver must have just missed seeing it, or his GPS had steered him wrong. He'd be here in minutes, and Guy needed to be ready. And—

Thump.

It came from somewhere behind him. Sharp and loud, halfway between a *thud* and a *boom*. His stomach, already clenched, wrung itself even tighter so all its acid shot up the back of his throat.

He had unquestionably heard a noise. There shouldn't be noises. Nobody else was in the house. Mae's car was gone, so she was still off somewhere. Luther had left. Guy was the only one here.

Thump.

He jumped. Again.

He was pretty sure it had come from the kitchen—behind him and past the basement stairs. Several possibilities scrambled through his mind. A cabinet door had broken off, or the weight of the countertop had cracked the wood beneath it, or some part of the framing had expanded. Whatever it was, he needed to know before the buyer got here.

He took another look out the window and saw that the car had stopped at the end of the driveway, but it hadn't turned in yet. Maybe he was trying to figure out if this was the right place, or just evaluating how it looked from the road. Whatever the reason, Guy had a moment. But *only* a moment.

He jogged to the kitchen and rounded the corner, expecting to immediately spot something out of place, or something damaged.

But the kitchen looked intact. It was quiet and unblemished. It still had the unnatural, muted silence and the unsettling, chilly, desaturated look. But that wasn't unusual anymore; everywhere in the house had looked like that since the hole was opened. There was nothing obvious in the kitchen that could have made a noise like what he'd heard.

He tried opening and slamming one of the cabinet doors (admiring, once again, how much they looked like $18,000 cabinets when in reality Luther had installed them for $4750 all-in) and it made a noise similar to what he'd just heard. So it could have been that. But he hadn't left any of the cabinets open. He'd double-checked them this morning. There was no way one of them had swung closed in a draft, unless it had first swung open in another draft. Twice. That was a lot of drafts.

He decided to be convinced that it was all in his head. Pre-show-ing jitters manifesting as auditory hallucinations. It was the first time in his life he'd ever considered hallucinations as the preferable alternative to anything.

He pressed the cabinets closed—*extra* closed—on his way past.

The buyer would be on his way up the driveway by now. Guy had to collect himself and look professional. Be a tour guide, not a salesman, he told himself. Be casual. Be detail-oriented. Don't let him in the basement. And above all, stop sweating and be calm.

He stepped out onto the porch and leaned against a post, trying to look casual. He could see that out at the end of the driveway it was a beautiful day. The dead trees, while corpses, were at least basking in the kind of sunlight normally reserved for Club Med commercials. By all rights, the sun should have been baking the front of the house and making Spielbergian light shafts in all the rooms on this side. Yet somehow, the entire front of the house was in impossible shadow. He wanted to run out to where the house held no sway, where the world made sense.

But he couldn't leave. The car was halfway up the driveway already, trundling with careful deliberation. He saw now that it was a Porsche Taycan, but clearly it was driven by somebody who didn't know how to drive a Porsche Taycan. Slowing down just wasn't something you did in one of those. It navigated delicately through the trees, careful not to let any of their twiggy claws scratch the paint. So, maybe the driver *did* know how to drive a Porsche Taycan.

Guy manhandled his breathing under control, put on his best everything-is-great face, and went down the porch steps to meet the car in the driveway. He was amazed at how much the temperature rose just a few feet from the house.

The Porsche parked just shy of the shadow of the house with its hood almost pressed up against Big Ugly Rock, and its two occupants got out. Guy realized that he had only ever spoken to the buyer on the phone or through email, so he had no idea what he looked like. He knew that he worked on Wall Street, and he now knew that he drove a Porsche. So he expected Cameron and whoever was with him to be a corporate hedge fund in human form, all Armani, Gucci, and cologne that smelled like a billion-dollar contract drawn up by an army of lawyers.

But they were adorable. Instantly huggable. Not at all the kind of people you'd expect to drive around Connecticut in a Porsche.

Cameron was at least two inches shorter than Guy, made out of jeans and cardigan and two days of stubble, and built like a plush Friar Tuck. The woman with him was virtually the same shape as Cameron but six inches taller, towering even over Guy, with a teal dress that defined the word "sensible" and glasses that defined the word "glasses." Both of them had an obvious chronic smiling problem, but Guy was okay with that. He could work with these people. As long as he could keep them out of the basement.

And keep cabinets from slamming, he reminded himself. That was harder. But he'd find a way. At least the two of them hadn't immediately recoiled in horror from the place.

"Good to finally meet you!" he said as he strode across the yard toward them. "This rock will be gone." He normally wouldn't have opened with that, but Big Ugly Rock was right there.

Both of them shook his hand and smiled at him, then at the house, then at each other, then at the house again.

The woman had a surprised look mixed with a kind of realization like she'd just figured out a secret. Guy had no idea what the secret was. But he expected he wouldn't have to wait long to find out.

"Wait a minute," she said, covering her mouth with both hands to keep all the joy in. "Cameron. What is this? What's going on? Is this a house?"

Guy still didn't know what was going on. Or how to answer a question like "Is this a house?" from someone looking directly at a house.

"Brooke, honey," Cameron said, turning away from Guy to face her. And Guy was happy to allow that any sentence beginning with "honey" likely didn't involve him, so he stayed silent. Cameron went on: "Remember how you said you wanted a big old house in the country, someplace with real character and not just one of those cookie-cutter suburban boxes?"

She nodded, still clutching her face. There were tears lining up to escape her eyes.

Guy didn't dare interrupt whatever this was. And he was starting to understand what it was.

He understood it even more when Cameron dropped to one knee and started fishing in the pocket of his cardigan.

Guy's heart skipped. Not out of the joy of what was coming for these two, which he cared exactly zero about. But because he could now see that the sale was virtually guaranteed. If Brooke already loved the house, which seemed to be the case, then Cameron couldn't very well *not* buy it. The way he'd planned this proposal, he was getting engaged to her and the house at the same time. No matter what happened inside and how many bottomless holes were in the basement, he was locked in.

As long as she said yes, Guy would win. The hole couldn't stop this. He thought he might be happier about this marriage proposal than Brooke was.

But Brooke put a hand on Cameron's shoulder. She shook her head. "Ask me inside," she managed to choke out around a mouthful of bliss. "In *our* house!"

Cameron smiled and nodded in agreement. "Yes! Perfect!" he said.

"No!" Guy blurted. They looked at him in surprise and shock. Why was this stranger making suggestions while they were enjoying the best moment of their lives? He had to quickly cover. "It's so nice out," he said, attempting to sound jovial. "Come on, you crazy kids. Just do it here. I'll take a picture!"

But Cameron jumped up, took Brooke's hand, and pulled her toward the house. "Let's go! I want you to see what Guy's done with this place! *Our* place. Right, Guy?"

"We could make that official," Guy suggested, patting his plaid coat where the papers were waiting. But they had already scampered off together toward the house.

Brooke exploded into the house ahead of them and wafted straight through the entryway, twirling in a kind of rapture all the way across the hall and into the living room.

She took a big whiff of the successfully freshened air. "It's perfect!" she said. She clicked on the chandelier and, to Guy's relief, it came on. It gave off the kind of gunmetal half-light that happens at the peak of a solar eclipse, but it came on. She clicked it off and on again a few times and he waited tensely for her to ask why it wasn't brighter. But she seemed to decide that the moment was too wonderful to ruin with questions like that. "Ask me in here!" she called to Cameron. "*Our* living room in *our* house!"

Cameron very nearly sprinted across the living room to her. He took her hands and dropped again to one knee.

Guy hovered in the entryway, watching and wringing his hands. Cameron was going to ask her. "Sunshine, Lollipops and Rainbows" would forever be *their* song. It was all going to work out. Guy was going to—

Thump.

It came from the kitchen again. And it was louder than the last time. Loud enough to reverberate down the hall and produce metallic echoes from the sconces. Guy hoped they hadn't heard it, though it was impossible that they hadn't.

They interrupted their bliss to look over at him questioningly.

Of all the reaction choices available to him, he chose the most obvious: pretend it hadn't happened. "Do you want the fire on?" he asked. "The fireplace is retrofitted with natural gas service."

Thump thump. Thump!

Three in rapid succession. The last one was loud enough to make Brooke startle so hard that her glasses flew off her nose and she had to snatch them out of the air as they fell.

Guy hurried over to the wall. "The wallpaper is period-inspired—"

"What's that noise?" she said, not interested in wallpaper, no matter what period had inspired it.

Guy floundered for an excuse and settled on one. He smiled apologetically. "One of the carpenters might be doing some finishing touches. I'll just ask him to wait. Be right back. You kids just get on with it! And don't wander off!" He said it jovially, but then decided that it was a point that needed to be emphasized. He couldn't have them exploring on their own when there were *thumps* around. "Seriously," he added without the joviality. "Don't."

He walked back to the hallway, and as soon as he was out of their sight he switched to a kind of tiptoe run. He did that all the way up to the kitchen door, marveling at how Luther had ensured no squeaks in the floor. From here, he could only see a sliver of the kitchen: the end of the island and a small section of counter. And there wasn't anything obviously making noise. He couldn't help feeling like he was being toyed with.

Slam!

It was even louder than before, and so close to him that it stopped his heart for a second. But he still hadn't seen anything move.

So he steeled himself and sprang around the corner.

For a moment, he saw nothing. The kitchen looked as pristinely gleaming as it had before. No supernatural entities were dancing on the island. Nothing was making noise.

But a hint of movement in the corner caught his attention, and he poised himself to leap at it.

It was the pantry door swinging slightly open. He got the sense immediately that it wasn't being pushed at this moment, but rather was bouncing. Something had slammed it, and now it was swinging back. As he watched, it drifted to a stop with an open gap of a couple of inches.

But what had slammed it? And how could he stop it from happening again? If he simply closed it so it latched, would that be enough to foil whatever invisible forces were so offended by its pantry door-ness? If he brought those people in here and they saw a door slamming by itself, they'd never buy the place. And surely, that was the hole's plan. Scare them off with a pantry door.

He crept forward, touched the door hesitantly with his index finger, and pushed it. A tentative test at first, just to see if it would move. It offered no resistance.

So he pushed it the rest of the way until it *clicked* softly. And then he dug into the cabinet under the sink where he knew some scraps of lumber still hadn't been disposed of, and grabbed the smallest one he could find with a sort-of wedge-shaped edge. He jammed the thin end under the pantry door.

He tugged on the handle and it stayed closed. Tugged harder, and it still wouldn't budge.

He breathed for the first time since he'd entered the room.

If he was cursed to keep the house, then it wasn't much of a curse. He'd beaten it by closing a door.

"Is that the best you've got?" he whispered into the air, with no idea who he was talking to. He wondered if he should direct his taunt into the pantry, or maybe down into the basement. Surely whatever entity was here in the kitchen would deliver the message, and the hole would know not to mess with the likes of him. "Pathetic," he whispered. "I'm selling this house. Today. Right now." And he meant it.

When he turned to go back to the living room, the screaming started.

Chapter 18

Mae spotted the flashing emergency lights from the road. From this distance, she could see only lights and not the vehicles they were attached to, so she couldn't tell if they were police, ambulance, or fire. It looked like a mix—certainly at least three sets. She had a twinge of worry about Guy. Had he stepped on a rusty nail, maybe? Or set fire to the place as an insurance scam? Both theories sat comfortably in the "plausible to likely" zone.

She accelerated. But not too much. Her car had taken enough of a beating the last time she did that.

Just before she reached the end of the driveway, she could finally see that the house appeared mercifully un-burnt, and the flashing vehicles were two ambulances and two police cars. She wondered what emergency at the house could possibly need so many responders. And for most of the way up the drive, she actually worried that Guy might be dead. By the time she pulled up next to one of the police cars, she'd convinced herself it was true, and was trying to figure out what it meant for ownership of the house. It could be legally complicated.

She scolded herself for thinking only about that and not feeling sorry for poor dead Guy, agonizingly killed by rapid-onset tetanus from stepping on his own rusty nail. Really only himself to blame, though. He'd probably bought the tetanus-infected nails because they were cheaper.

But she was relieved to see Guy on the porch talking to an officer. So he wasn't the person she could see lying in the back of the nearest ambulance, being fretted over by paramedics. Or the person she could see lying in the back of the other ambulance being fretted over by different paramedics. She could only see their feet, and she had no idea who they were or why they needed separate ambulances.

Nobody stopped her as she hurried past the parked vehicles to the porch. Guy spotted her coming and inclined his head toward her in greeting, but didn't stop his conversation with the officer. Mae stopped at the bottom of the porch stairs to listen, and noticed that, for some reason, an awful song about rainbows was playing inside the house. She also noticed that Guy's jacket had a wide splatter of red across the front.

Had Guy murdered somebody? That theory, too, was right in the same zone as the others.

The uniformed police officer interviewing Guy sounded impatient, like she was annoyed that he had been briefly distracted by Mae. "Sir?" she said to re-claim his attention. "You said she attacked him first?"

"Attacked him?" Mae blurted, shocked. "Who?" Mae's mind floundered for explanation and finally settled on the house buyer. One of the people in the ambulances was the buyer that Guy had been talking about for months. But who was the other? And what did Guy do to them?

The officer shot her a scowl for the interruption. Guy pointed half-heartedly at Mae. "Sorry, this is my..." He had to pause and think about what to call her. "She co-owns the house."

"I wasn't here," Mae added, trying to be helpful. "Whatever this is, it probably wouldn't have happened if I was here."

The officer didn't care. "I'm talking to you, sir. She attacked him first?"

"That's what it looked like," Guy said, rubbing his eyes. He looked like he'd been through this story already and didn't want to go through it again. He switched topics to something more on his mind. "Hey, can we move all these cars and stuff around back? We're trying to sell the house. This really doesn't help."

"She attacked him with the glass flower vase?" the officer asked, writing notes and ignoring Guy's question.

"At first, I guess. That was already broken by the time I got there. I only saw her with the fireplace poker. And then the chair." He scrunched up his face, recalling. "No, wait, the chair was after the lamp cord."

Mae realized her jaw was hanging slackly open, and closed it. No matter where in her logical mind she looked, she couldn't find an explanation for this. Was Guy so terrible a salesman that he'd caused his buyers to attempt murder? That, too, wasn't far outside the realm of what Mae could imagine. But then why hadn't this woman attacked Guy instead of whoever she was with? Attacking Guy was something Mae could at least see as justified and plausible. And, possibly, enjoyable.

"And then he fought back?" the officer asked. "Attack her? The wounds on her head—"

"No, he never really fought back. She did that to herself. She picked up the poker again after she was done with him."

"She hit herself with the poker?"

"A bunch of times, yeah. I took it from her to make her stop, but then she found this candelabra, and—"

"Did she say anything?" the cop asked. "Give any reason?"

"She was screaming something at him, but I didn't understand it."

"Why not?"

"I don't think it was English. Some language I've never heard before."

An explanation reached up and grabbed Mae's mind to stop it from spinning.

The hole. The hole had done this to prevent Guy from selling the house. Exactly as Honest Bob had claimed it would.

Mae shivered with the realization, and suddenly felt like she could feel the cold air seeping up from the basement. Could the hole do that? Infect someone's mind? *Possess* them and turn them psycho? It explained some of what she'd found in her hours of gazebo Googling.

Mae was suddenly very sure she'd be sleeping in her car again tonight.

The officer stared at Guy for a lengthy pause but didn't press him. "How did they seem before the attack?"

He shrugged. "Happy. Like, really *really* happy. It was a little nauseating, honestly."

"Can you think of anything—anything at all—that might have prompted them to suddenly attack each other?"

He thought for a long time before answering. Or rather, he tried to *appear* to be thinking. Mae had known him long enough by now to tell the difference. "They must have had a fight while I was in the kitchen," he said.

But no, Mae knew that wasn't it. He was hiding the real reason.

The officer didn't appear satisfied with what he'd told her. She looked, in fact, very suspicious. And Mae couldn't blame her for that. But the officer flipped her notebook closed and seemed ready to move on. "Alright," she said, "we'll be in touch if we need more information." She had a tinge in her voice that confirmed for Mae that yes, she was suspicious.

As the officer descended the porch steps, Mae considered telling her about Honest Bob and the abandoned car in the ditch. But it seemed like a can of 30-year-old murder-worms not worth opening. It was a lot to hit a cop with after she'd just finished wrapping up an inexplicable violent assault. So Mae let her go and climbed up onto the porch. She stood with Guy and they watched the ambulances and police cars roll away and down the drive in an emergency convoy. Neither of them said anything until the convoy reached Whitemarsh Road and the ambulance lights faded into the distance. Then it was Guy who spoke first.

"We're never selling this house, are we?"

She almost felt sorry for him. Almost. "Do you want to tell me what really happened?"

With the officer gone, he dropped what had plainly been an act. His eyes took on a haunted look, and he kneaded his fingers as if trying to squeeze toothpaste from their tips. "I've never seen anything like it," he said. "She was... she was... I don't know *what* she was. She had this voice. And these eyes." He became lost in some horrible mental replay for a few seconds. After a long pause, he looked at Mae sideways. "How is this possible? It's *not* possible."

She decided that now was the best time to tell him what she'd dug up. It couldn't make him feel any worse. Well, not much. "It might be possible. I looked up the history of this house today. 41 people owned it before us."

Guy's eyes flickered. Maybe he was doing the same mental math that she had done. "That's a lot," he said dimly.

"Yes it is. I couldn't find much information about most of them. Especially the early ones. But I found a little."

He sighed. "Is it bad?"

"It's not good."

He sighed again.

"I found records for only about sixteen of them, mostly from the 1940s onward. Of those... four were reported missing and never found."

He sighed.

"Three committed suicide."

He sighed.

"Five were committed to institutions. As far as I can tell, they never left them."

She waited for him to sigh.

He sighed.

"And—"

He interrupted her so abruptly that it startled her. "Don't say it."

She said it anyway. "And four went to jail. For murder." That number included the builder of the house, Arthur Desmond Hole himself.

She could only guess about the ones she'd found nothing on. But the pattern was clear. Guy saw it too, and summed it up.

"So," he said, "our choices are: kill ourselves, go broke, go crazy... or kill somebody?"

"Seems that way," she said softly. It seemed that Honest Bob had been completely honest. There was no way out of this place without throwing someone down the hole. So there was no way out.

Guy stood up suddenly. "I'm selling this house," he said. "I don't care what it takes." He turned and pointedly marched into the house.

Mae sat on the porch for a while after and tried to decide what he meant by "whatever it takes." Because it could mean a lot of things.

Chapter 19

G uy wasn't ready to put up a "for sale" sign out front. That was the same as putting up a "this house sucks" sign. And if he did eventually resort to that, the only consolation would be that nobody would ever see it, because Whitemarsh Road had literally zero drive-by traffic. It would be both humiliating and useless.

But he did list the house in every "for sale by owner" listing service he could find. Some of them were expensive, especially for someone like him with every credit card well beyond maxed out. But those fees were easier to swallow than the commission an agent would take. And how would he ever explain to a real estate agent why people who came into the house wound up murderously possessed?

He had a few nibbles on the first day the ads were up. And he even scheduled two more showings, promising himself that he wouldn't let them out of his sight as long as they were in the house. As soon as he saw one of them get that look in their eyes and start to pick up the nearest weaponized decoration, he'd usher them quickly out the door.

The first showing was for a couple who said they'd flown in from San Diego to look at places, and wanted to squeeze in a look at this house before they got on the plane home. And after the first half hour of them strolling around the house like it was a museum of shining wonders and complimenting him on his renovation job, he allowed a bit of optimism to creep in. Maybe the hole had brought its A-game for Cameron and Brooke, and had nothing left for anyone else. It couldn't even stop these people from liking the floors, which they did.

At first.

They liked the floors much less when they came back downstairs from looking at the bedrooms and found a burbling stream of blood flowing along the entire length of the main floor hallway, feeding into a blood waterfall down the basement stairs. An unnecessary amount of running and screaming followed. But none of it was from Guy, partly because he had expected something like that to happen, but also because he knew the floors were laminate and would mop up more easily than hardwood. He needn't have considered it, though, because by the time he got back into the house after apologizing to the back of the California couple's car as it sped away, the blood was gone. There wasn't even a drop on the wallpaper.

The second showing, later the same day, was for a man from Manhattan who gave no personal details and made no small talk, but exuded essence-of-attorney. Guy was anxious about a possible repeat of the blood creek, but that turned out not to be a problem. This new visitor didn't make it past the front door. Because as soon as Guy opened the door for him, an enraged swarm of flies erupted out, whirling like a black dust devil, and engulfed the visitor. They didn't bother him for long—a few seconds at most. But Guy understood that, when it comes to fly tornadoes, any amount of time is too much. When the attorney peeled out down the driveway, he was still trying to expel bugs from one of his nostrils. Guy hoped there was no way he could sue for flies.

The flies, too, were gone when Guy went back inside. The hole had no interest in harassing Guy; it only toyed with anyone Guy brought in to look at the house. When it was only him, or him and Mae, the house was quiet. Dim, cold, and tomb-like. But quiet.

So Guy was already demoralized when one of the banks decided to brighten his day by emailing him about several overdue interest payments.

Or, at least, he assumed that's what it was about. He deleted it without reading it. And, to make sure he wouldn't ever have to read it, he decided to throw his phone down the hole, emails and all.

The hole exhaled and moaned at him. And it had never sounded so much like laughter.

Guy stood on the edge, holding his phone out over open space and seriously thinking he would drop it.

The house was unsellable. He couldn't book anyone else to look at it, because who knew what horrors the hole would dream up to chase them away? Two people had already been physically hurt; three if you counted flies up the nose. What was the point of bringing in more?

The hole was going to win. And that enraged him more. Not only was he going to lose everything, he was also going to *lose*. To a hole in the ground.

"Fine," he said out loud. "You win."

The hole didn't reply. It groaned and moved the dust in the air around him. He gazed down into its shocking depths, wishing it had somewhere he could punch.

And for the first time, he thought, "What if I just give it what it wants?"

He wasn't about to murder someone, of course. That wasn't him. He couldn't just go grab someone off the street, throw them in the back of his truck, and toss them down the hole. He wasn't Ted Bundy.

But what if it was someone who deserved it? What if he could find a Ted Bundy, and throw *him* down the hole?

The thought intrigued him uncertainly.

Instead of dropping his phone, he dialed it.

"As I was not scheduled to be on-site today," Luther answered without saying hello, "the duration of this call will be added to my invoice as an expense line item. Beginning now. Go ahead, Mr. Gillis."

Guy pushed past his annoyance. "Luther, I need to ask you something. It's kind of an unusual question."

Luther said nothing. Guy could hear him breathing.

Guy couldn't believe he was going to ask this. But he reminded himself it was just a question. It didn't mean he was going to do it. "In your job, do you sometimes have to deal with people who are a little... unsavory?" He meant criminals, perhaps the Providence Mafia members who were probably even now lounging on the deck Luther had built for them. But he didn't want to say it out loud.

"I don't know what you mean, Mr. Gillis," Luther said flatly. There was a pause. Then: "But, yes."

Guy thought about backing out, but again reminded himself that he was just asking questions. The hole breathed frostily at him, prodding him on. "And do these... 'unsavory' people ever need to make things disappear? Like, say, accounting records? Or..." He gulped. "...associates?"

Luther didn't answer. Guy could still hear him breathing. It was almost as ominous as the sound from the hole.

Guy waited for him, hoping that Luther would put it together and not force him to say it.

Luther took three more breaths, and then finally answered. "Just so we're clear..." There was another infinite pause as Luther searched for words."Are you asking me to provide you with criminals to be thrown down the hole by other criminals?"

Guy didn't respond. Spoken out loud like that, it sounded worse than he'd thought.

"Because if you are," Luther said, "then yes, I can provide that. What time is good for you tomorrow?"

It was suddenly far too real for Guy to deal with. His blood felt like it could feed a glacier. His heart stopped beating so it could listen to his next words and not miss any.

"No," he said. "Never mind." And he disconnected the call.

He wanted to forget that he'd ever had that idea. He couldn't believe it had ever even crossed his mind. It would certainly never have crossed Mae's. How could he look her in the eye knowing he'd suggested something like that?

Before he got his phone put away, he glimpsed the subject line of an email that had come in during his call. It was from another bank. About another missed payment.

He swung his arm back to finally hurl the phone into the hole. But he needed the phone. So he leaned his head out over the hole and screamed every ounce of pent-up rage and frustration out of him, hurling all of it down the hole with such force that whatever was down there would surely hear it.

Even though it was a phone call, Mae could hear the deep look of bewilderment on her mother's face. "You're still in that mansion? I thought it was done."

"It *is* done," Mae said patiently. "But we've had some problems." Most of what she used the kitchenette on the third floor for was making tea, and she was doing that now to help her through this call. She reminded herself not to stir so hard.

"We? You're still living with that man?"

"I told you, I'm not living with him. Well, I am... but not like how you're saying it. It doesn't matter. All I wanted to say is, I'm not sure how long I'm going to be stuck here." It could be forever, she thought. But now was not the time to attempt that explanation. "It could be a while. But I'll come out this weekend—"

A faint wisp of air brushed against her ear.

She stopped mid-sentence. Had she felt that? She knew not to doubt herself, but doubted herself anyway. A window might have been left open. The HVAC might have just come on.

She stood perfectly still.

"Mae?" her mother said from the phone.

"Shh," Mae said, knowing her mother would find it rude.

She waited.

And there it was. The unmistakable feeling that someone was standing right behind her, inches away.

Mae had developed a theory about this presence, and she was going to test it. It was based mostly on the fact that she only knew the name of one person who had certainly died in the hole—Arthur Desmond Hole's wife. So, by default, Mae thought the presence might be her. It wasn't scientific, but neither were ghosts.

"Gretchen?" she said softly.

"Who?" Mae's mother said from the phone.

Mae didn't answer. She waited.

A silent moment dragged on while Mae's tea cooled around her spoon.

And then there was a voice, unmistakably feminine, and delivered so close to her ear that Mae almost panicked and screamed.

There was a murmured, slurred syllable and then, much clearer, a single word. "Them."

Mae kept her head still, and tried to keep her heart still. "Who them? What about them?"

"What?" her mother said from the phone. Mae could hear the look of offended impatience on her face.

But the other voice in Mae's ear did not repeat.

"Who them?" she tried again. "Don't do this to me again, Gretchen. Use more words!"

But no more words came. And the electric presence she had felt leaning over her faded away as the air around her turned cool.

And then, from outside, the slam of a car door.

"Mom, I'll call you back," she said, and disconnected without waiting for her mother's protest.

She gave the counter a strong heave and the concealed door it was attached to swung open. She stepped out onto the balcony beyond and looked down into the driveway.

It was Guy's truck. And she couldn't imagine how that had anything to do with "them." What "them" would that be? House flippers? Bearded men? Trucks? Why did the spirits of the dead have to be so vague?

She watched the truck roll all the way down the driveway, disappear into the trees, and then reappear near the end of the driveway. It stopped at the edge of the road and pulled off onto the grass. Then the tiny figure that was Guy climbed out of the cab, dropped the back of the pickup, and lifted a "for sale" sign out.

Even from her great distance, he looked half-hearted about it. He had a slouch that he didn't usually have. He carried the sign to the edge of the road like he was putting out the trash. She watched him try to drive it into the ground just with his hands, then check to see if it would stay up. It fell, so he caught it and tried to drive it further into the ground using his elbow as a sledge. He tested it again, and it fell. Now with obvious resentment in his movements, he ripped it out of the ground again, hoisted it high above his head and drove it down over and over again, trying to spear it in with sheer brute force. When he stopped, it seemed like it might hold. He wiggled it as a test, and it fell crooked, but stayed up. A stiff wind would blow it over, but it seemed to be good enough for him. She wasn't sure, but she thought she saw him yelling at it, maybe telling it that if it fell over again, he'd burn it and roast marshmallows over its corpse. The threat seemed to work because it stayed up.

He slouched back to his truck. And from the way he moved, Mae could tell that he thought the same thing she did about that sign. Even if it stayed mostly vertical, it wouldn't work. Even if there wasn't the threat of potential buyers becoming possessed and murdering each other, nobody would see the sign. Nobody drove on Whitemarsh Road. And anybody who did was unlikely to be in the market for a Queen Anne Victorian mansion with a seven-figure asking price. The sign was utterly futile, and they both knew it.

Mae was about to go get her tea when some distant movement caught her eye.

It was a black minivan on Whitemarsh, flashing in and out of existence through the trees. She kept an eye on it, fascinated, as it approached the end of the driveway.

She could see Guy still standing with his hand on the door of his truck. He'd seen the van too, and was watching it.

It slowed.

And, after a ponderous few seconds, it turned into the driveway.

The sign, by some wildly improbable miracle, had already worked.

Chapter 20

The driver of the van didn't seem to have noticed Guy parked at the side, because they drove right past him while he stood there with his mouth hanging open.

The sign had worked. He had expected it not to work at all, and it had worked in less than a minute. He had a whole new respect for signs and the sign-making profession in general.

He looked up and down Whitemarsh Road, wondering for a moment if a whole rush of buyers was coming. Was the minivan just one of many? Had word-of-mouth spread already? But the road was, as usual, empty. It was just the minivan, which was quickly getting away from him up the driveway.

Guy jumped in his truck and followed it, keeping back far enough to not make them think he was chasing them. By the time he pulled up behind the van, it had parked next to Big Ugly Rock and its occupants were climbing out. Guy parked hastily and rushed toward them. Again, trying not to *look* like he was rushing toward them.

Out of the passenger side came a man: tall, immaculately groomed, a young-looking 30-something, with short-cropped bleached blond hair that looked like he had it professionally styled every morning before breakfast. He was dressed in a bright yellow turtleneck that seemed to push his head even higher, and matching yellow slacks down to shoes that were mercifully white. His long, pointed face had the delirious look of one who had achieved the purpose for which he was born and was now ready to attain another level of illumination. But the eyes were wrong, too intent and piercing, the blackness of the iris empty and cold. When he smiled—which he was already doing—it was not like someone happy to meet you, but like someone happy he'd soon be eating you. Guy found it hard to look straight at him.

The driver, who got out next, was a short, intent woman, innocent-looking, and strangely doddering like an extremely young grandmother. Her hair was pulled back into a ponytail and tied with a blue ribbon. Her small frame was draped in a yellow dress—the same yellow as the man's turtleneck—with a high collar and cap sleeves. She appeared not so much deliriously happy as deliriously okay.

"Hello!" Guy said, waving in a way that he hoped didn't make him look desperate. "I'm Guy! This rock will be gone."

The man turned toward him, and his smile cranked up from a seven to a nine. "It is beyond a delight to meet you," he said in a voice like a honey-coated icicle. "I'm Ansnorveldt."

Even having heard it, Guy had no sense at all of how to pronounce it. "Sorry... Ansor... velt?"

"Ansnorveldt. It's Dutch or something." He held out a hand to indicate the woman next to him. "And this is Ruby. She's my..." A pause. "She's also here."

The woman took half a step forward. "I won't be speaking," she said. Her voice was so nasal, Guy wondered if she was actually talking through her nose. "Not after this that I'm saying now."

Ansnorveldt gave her a smile of appreciation. He seemed to have a spectacular range of smiles with slight variations that were a whole language unto themselves. This one was wide, symmetrical, and had a slight movement to it like it was silently mouthing the words, "thank you."

Guy shrugged it all off. No sense in getting bogged down right at the start trying to understand things. He filed Ruby away as Ansnorveldt's assistant and/or wife. "Okay then. Well, very nice to meet you both."

Ansnorveldt looked past Guy and rubbed his hands together in anticipation. "So you're selling this magnificent home?"

Guy noticed that Mae had emerged from the house and was standing on the porch, looking at these new arrivals suspiciously. If she got in the way of this showing, then he thought he might throw her down the hole himself.

"That's right!" he said, trying to block their view of Mae's dark expression. "Were you just passing by, or...?"

"Sort of!" Ansnorveldt said. "We drive by here all the time and we keep seeing the sign, and every time we say to each other, 'We should really go have a look.' And this time we finally decided to just do it. Right, Ruby?"

She nodded and tried to shape her smile to look like his. It was a pale imitation at best.

Guy tried not to let his own welcoming smile flicker. But he was baffled by the lie. They were lying to his face. The sign had been up for ten seconds. Why would someone lie about that?

But did it matter? They were here to look at the house and maybe to buy it. What did it matter how they got here?

He flipped into salesman mode. After the nightmare with the other showings, he decided that his best tactic was some small measure of honesty. Maybe if he could remove some of the surprise when dark things started happening in the house, they wouldn't be so put off by it. It was worth a try. "Look," he said, "I gotta warn you. This house is beautiful. It's expertly restored. That's been my thing the whole time. Spare no expense." He heard Mae snort from the porch. "But... it has some quirks. Some things that you probably wouldn't expect."

"Oh, you'd be surprised what I expect." Ansnorveldt gave him a slightly different smile, a little narrower than the last one, and crooked. It gave the impression that he had recently beheld the loving face of his creator, while also loudly saying "shut up and get on with it."

"Alright then," Guy said. "Shall we?" He walked alongside them toward the porch steps and tried not to be astonished at how little Ansnorveldt's head bounced when he walked. Guy had to check to make sure the tall man's feet touched the ground.

"Hello," Mae said frostily as they approached. "I'm Mae."

"Yes!" Guy tried to be extra cheerful to make up for her attitude. "Mae is also here."

Mae scowled at him. "Guy, can I talk to you privately for a second?"

"Nope," Guy said pointedly.

"No no, please," Ansnorveldt said, "have your chat. We understand. We'll take the moment to just..." He inhaled deeply and gazed up at the tower looming darkly over the porch. "... take it in."

Mae dragged Guy into the house and closed the door. They could still sense Ansnorveldt hovering outside the door.

"Does anything about these people seem weird to you?" Mae whispered. "No, let me rephrase that. Does *everything* about these people seem weird to you?"

"They're buyers, Mae," Guy replied in the same whisper. "I don't care how weird they are."

"Why are they even here? Because they did *not* see the sign."

"Who cares? They're here to look at the house. I'm going to show it to them."

He reached for the door, but she held up a hand to stop him. "Wait! We need to be careful. I heard the voice again."

He almost rolled his eyes, but at the last second decided that the reaction to that wouldn't be worth it. So he stopped them mid-roll. "What did it say this time?"

"It warned me about 'them.'" She paused. "I think. I may have missed a word or two."

"Awesome," he said. "Very helpful." If dead people were going to talk to her, the least they could do was be specific. Before she could protest more, he pasted his smile back on and ripped the door open. "Please! Come in!"

Ansnorveldt, who didn't appear to have moved since they left him, wafted through the door, stopped just a few feet inside, and gazed at his surroundings as though entering the Sistine Chapel for the first time.

"Astounding," he said breathlessly. "It's everything I imagined."

Ruby came in after him, and her hard shoes *clacked* on the floor. She looked surprised at the sound. "Laminate," she muttered.

Guy didn't need to see the look Mae gave him. He could feel it without looking at her.

"Yes," Ansnorveldt said. "Isn't it wonderful?"

Guy almost let out a little laugh of glee, but barely managed to suppress it. He thought about giving Mae a triumphant look, but suppressed that too. She'd know without him doing it.

Ansnorveldt looked to Guy. "May I?" he asked, motioning toward the hall and the living room beyond.

Guy's voice cracked with joy when he said, "Yes please!"

Ansnorveldt floated into the hall and turned his head slightly to glance toward the stairs and kitchen, but drifted on through to the living room. Ruby clacked along behind him, her arms clutched to herself as if she was hugging a precious file folder or clipboard, but she wasn't. Guy stayed behind them, giving them space. And he could see Mae staring hard at them, just waiting for them to do something weird.

Guy realized too late that he hadn't had time to plug in the air fresheners or start up the music. The air in the house was heavy and still, and it smelled like a crypt. He thought about running around and plugging them in now, but it was impossible not to be spotted. He was suddenly tense again. Any minute now, he expected these people to notice the dead air, and/or to kill each other, and/or to be engulfed by supernatural horrors.

Ansnorveldt stopped in the middle of the living room and turned in a slow circle. He closed his eyes and took a deep whiff of the air.

Guy tensed more. This could be it.

And Ansnorveldt's face shifted to a different smile, like he'd just remembered what it felt like to be a child. "Such ambiance," he said rapturously. "You can feel the years in the air."

All of Guy's tension was forced out of him by an explosion of triumph. The perfect buyers for this house had fallen into his lap. He didn't know how, but here they were. He didn't have to do anything but wait and watch. He didn't have to lie. He didn't have to hide anything.

He launched into his pitch with gusto. "It's 5,200 square feet, eight bedrooms, two and a half bathrooms, with a full kitchen on this floor and a kitchenette on the third—"

"Do you think we could see the basement?" Ansnorveldt interrupted him. It came out of nowhere, in a blurt, like he'd been holding it back this whole time and it finally burst out of him.

Guy's tension seized him again all at once. Even these people had to be put off by the hole. *Everyone* would be put off by the hole. And Mae took a step forward into the room, alarmed that the subject had come up. She shot him a hard look of alarm. It intensified his tension.

"The basement is unfinished," he said. He sounded like he was reciting a prepared excuse. So he decided to go with it and recite a few more of them. "It's not well-lit. You won't need to go down there very much. And the floors—"

"Still, we'd like to see it," Ansnorveldt said, gazing at Guy liquidly.

"We just treated the stairs," Guy went on. "They can't be traversed right now. But I can show you the old carriage house—"

"The basement," Ansnorveldt said with a stab of impatience. He quickly attempted to erase it by switching his beatific look back on. "Please," he added with syrupy gratitude, like he was asking Guy to be the godfather of his children.

Guy floundered for another excuse. Anything. He couldn't say it was flooded; that was almost worse than the hole. He couldn't claim there wasn't a basement at all. Could he pretend he'd lost the key to the basement door? Could he claim a heart attack? He wouldn't have to fake most of the symptoms because he was experiencing several of them already.

But he knew none of that would work. And he could feel the sale slipping away. Nobody could forgive a bottomless hole in the basement. Not even people as zen-like as these.

He forced a smile. It was by far the least sincere facial expression he'd ever made. "Of course," he squeezed out. "Follow me."

Ansnorveldt paused at the bottom of the basement stairs, then lowered his foot onto the clay floor like an astronaut taking the first step on a new planet. Guy could hear his breath catch in his throat, as if that step was the most profound experience Ansnorveldt had ever had.

And then he saw the hole, and the rapturous look he'd had until now became fully euphoric. He let out a gasp of wonderment. And he floated all the way to the edge of the hole without hesitation.

Guy started to feel pretty euphoric as well. Because, far from being put off by the hole, it seemed like Ansnorveldt was in love with it. Guy was glad Mae hadn't followed them down the stairs, because she would probably find a way to make this into a negative.

Hypnotized, Ansnorveldt barely seemed aware that the hole had an edge at all. He stood with his toes out over open space and gazed down into the emptiness. He leaned out over it at an angle that by all rights should have meant he fell in, and held his hands over it like he was warming them over a fire.

"It's amazing," he whispered.

"It is?" Guy said before he could catch himself.

Ansnorveldt didn't answer. He closed his eyes and let the cold air rising out of the hole flow around his face. Then he turned his head sideways so his left ear was aimed at the hole. He seemed to be listening, and he did it for more than a minute. Guy didn't interrupt him. Both he and Ruby watched silently from nearby, and he was surprised that she seemed as puzzled by Ansnorveldt's behavior as Guy was.

Ansnorveldt finally pulled back and turned to Guy. "Guy, perhaps you could remind me of the asking price."

Guy started to legitimately believe this was a dream. "You want to make an offer?"

Ansnorveldt didn't nod or shake his head. He betrayed nothing but a profound sense of universal love. "The asking price?"

Guy gulped. "$1.75 million," he choked out.

Ansnorveldt put an appreciative hand on his shoulder as if Guy was a doctor who'd just cured him of a terminal disease. "Thank you," he said.

He took his wife-slash-assistant by the arm and the two of them moved far enough away from Guy that he could no longer hear their whispers. He watched them confer for a few moments. There seemed to be no disagreement between them. The rapturous look never left Ansnorveldt's face, and the okay look never left Ruby's. They might have been discussing baby names and agreeing on every one.

Finally they nodded to each other and stepped back over to Guy.

Ansnorveldt touched Guy's shoulder again. "Thank you for waiting," he said. "You've been very kind. We deeply, deeply appreciate you taking the time to show us the work you've done on this beautiful house. You've treated it with care, and respect—"

Guy missed a few of the sentences that followed because, with the note of finality in Ansnorveldt's melodious voice, Guy was thinking, "I've lost them. The asking price was too high. I had them and I lost them."

"—very proud," Ansnorveldt finished.

Guy wondered what he'd missed. But at the same time, he didn't care. "Uh huh," he said. His mind flailed around for a number that would win them back. How much should he reduce it by? Would one point five do it? That would still be a profit. Not much of one, but he'd be out of this mess and back on his feet. Maybe that would be enough to entice them. Maybe they could afford—

Ansnorveldt interlaced his fingers in front of him. "Mr. Gillis, we're prepared to offer you $2.5 million."

Guy's knees almost went out from under him. The only thing that kept him standing was his fervent belief that he'd misheard. "But... that's..." he stammered. "That's... that's *more*..."

"$2.5 million," Ansnorveldt repeated. "But we need a closing date this week."

"Before Saturday," Ruby, his assistant-slash-wife, clarified.

Guy very nearly passed out and fell into the hole himself.

Chapter 21

Mae was accustomed to identifying her whammo moments, when the unequivocally right thing to do slapped her in the face and she would stop listening to any other suggestions her brain came up with.

She was less accustomed to moments like this, when she knew she was doing the *wrong* thing. She would have to audition names for it, because so far she was calling it a ding-dong moment, and that just sounded dorky. So did whammo, but she wasn't to blame for that; her mother had come up with that one when Mae was nine and dorky stuff worked on her.

What she was doing right now to earn the *ding-dong* was breaking into Ansnorveldt's minivan. He and his weird little assistant were in the house with Guy, and Mae had sneaked away from the tour while they were distracted.

She'd never done anything remotely like this before, and it was practically causing her physical pain. Just opening the passenger side door, which they had conveniently left unlocked, caused her to close her eyes and wince like she was being jabbed with an extremely long needle. Her mind kept repeating as she did it: *ding-dong, ding-dong, ding-dong.*

But she did it anyway. She checked the front door of the house to make sure they weren't coming out yet, and scrambled into the passenger seat.

She didn't know what she was looking for. She just knew that Ansnorveldt was wrong. He looked wrong. He smelled wrong. The way he fawned over the house was wrong. His hair was wrong. Everything about him was wrong. She needed to find out... anything. But all she could tell so far from her break-in was that he kept an immaculate van. Even that was wrong in its way. These people were monsters—who kept a van so clean? There should at least be gum wrappers.

Ding-dong, ding-dong. She ignored the relentless chiming of her conscience and opened the glove compartment. And she didn't even get anything useful for all the discomfort it caused her. Just the bare minimum glove compartment stuff. And again, that felt wrong. Who didn't keep at least some wet wipes in there? Monsters, that's who.

Any minute now they could come out the front door, catch her in their van, find out she was a terrible person, and have her arrested, tried, and executed. And she had nothing to show for it. If nothing else, she should at least get their address.

She flipped open the car registration wallet and, growing more tense by the second, scanned the documents.

Even those were disappointing. The car wasn't registered to anyone named Ansnorveldt. Or to any person at all. It was registered to something called COTOWWHF INC. So it was a company car. Why were these weirdos out cruising for real estate in the middle of rural Connecticut in a company car?

Mae pulled out her phone to take a picture of the New Haven address on the registration. But before she could get it lined up, she caught movement in the entryway.

The door was opening.

She panicked.

She hurled the big wallet into the glove compartment, slammed the compartment closed so hard that it shook the van, and crawled to the driver's side door, which faced away from the house. She shoved it open and rolled out into a crouch. But she couldn't let them catch her anywhere near the van. She'd look guilty standing there. She'd look guilty walking away from it. She would look guilty just generally.

Her car was parked beyond the minivan, in a spot where she might be shielded from view if she ran to it. So she dashed across the space, dove into the passenger seat, and made herself as small as she could so they wouldn't see her.

She could hear their voices as they crossed the yard to their van, but she couldn't catch many words because her windows were rolled up and she was practically on the floor. After a few minutes, she heard the van start up, and saw the roof of it pass through her view as it executed a three-point turn. Then it was gone.

Half a minute later, Guy knocked on her car window.

She didn't sit up. Admitting that she was hiding seemed somehow more embarrassing than continuing to hide. "How'd you know I was in here?" she asked.

"I saw you."

Great. "Did they see me too?"

"Yep. They asked if you're okay."

Mae swallowed her humiliation and sat up, but refused to look at him.

"I have news," Guy said.

She refused to ask what it was.

"It's done. They bought it," he said. "We're out of here on Saturday."

Involuntarily, her head snapped around to look at him. His grin almost completely overtook his beard. He evidently expected her to leap out of the car and do a touchdown dance with her.

But she stayed in her seat, uncertain and dazed. The house had very nearly murdered the previous people who considered buying it. Whatever was in the hole didn't *want* the house sold. It wouldn't allow it. So how had these people bought it?

"That's not even the best part," Guy said. "Guess how much."

"I don't know."

"Not even close." He flicked his eyebrows at her like he was about to reveal a truly juicy secret. "2.5," he said. And he waited for what he expected to be an explosion of happiness.

Mae blinked. In her dazed state, the number meant nothing to her. It didn't seem like very much. You couldn't get a decent coffee for that. Was it some obscure foreign currency that let you buy a house with only two bills and some coins? "2.5 what?"

Guy opened her door like a concierge. "Million," he said, grinning. "You get your $80,000 back, and I'll throw in $20,000 more. No, make that $40,000. Get your mother a better house than she needs. All I need is your signature."

She stood out of the car, still unable to process the numbers. $2.5 million. That made no sense. That was more than the asking price. A lot more.

She looked at the house. As usual, despite the bright afternoon sun, the house lurked in a swamp of its own shadow. It seemed to exist in a different, darker universe that somehow overlapped this one. Just looking at it made her shiver. "Those people want to pay $2.5 million? For this?"

"Yes! And they didn't try to even murder each other. I watched."

"And you showed them the hole?"

He bounced like an excited child. "They loved it!"

"But you didn't tell them about the curse?"

Guy refused to abandon his enthusiasm in the face of her question. "Well obviously that's not real, because I just sold the house! In fact, they don't just *want* to buy. They're straight-up jazzed about it. I've never seen anybody want a house this much."

The question scratched at Mae like a cat wanting in: why? Why did these people want it so badly? Why did they lie about the sign? What kind of person would want to live in a house like this? Who would not be bothered by a bottomless basement hole that leaked frigid air from the center of the Earth and demanded human sacrifice?

She closed her car door and leaned against it, gazing at the house. It gazed back, sullen and dark.

"What do you know about them?" she asked.

"Nothing. But they're very nice. Some of the most positive people I've ever met. He hugged me before they left."

"How do they have $2.5 million?"

"Why does that matter?"

"Are they rich?"

"I guess they must be."

"What are they rich from? Are they doctors? Lawyers?"

"I didn't ask."

"Well, shouldn't we look into them? Do a background check or something?"

"Are you worried that they don't actually have the money?"

"No."

She hadn't dampened his enthusiasm at all. He was practically tap dancing. "Then what? If anything, you should be *done* worrying. You can finally leave this place, and nobody has to get thrown down the hole!"

Mae frowned. "Nobody has to get thrown down the hole... by *us*," she corrected him. "Aren't we just passing the curse off to somebody else?"

"It's not real. We know that now."

"Do we?"

Guy seemed to sense that his giddy tone wasn't winning her over, and turned practical. "Mae, this isn't just win-win. This is, like, win-win, win-win-win, win. Win. Maybe more wins than that. I lost track of how many people are winning here. You, me, those people buying the place. Luther. The house. Whatever lives in that hole. The bank. Your mother. Everybody wins. Everybody. There is literally no downside here."

That we know of, Mae thought.

Guy seemed to think she was negotiating. "Let's make it your $80,000, plus another $50,000. That's $130,000! That's a huge down payment on the perfect house. Brand new, not a fixer-upper. No holes in the basement. Or get a small house and, I don't know, a hot tub. Some art. A kangaroo. Whatever she's into. Think about that."

She did. She thought about it. And despite herself, she started to think that maybe he was right. Why did they need to be saddled with the problem of this house? They hadn't asked for it. It had fallen on them by accident. These people knew about the hole, and wanted it. Why not let them have it, and earn enough to keep her mother happy at the same time.

To her great surprise, it began to seem like a good idea.

Guy sensed that he was winning, and turned earnest. "Please, Mae. I need this. You have no idea how much I need this. If we don't sell the house to these people, we'll never sell it. Never. And I'll be ruined. You understand that, right? Ruined. Every dime I have, plus literally millions of dimes that I *don't* have—they're all tied up in this place. If it doesn't sell, then I'm in debt for the rest of my life. I do not recover from that. I need you to understand. Please. Please, can we close the sale?" It was more earnest than she'd ever seen him. For a minute, she thought he'd get down on his knees and clasp his hands together. He was already doing that with his eyes.

Mae's mind went in circles. She still had a gnawing sense of dread that Ansnorveldt was wrong. But maybe it was her imagination. Maybe they legitimately just enjoyed the novelty of living in a house that was inhabited by supernatural forces. Or maybe they didn't believe in it, and so the house had no power over them.

But whatever the case with the buyers, the look on Guy's face moved her. If she refused to sell, she could ruin him. And as much as she'd disagreed and fought with him during this seemingly endless project, she didn't hate him. And she certainly didn't think she could hurt him like this. Not knowingly.

Her mind stopped whirling, and locked in. Not a solid lock, but enough to make a decision.

"Okay," she said, after a lengthy pause. "Where do I sign?"

Somewhere in the back of her mind, a tiny voice said, "*Ding-dong.*"

Chapter 22

As Guy tossed another armful of scrap into the back of Luther's truck, Luther asked him for the third time, "Are you sure?"

"I don't need it," Guy replied. Also for the third time.

"You understand, you wouldn't have to push him in yourself. They will send someone to do that."

"Doesn't matter. Forget I ever asked."

"Alright. But if you change your mind—"

"Let it go."

Despite Luther's continued enthusiasm for the plan, Guy no longer needed any help from Luther's shady friends. Not that he'd ever seriously considered asking for that help. Not really. Not in so many words.

It didn't matter. The house was sold. For $750,000 more than he'd ever hoped to get. Even with the bonus he had offered Mae, he was making an absolute killing. Supernatural beings and ancient curses be damned; he was leaving this house, and it was making him more financially liquid than he'd ever been in his life.

He brushed off his hands and didn't even care that the scrap lumber had left him with a dozen or so splinters deeply embedded in both palms. With the proceeds from the sale, he could buy lots of tweezers to pull those splinters out. Good ones. Or, he corrected himself, he could pay somebody to pull them out of him with really good tweezers while he sipped sangria on a Mediterranean beach. It was time to start thinking big.

Luther's truck was almost full. Guy guessed that he could get two more armfuls from the bits of scrap still scattered around the back of the house. Cleanup after the end of a job had never been so satisfying or felt so final. Maybe because he'd never helped with it before. But this time, they needed it done at the speed of light, so he pitched in. And it would mean he could leave the house that much sooner and never come back.

"When are the painters taking the scaffold?" It was still propped up against the back wall, serving no purpose other than making the back of the house ugly.

"Today," Luther replied.

"You said that yesterday." And the day before. And the day before. And the week before. But he found it hard to care right now.

Because the house was sold.

He was tempted to go to the basement and raise a triumphant middle finger at the hole. He was sure it would feel good, but he was also worried it would cause some kind of earthquake that might crack the walls and spoil the sale. It wasn't worth it. Almost, but not quite.

Mae had been pitching in too, without Guy having to request it. She finally seemed willing to take the money and run, so he'd put her in charge of moving out the rental furniture. Luther assigned her a couple of guys and a cube van to help, and she did the work diligently over two days, working mostly in silence and mostly far away from Guy. She was obviously preoccupied, and it worried him. He wanted to see her skipping and dreaming of beaches like he was, but instead, she was distant and distracted. He'd often see her sitting in the corner of a room, typing or searching on her phone. He feared that she'd still do something to ruin the sale. He didn't know what, or why. But something.

On Wednesday evening, after all the cleanup had wrapped for the day, he decided that he'd head off any potential derailments by reminding her how great a deal she was getting. No harm in making sure she remembered that this was all good, both for her and for him.

He intended to buy her a cake and have somebody write "House Flipped!" on it with icing. But the bakery he went to in Woodbury said he needed to book a cake like that several days in advance. So he bought a cupcake with caramel drizzled on it, and wrote on it by dragging a coffee stir stick through the frosting. But, since it was a cupcake, he only got as far as "Hous" before he ran out of space. Still, it looked like a good cupcake and he couldn't afford anything else until the deal went through, so it would do.

Celebratory cupcake in hand, he prowled through the house looking for her. All the furniture had been removed now, so the house was emptier than usual, and his footsteps echoed. The house had a different atmosphere since they'd sold it. The air was lighter, more alive. Sound traveled better, and it no longer felt like an underwater mausoleum. More like a house. Maybe the hole was admitting that it had lost. It had no reason to fight him anymore.

He found her in the basement, sitting cross-legged in the faint amber light from the west-facing foundation windows, scrolling through something on her phone. She barely seemed to notice anymore that there was a bottomless drop in front of her, breathing primordial air at her.

But Guy still noticed. The memory of dangling over that pit, inches away from death (a *lot* of inches, but still), was fresh in his mind. He stayed back a few feet and waited for her to notice him. When she didn't, he said, "Hey."

He expected her to be startled, but she seemed unsurprised that he was there. "Hey," she said distractedly.

He held up the cupcake. "I thought we could have a little celebration. We did it, yay! Selling a hole house has got to be worthy of a cake. But I got this instead." It all felt goofy and he wished he hadn't said or done any of it.

But she smiled at him, and he wondered if she'd ever done that in his direction before. Suddenly he didn't feel so goofy, and instead wished he'd brought *two* cupcakes.

"That's sweet of you," she said. "And you wrote 'house' on it, sort of. How did you know caramel was my favorite?"

He didn't. It had been the cupcake closest to the front of the bakery cabinet. "You live with someone a while, you get to know things about them," he said. It made him realize how little he actually did know about her. He'd made no effort at all to find out anything, and now that the project was finished and they were on the same side, she didn't annoy him so much anymore and he felt bad about all the ways he'd treated her. Especially since she'd very recently saved his life.

He sat down almost next to her but further back from the edge of the hole, and set the cupcake between them. It had held her attention for about five seconds. Now she was fully focused on her phone again.

"Look," he said, "I wanted to say I'm sorry for—"

"Do these letters mean anything to you?" she interrupted. "C-O-T-O-W-H-H-F?"

He shook his head. "Don't think so."

"They don't mean anything to Google either. I'm sure about C-O-T-O, but maybe it was W-F-H-F-F." She typed quickly, then frowned in disappointment.

"Let me guess," he said. And then he realized that he couldn't. He had no idea. "No, forget that. Just tell me. What are they? They're not words."

She lowered her phone and looked at him like she was trying to figure out what celebrity he most resembled. Then, without answering his question, she picked up the cupcake and peeled the paper wrapper off. "I'm eating this now," she said. "Because I'm not sure you'll want to give it to me after I tell you."

That didn't sound good. It made him tense the whole time she was eating it. But he kept telling himself there was nothing she could do to kill the deal now. It was done. So there was nothing to worry about.

"It was the name on the registration for their van," she said around her last bite.

"Whose van?"

She screwed up her face like she didn't want to tell him. But she told him. "Ansnorveldt. The registration wasn't in his name It was C-O-T-O-something Incorporated."

Guy was unmoved. Had no desire to be moved. Couldn't be moved if he wanted to. "So what?"

She leaned toward him, grabbed his forearm, and squeezed. "I'm not saying there's anything wrong with him. It's just that there's something *wrong* with him. I'm doing a little background check. That's all."

Guy wanted his cupcake back. "You should let it go. The house is sold. The papers are signed. You can go back to your mother and be happy. This house is not your problem anymore."

She let go of his arm and leaned away. And her gaze inevitably fell on the hole again. She stared deep into it and he could see the cold air coming up from below moving the loose hairs dangling over her forehead. "It's weird," she said. "Have you noticed the house feels different?"

So she had noticed too. He'd wondered, but he should have guessed that she would.

She leaned forward more to look even deeper into the hole. "It's like it's waiting for us to leave. Like..." She paused. The air flowed around her face. "Like it *wants* to belong to them."

Just as she said it, Guy thought he heard the constant low moan of the rising air stutter. The flow of air grew stronger, just for a second, like a bubble of pressure had risen and popped, and Mae's loose hairs were lifted vertically, only for a second, and then dropped again. It was a gust, a sharp exhalation. A scoff from miles below the surface.

It felt—almost—like the hole was answering her.

But was it a confirmation or a denial? Guy couldn't tell, and wasn't even sure it had happened at all. But the way Mae turned slowly to look at him let him know that she'd noticed it too. And that she wanted Guy to acknowledge what it meant. He just didn't know what that was.

"What is it about these people?" Mae whispered, maybe so the hole wouldn't hear her. "Why does it want them? Don't you want to know? I do."

Guy shifted himself back from the hole a few more inches. He didn't know what answer to give her. She wasn't wrong—it *was* weird, and maybe a little concerning. But it just wasn't his problem. The deal was done. He had beaches to get to and umbrella beverages to drink on them. Anything he did with her seemed likely to put a damper on all that.

Mae stood up and brushed herself off. "I almost remember the address on the registration. I'm going to go find it. Come with me." She said it like a suggestion. Like he didn't have to, but it was really in his best interest.

He stayed on the floor. "The deal is done," he said. He wanted it to sound definitive, but it sounded weak and desperate. "They're moving in on Saturday. There's nothing we can—"

She turned away before he even finished the sentence, as though she'd been expecting exactly that answer and had already primed herself to turn and walk up the stairs. Which she did, loudly.

Guy sat on the edge of the hole and listened to it breathing. He didn't move for a long time, even after the sunset faded in the windows and the basement got completely dark.

He only went upstairs when he thought he was starting to hear whispers from below. It was probably his imagination. It might have been the hole whispering at him. Or it might have been his conscience. Either way, he didn't want to hear it.

Chapter 23

The fifth address that Mae tried couldn't possibly be the place. It looked like an abandoned Burger King. It was a squat, square, brick box shoved into the corner of a parking lot like it had been hurtfully rejected by the strip mall just a hundred feet away. It had no signage at all, and the windows were covered on the inside with what looked like newsprint paper. Anybody who noticed it was likely to wonder why it hadn't been torn down and replaced, maybe with a Chipotle.

But she could see that, behind the paper, the lights were on. And in the five minutes she'd been sitting in her car looking at it, two people had gone in. That was odd, and it gave her pause. Why would anyone be going into an abandoned fast food place at 8:00 on a Wednesday night? Or at any other time of any other day?

She tried again to remember what the address on the registration had looked like. She was sure it had started with 33, but couldn't remember if there were one or two digits after that. And she thought that the street name had started with D, and that it was a short word, but she was less certain about both of those. This place was 322 Duff Avenue. So maybe she was wrong about the 33 and right about everything else.

And another person had just gone in while she was thinking about it.

She slipped on her painter's cap and opened her door as quietly as she could, for no reason other than she felt sneaky. And she checked to see if anybody else was approaching who might see her. There were a few people in the parking lot, but they were all more interested in the strip mall than in her. She had a clear path to the door. She was surprised how good she was at sneaking. She would get to the door without being spotted, and then—

When she was almost there, a bald man in his 50s wearing a raincoat in its 30s came around the corner of the building and spotted her immediately.

She froze like someone caught shoplifting gum. It took all her self-control not to immediately flee back to her car and peel spectacularly out, and she fully expected a car chase.

But instead of sounding an alarm or hurling a net over her, the man smiled and held the door open.

Thrown off-balance, Mae recovered as quickly as she could, smiled back, and stepped inside.

The place was a single room, and mostly empty. It had a cloak-room next to the door, but it was really more of a cloak-corner with a rack and some hangers, one of which, surprisingly, held an actual cloak. The lights were institutional fluorescents that were painful to exist beneath, and the carpet was that thin, threadbare, gray builders' stuff that was barely softer than concrete. A card table sat at the far end of the room to serve as a kind of podium, and another card table at the side supported a coffee machine, some paper cups, and a few croissants on a plate. The rest of the space was filled with rows of folding plastic chairs, many of which were presently occupied by a mix of people who looked mostly impatient for something to start.

Trying to look as though she belonged, Mae chose a seat behind a broad, bearded man who seemed to regard her seat choice as a grievous breach of protocol. He shifted several chairs over and she decided not to follow him. She sank down into her collar instead and pulled her hat so far over her eyes that she could only see the carpet.

For a while, she sat and listened to the murmur of conversation, and began to wonder if she was in the wrong place. Everyone was talking about sports, work, the weather—none of it different than what you'd hear at work or at a restaurant. She had almost convinced herself to leave and try another address.

And then Ansnorveldt walked in.

Or rather, he floated in. And his assistant/wife/sidekick Ruby scurried along two steps behind him just as she'd done at the house.

But it was Ruby who spoke first. "Everyone! If we could—"

"I apologize for being late!" Ansnorveldt cut in. His face beamed like a lighthouse. Right away, everyone rose out of their chairs as if Ansnorveldt was the bride coming down the aisle. Mae jumped up with them but still tried to keep her face low. "As you can imagine," Ansnorveldt went on as he glided up to the card table at the front, "there are a lot of preparations. But that is no excuse for tardiness. And I apologize."

He took his spot behind the table and folded his hands in front of him, and Ruby stood just behind and to his right, pursing her lips like she was trying to keep herself from speaking. Ansnorveldt swept the loving beam of his smile across the standing crowd. It struck Mae that he looked very much like a preacher about to deliver a sermon.

And as soon as she had the thought, her brain clicked.

Oh God, she thought, is it a cult? Please don't let it be a cult.

"Now then," Ansnorveldt said. And then he raised his voice to an echoing bellow. "We pay homage to The One Who Was Here First! The original, the precursor, he who has dibs on the Earth and all upon it!"

"We follow after!" the crowd said back to him in unison, like a chant.

Yep, Mae thought. We sold the house to a cult. And not even one of the good ones.

Her mind clicked again, and she thought: The One Who Was Here First. TOWWHF. Add a CO on the beginning, and that was the van registration. Her mind raced, hunting for what the CO could be, and landed on "Church Of." It wasn't much of a church, but it made sense.

"Be seated," Ansnorveldt said.

There was a great sighing of clothes and creaking of folding chairs as everyone descended back into their seats. Mae tried to keep pace with the others and remain unnoticed.

"For those who don't know," Ansnorveldt said, "I... am Ansnorveldt." He lifted his arms out from his sides as though he was walking on water and intended to make sure they witnessed it. "Do not be frightened. I am as human as you. Perhaps more so." He motioned behind him, vaguely in the direction of Ruby. "I'll be taking over from your Chapter Ovate, Ruby, until the ascension is complete. After which... well, who cares? Right?"

That was apparently an inside joke, because it was met with smatterings of knowing laughter from around the room.

"Now, a couple of housekeeping items first," Ansnorveldt said. "If you haven't got your smock yet, get one from the boxes in the back before you leave." He waved a hand as if conjuring the boxes out of the ether. But the two cardboard boxes didn't need conjuring; they were already stacked in the back corner. Based on the logo printed on its side, one of them had recently contained toilet paper.

"They're one size fits all, and they're all the same color. So there's no need to dig," Ruby said from behind him.

"Yes, thank you, Ruby," Ansnorveldt said irritably. "Second item: we need more vehicles for Saturday. The van is only so big and we have a lot of things to move." His voice rose and some frustration crept into it. "As you know, Saturday is a big day. The biggest day since before time began. We've waited a millennium for this, and it will be another millennium before we get another chance. So surely somebody in the Community can spare a truck or a trailer. Something. Come on, people." He seemed to realize his frustration was showing through, so he re-lit his smile. "No judgment. You are all wonderful."

"We follow after," the crowd chanted.

Mae didn't know how to process some of what he was saying. The biggest day since before time began? What did that mean? And why was it Saturday, the day they were moving into the house? Obviously, the cult was crazy, but she hadn't begun to guess exactly *how* crazy.

She started to feel uncomfortable among these people, a heretic among the faithful. If they spotted her, what would they do? How fanatical could a cult be if they met over croissants on Thursday nights? Still, she wanted very badly to leave, but didn't think she could do it without being noticed.

"Third," Ansnorveldt went on. "Ruby tells me that some of you still haven't learned the chant. You were all emailed the lyrics. Yes, I understand, they're in an ancient tongue that has never been spoken aloud. But that's no excuse not to memorize them. Rehearsal is tomorrow night, so... be ready. Thank you."

"We follow after," everyone repeated. Their robotic repetition was starting to annoy Mae.

"And finally," Ansnorveldt said. "Most importantly. I don't see very many names on the sign-up." He pointed at the side wall where a single piece of paper was taped at eye level. A ballpoint pen dangled from a string next to it. As far as Mae could tell, all the lines on the paper were blank. "In fact, I don't see any names on it at all. If nobody's going to sign up to be a sacrificial victim, then what are we doing here?"

Mae gripped the edges of her chair until her knuckles almost burst through her skin.

Sacrificial victim. That's what he had said.

Sacrificial.

Victim.

Mae risked a glance around the room. Everyone was avoiding Ansnorveldt's stare, studying their shoes, deeply considering the meaning of the ceiling tiles.

Ansnorveldt went on before she could fully digest what he'd already said. "Can we even call ourselves a cult if nobody's willing to die? Frankly, it's a little embarrassing." He re-calibrated his face again and shone it at them. "No judgment. But please, friends. The ascension is Saturday. Let's get some names on that list. I'm looking at you, Gary." He locked his gaze on the bald man who had let Mae in. Gary sank so far into his chair that Mae thought it would snap closed and swallow him.

She didn't know what insanity these people believed, but it didn't matter. Because she now understood why they'd bought the house, and it was her worst fear realized. They weren't afraid of the hole, or of the curse, because they *wanted* to throw someone down the hole.

She couldn't stay here any longer. Things were snapping into focus and they were making her feel ill. She couldn't believe none of these people were as horrified as she was. In every face she looked at, she expected to see anger, disgust, horror. Instead they nodded passively, each of them trying to wordlessly indicate that they were planning to sign their names on the sheet but just hadn't gotten around to it yet.

Mae tried to shift inconspicuously out of her chair, ducking low to stay hidden behind the shoulders of the people a couple of rows ahead.

It didn't work.

"Is that..." Ansnorveldt said. She looked sideways and saw him leaning at an angle for a better look at her. "Mae, isn't it?"

Every face turned toward her, though they seemed unclear on why she was interesting.

Mae shrank under their stares, and her mind raced. She could envision three possible reactions. One was to just nod, smile, and indicate that she was only here out of mild interest and not in any way disgusted by his entire cultish organization. That was the middle reaction. To one extreme side of it, she could throw a chair at him, spill the coffee machine onto the floor and storm out, raging that she was going to torch his organization to the ground. That option was appealing but probably not realistic. To the other extreme side, she could pretend to be a prospective new member, and maybe even sign her name on the list as a sign of goodwill. But she didn't think she could manage the performance. Not when panic was trying to wring out the contents of her stomach.

She realized that she'd been standing there considering her options for an uncomfortably long time, and everyone was still staring at her.

"Friends, this is Mae," Ansnorveldt said, every word dripping honey with shards of broken glass suspended in it. "We owe her our gratitude. She helped refurbish our new temple and bring it up to its present glory, which you will all be able to enjoy on Saturday. Thank you, Mae."

He waited for a response. Maybe a "you're welcome." But she didn't feel like giving him that.

She wondered what she was afraid of. These people were weird, but they didn't seem to be frothing at the mouth. So why back down? Why pretend? What was the worst that could happen?

She straightened, and lifted her cap a little so it no longer hid her eyes. And she turned them straight at Ansnorveldt. "We're not selling," she said.

Ansnorveldt's semi-permanent look of rapture flickered. It transformed him. He suddenly looked less like an incandescent beacon of enlightenment and more like a bleached-blond human man in a yellow turtleneck. "You already did," he said.

"Well, we're backing out. You'll have to find somewhere else to have your little sacrifice party."

"You can't do that. It's illegal."

"So is this," Mae said. And she marched past empty chairs to the end of the aisle and ripped the sign-up sheet off the wall.

It produced shocked gasps from around the room as if she had just brushed white-out onto a Bible and changed the words in pen.

A couple of people stood. They didn't move toward her, but from the rabid looks in their eyes, she could tell they wanted to. She suddenly didn't feel so confident and rebellious anymore.

But she crumpled the paper anyway. As slowly and loudly as she could.

There weren't any names on it, so the gesture felt slightly empty. But they got the symbolism. She could tell because they stood up. All of them. Their eyes stabbed into her and they looked like, if Ansnorveldt said the word, they'd tear her to pieces, maybe with their teeth.

"Friends," Ansnorveldt said. His voice had lost all its honey, but still had the broken glass. "I take back what I said about owing Mae our gratitude. You're not going to be a problem, are you, Mae? We have an important task and not very much time to achieve it. We can't afford to have anyone in our way."

The room balanced on a knife's edge. Mae felt that if she said anything at all, they'd be on her like she was a Thursday croissant.

It occurred to her that if these people thought some major cosmic event was happening on Saturday, they might not fear consequences. They could bury her in a repurposed toilet paper box under that card table and never worry for a second about being caught.

Her mouth went dry. Her knees went soft. She held the crumpled paper tight in her fist and wondered if she could take one of them out by throwing it at them.

Nobody moved. Not her. Not them. Not Ansnorveldt. She didn't know for how long.

And then, finally, somebody did.

"I'll show her out," Ruby said.

She shuffled past Ansnorveldt and around the card table, and took Mae gently by the arm. "Leave," she whispered.

There was no attack in her posture or her voice. And everyone seemed to have deference for Ruby. A couple of them even stepped aside to clear a path to the door.

So Mae let Ruby escort her, and they moved in silence to the exit. Mae turned and walked backward so she could keep an eye out for attackers. But everybody stood still and watched. And Ruby pulled her arm harder.

"Thank you, Ruby," Ansnorveldt said. "Mae, we'll see you on Saturday, perhaps. When you hand over the keys." And he smiled that exultant smile straight at her, so hard that she could feel it burn.

Ruby took her right out the door, then released her arm and made a "shoo" motion with her hands. "Don't stop," she whispered. "And don't get in the way."

"Ruby..." Mae pleaded.

But Ruby didn't stop to listen. She disappeared inside and pulled the door closed. And Mae heard the hard *thunk* of a deadbolt from the other side.

Chapter 24

G uy reclined the seat and lay back in the cab of his truck because there was nowhere else to sleep. All the rental furniture in the house had been returned, and he'd even cleared out his air mattress from the bedroom on the second floor. He still had two nights to spend at the house, but he wanted everything out just so the job could feel complete. So even though it was still early, he was exhausted from carrying scrap and he stretched out in his truck, looking at the house and thinking about what Mae had said.

What is it about these people? It's like it wants *to belong to them.*

It was crap, obviously. But he couldn't stop thinking about it. The house had definitely changed its tone since he'd sold it. There was no question about that. But was it a stretch to think that meant something sinister? Maybe it was a good thing. A supernatural hole in the ground that liked its owners was bound to be better than one that hated them. Wasn't it?

He fell asleep with Mae's voice echoing in his head.

And then he woke up with Mae's actual voice yelling in his ear.

"Guy, we need to cancel!"

It took him ten seconds to figure out that he was awake, five more to discern that it was still night, and another five to calculate that he'd been asleep for a couple of hours. Mae spent all of those 20 seconds repeating what she'd said.

"We need to cancel!"

He tried to roll the window down, but the truck wasn't started and in his foggy state he couldn't remember how trucks worked. So he opened his door instead. "What?" he said, cotton-mouthed.

"We need to cancel the sale," she said. She looked the exact opposite amount of awakeness that he felt. She was agitated, even jittery.

It was too much for him to handle in his present state. "Why?" he managed to ask, rubbing his eyes.

"Those buyers... they're worse than we thought."

Guy waved it off. "I get it. They're weird. But even weird people have the right to own a quality home. That's probably in the constitution or something." It probably wasn't, but he still couldn't wake up to think about it. He wanted very badly to be asleep again. He laid his head back on the headrest and tried to find the way back into his dream.

"They're not just weird, Guy. They're a cult."

Guy thought at first that she was exaggerating, but the more he pictured the couple with their impeccable hair, oddly monochromatic outfits, and unflappable expressions of joy, the more sense it made. "Yeah, that tracks," he said. "But still, if they need a place to live..."

She stepped closer to the open door. She was within punching-him range now, and he didn't like it. "They're going to sacrifice people."

"How do you know that?"

She held up a crumpled sheet of paper that he hadn't noticed she was holding. And, with admirable dramatic flourish, she uncrumpled it and showed it to him.

He could dimly make it out in the faint illumination from the truck cabin lights. The paper was mostly blank except for parallel rows of black lines. He had no idea what it was supposed to mean, and he told her so by giving her his best puzzled look.

She turned the paper back to herself and looked at it. And made an exasperated noise. "Agh. They could at least put a header on it. It's a sign-up sheet. For sacrificial victims."

He blinked at her, because nowhere in his mind could he find anything that felt like an appropriate response to that.

"It's crazy!" she said, pacing in an exasperated circle. "They have some kind of once-in-a-millennium ceremony on Saturday that they think is going to change the world, and to make it work, they need a human sacrifice. So they're going to sacrifice some of their members. Maybe all of them. I don't know. Nobody is signing up, so he's trying to coerce them. I saw it, Guy."

It sounded nuts. And he said so. "That's nuts. What do they think is going to happen?"

"I don't know! But it doesn't even matter! *They* think something will happen. *They* think it needs a sacrifice. So they're going to throw some of their followers down the hole. How do we cancel the sale?"

Guy finally felt awake enough to get out of the truck. He was almost able to see her point. But he didn't want to see her point. He wanted to sell the house. And, in fact, he already had. "We can't. Even if we wanted to, we can't. It's a binding agreement. It's signed. You can't just back out of a purchase agreement."

"Tear it up." She said it like it was obvious and he should have done it already.

"It doesn't work that way. You think if we just tear it up, it ceases to exist? It's already on the books. They'll sue."

"There has to be a way!"

The truth was that he didn't know. Maybe she was right and there actually was a way. But if there was, it would likely mean a protracted legal battle with lots of lawyers that needed to be paid.

And even if they won, it meant he wouldn't get any portion of the $2.5 million sale price at the end of it. None of that was appealing. So he said: "No, there's no way. It's done. As of noon Saturday, the house is theirs."

She balled both her fists and pressed them to her face, and for the first time he saw past the dollar signs that had filled his vision all day, and started to worry about her.

She dropped her hands and looked at him like he was a drink she'd just noticed had a bug floating in it. "It doesn't matter to you that they'll be throwing innocent children down that hole?"

"It's children now?"

"Maybe! If nobody signs up, kids are easier to catch!"

He worried about her even more. "I gotta tell you, you're going a little nuts right now."

Anger flashed across her face. "Yes! I am! And I don't know why *you're* not!" She stormed away down the driveway and climbed onto the hood of her car. She sat there with her face buried in her hands.

He didn't think she was crazy. She was acting crazy, but that didn't mean she was. He believed everything she was saying, and that surprised him a little, given how much of a fruitcake he'd thought she was when they first met. He now recognized that what he'd interpreted as fruitcakery was just an excess of conscience, which he couldn't really convince himself was a bad thing.

So if he believed what she was saying, then selling this house to those people meant somebody was going to die. Maybe several somebodies. He didn't believe for a second that their sacrifice meant some cataclysmic supernatural event would take place, but Mae was right—it didn't matter. People would die either way.

The question was, could he live with that?

The other question was, could he live without his share of the $2.5 million?

He didn't know the answer to the first, but the answer to the second was a loud and emphatic "nope."

He couldn't live without that money. He'd be ruined. Bankrupt. In debt forever. No matter what, he could not interfere with the sale. If people were dying, they maybe should have considered that before they signed up for Ansnorveldt's freaky death cult. That kind of thing was exactly why it was called a death cult. It was right there in the name.

As vehement as he was about that answer to the second question, he still could not shake the first. Would he be able to sleep at night, even on a pile of cash, if he could have saved people from dying, and didn't?

He still didn't have an answer. He liked thinking about sleeping on the pile of cash, though. It seemed comfortable.

He looked over at Mae again. She hadn't moved from the hood of her car, and hadn't broken her pose at all. She seemed to be wrestling with mental anguish. So he had that to live with as well. That didn't help.

And suddenly he had an idea.

Bridgeport.

That could work.

He saw it with such clarity, he didn't know why he hadn't thought of it before. It didn't require him to answer that first question, or to change his answer to the second. But it was still a risky, probably illegal plan. Did he want to go down that road? He wavered on the edge of convincing himself for a long time, teetering to one side and then the other. Then he decided to see if Mae would push him over. He could put that excessive conscience of hers to work for him, because his had atrophied from under-use.

He walked over to Mae. She showed no awareness at all of his approach. "You said this ceremony is once-in-a-millennium?" he said.

She lowered her hands from her face and looked at him wearily. "That's what they said. They've waited a millennium."

"So if they don't get to do it on Saturday, they'll have to wait another 1000 years?"

"They said that too. Is this going somewhere?"

He wrung his hands. "I don't know. Maybe. But here it is: we can't cancel the sale, but we *could* make sure they can't do their sacrifice on Saturday. After that, the house is no use to them for 1000 years. But they can't back out of the deal any more than we can. The deal will already be closed."

That made her pause for a blink or two. It hadn't occurred to her. "How do we do that?"

"Simple. We don't leave."

She waited for him to elaborate, and he relished the few seconds when he knew more than she did.

He let it go on too long, and she got impatient. "We don't leave? Can't they just have the cops come in and drag us out?"

"No! That's the beauty of it! Just like the guy in Bridgeport! I mean, before he died. The deal was closed; the house was mine. But he refused to leave, and I couldn't legally make him. Not without a trial, and that was going to take at least a month."

"So we just... stay in the house? What if they break the doors down?"

"If they were that kind of cult, they could have done that without paying $2.5 million. Not needing to smash their way in was worth that much to them." He jumped up on the hood of the car and sat next to her, forgetting how small the car was. They were practically cozied up together, but he went with it. "We only need to delay them for a day. They'll get a lawyer and demand that we leave, but by then it's too late. Their little ceremony doesn't get to happen. On Sunday, we hand them the keys, and they take over the house they already paid $2.5 million for."

"They'll cancel the deal."

"On Saturday at noon, their money is in my bank. After that, if they don't want the house anymore, they can sue us—which they will lose. Or they can try to sell it. And you and I both know how much fun that is."

She stared at him hard for a long time. And with every passing second, he became more certain she would tell him it was crazy and they shouldn't do it. He was on the brink of saving her the trouble and saying it himself.

But instead, she said: "Whammo."

So he decided that his plan wasn't so nuts after all.

Chapter 25

Noon on Saturday came and went. Mae, who had already been anxious all morning, went into anxiety overdrive. She paced the third floor, going into every room and looking out every window, every time expecting to see the cult arriving.

After an hour, Guy came upstairs and reminded her to eat something. He had been focused and helpful all day Friday while they'd prepared. She'd formed brand new, positive opinions of him, and wanted to believe that it wasn't just because he was finally agreeing with her about something. Maybe it was. But whatever the case, they felt more like a team now than they had in the months of renovation. She had to admit, she was glad he was here. But she still didn't take his advice and eat anything. She kept pacing until after 2:00 and then finally sat on a window sill instead and stared at the road.

For a cult about to usher in the end of the world, they sure weren't in a hurry.

Just before 2:30, she heard Guy talking to somebody downstairs and she ran to the landing. He yelled up from below that Ansnorveldt had called and arranged to meet at 4:00 to pick up the key. Guy had played nice, pretending that all was fine and good and he'd be there to do the hand-off.

Mae couldn't quite convince herself to relax until 4:00, though, so she kept alternating between pacing, fidgeting, and standing on the turret balcony doing mindfulness exercises that didn't work.

A few minutes after 4:00, they appeared.

Mae watched from the balcony as their vehicles rolled up Whitemarsh Road like a troop convoy. Guy had decided to stay down near the front entrance, but Mae really wanted to be up high because when you were about to be under siege, a turret in a tower seemed like the place to be. She felt like she should have a bow in hand and maybe a cauldron of boiling oil to pour, and she almost wished she'd thought of those sooner.

Ansnorveldt had been persuasive asking his followers to bring their own rides. The black minivan led the way, followed by two SUVs, one of them towing a trailer full of stuff—she didn't dare imagine what that stuff was—with a tarp over it, then three smaller cars, and finally a 16-foot U-haul cargo van. They were precisely spaced on the road like they were tethered together, a hive mind of cult drivers. They seemed unhurried, approaching at a leisurely pace that somehow made them more intimidating. Like they didn't need to hurry because they would get this done on their own time no matter what stood in their way.

The convoy reached the end of the driveway and for a moment, Mae wondered if they might have forgotten where the house was. But it was wishful thinking. The van made the turn confidently and disappeared into the trees, then re-emerged moments later. It looked like the head of a huge snake writhing toward the house, with all the other vehicles as its serpentine body.

"They're here," she said into her phone. She'd kept a line open with Guy so they could coordinate their plan. Which seemed slightly unnecessary given that they didn't have much of a plan at all. At least she wanted him to know that the wait was over.

"I see them," he replied from the phone.

She could hear in his voice that he was on edge, anxious. She didn't know how to reassure him because she was on edge and anxious too. She wasn't sure what these people were capable of, or how they would react when they found the place locked up. They'd certainly been none too friendly with her at the cult meeting, but would they smash windows and batter down doors? At least she was up in a tower and they'd get Guy first.

She scolded herself for the thought.

The vehicles parked in a tight grouping between the big chunk of rock and the house. They left enough space for the cube van to get around them and back up almost to the front door like it expected to dump its contents on the porch and be on its way. By the time they stopped, they were almost directly below Mae and she had to lean over the railing to peer down and see them.

A few of the cultists got out of the SUVs first and lingered awkwardly around the cargo van like kids waiting for their father, reluctant to approach the house until he was with them. Mae noted that they had obediently dug into the boxes at their meeting, because all of them were draped in what looked like billowy, lemon-yellow artist smocks. Even from this height, Mae could tell that they were embarrassed to be wearing them. And with good reason—they looked stupid.

When Ansnorveldt finally glided from the passenger seat of the minivan, they all immediately fell in behind him, moving with him but always letting him stay in front by half a step. Six more emerged from the minivan after him—Ruby among them—and still more out of the other vehicles until Mae counted nineteen altogether. They formed up behind Ansnorveldt like disconnected bananas trying to get back into their bunch.

Ansnorveldt looked around the yard and seemed disappointed. Maybe he'd been expecting press coverage to make this more of the big moment he probably wanted it to be. But, finding that it wasn't any bigger than just getting out of a van and walking through the dirt to the porch, he decided to add some gravitas by giving a speech. He turned at the top of the porch steps and addressed his banana congregation.

"Friends," he declared. She couldn't see his face but could hear the beatific smile in his voice. "Our long wait is at an end. More than a century ago, Arthur Desmond Hole set out to scour the Earth in search of the Great Passageway. And, as luck would have it, he found it in the first place he looked. Right here. And he constructed this magnificent temple upon it. It is one of many such temples built by many such devoted people over the centuries, all of whom believed they had found the Great Passageway. Most were stupid and wrong, and we don't talk about those ones and never did. Because we now know that Arthur Desmond Hole was right, and had found the one, true Passageway... right here."

Somehow Mae hadn't put together that this cult and Arthur Desmond Hole were connected at all, but now it seemed obvious. It was practically right there on Wikipedia. *Hole was widely reputed to have a lifelong fascination with the occult...*

"But though Arthur Desmond Hole opened the Passageway with his sacrifice, he lacked the courage to stay and nurture it. Many others were forced to come after him and make similar sacrifices. It was a big, century-long, sacrifice-a-palooza. And now, only one more sacrifice remains." His voice rose. "Tonight, The One Who Was Here First Returns! Tonight, at 8:47—the exact time of the Galactic Conjunction Or Something, when all the galaxies are in alignment... or something—there will be a bright new dawn!" He paused. Mae wondered if he was wishing he'd written this in advance. "Metaphorically! The actual dawn will still be in the morning at the usual time! But tonight at 8:47, a new age begins! As he who has dibs on the Earth comes to claim it! He who called shotgun on the universe comes to take his seat! He who was the first come shall be the first served! By us, and by all of humanity!"

"We follow after!" the whole congregation repeated, raising their fists into the air.

Then Ansnorveldt turned and went for the front door. They were coming inside.

Mae bolted for the stairs.

The doorknob was rattling when she reached Guy at the bottom of the stairwell. From there, they could watch the front door without being visible through any of the windows.

Mae and Guy had agreed that, at first, they would try to keep their presence a secret. They'd squeezed Guy's truck into the carriage house at the bottom of the hill, and buried Mae's car in branches near the other, much older hidden car. And then they'd locked themselves in the house. They hoped this would create confusion outside and lead to hours of delay while Ansnorveldt tried to locate Guy and acquire the keys.

They hoped.

They both stood on the stairs and watched the doorknob, almost expecting it to fall off. Shadows and reflections shifted across the floor as Ansnorveldt and some of his followers tried to see in the windows. But Mae and Guy stayed close together in the hall, blocked from view.

"You hear the speech?" Mae whispered.

Guy nodded. "So there's, like, an ancient god in the hole? Coming to take over the world?"

"I guess."

"That's a little crazy."

It's a lot crazy, she thought. But she didn't have the chance to answer.

The knob stopped rattling, and there was a pause. Then it rattled again with more urgency. Mae could feel Ansnorveldt's annoyance even through the door.

They heard a muffled discussion. Just bits and pieces. "...locked... give... supposed to... key..."

There was a pause.

And then Guy's phone buzzed.

He immediately silenced it.

Another quiet minute passed. And then another muffled discussion outside.

And finally, somebody said "...another door..." And footsteps moved off the porch.

So far, their minimal plan seemed to be working. But neither of them had much idea of what to do after that. It depended heavily on what Ansnorveldt did. If he showed any sign of preparing to break a door down, that's when Mae and Guy would be forced to reveal themselves. And that would force Ansnorveldt to back off.

Again... they *hoped*. Mae was entirely uncertain how stable Ansnorveldt was.

Guy motioned down the hall toward the kitchen, and they crept that way together. Mae caught a glimpse of yellow moving outside the dining room window as she passed, but it was dark enough inside that nobody would be able to see in without pressing their faces to the glass. She hurried past without stopping and turned into the kitchen just before the doorknob on the back entrance started rattling.

After their failure at the front door, they gave up more quickly on this one. And, again, there was a muffled discussion outside. The voices were rising now, getting angrier.

Guy's phone buzzed again. He silenced it.

A face appeared in the kitchen window, a gaunt man with his hands cupped around his eyes to see in.

Mae ducked back and shoved Guy ahead of her, and as they fled into the hall she could hear the man at the window saying, "It's dark."

They crept back along the hall toward the dining room. Guy pressed his back to the wall and peeked around the corner at the dining room window, and Mae dared a look over his shoulder.

Ansnorveldt was still on the porch with his phone to his ear. He waited a few seconds, then shut it off angrily. She could see his followers watching him from the ground, looking a little lost. Their world, which included ancient subterranean gods, stopped making sense when their infallible leader couldn't get a door open.

Ansnorveldt motioned for Ruby to join him on the porch, and she hopped up with a worried look. He whispered something to her, and she went back down the steps and whispered to someone else, a broad, curly-haired man who had rolled up the sleeves of his yellow smock in a failed attempt to make it look cooler. He nodded and pushed through the crowd, then walked all the way over to the covered trailer.

"What are they doing?" Guy whispered. "I liked it better when they weren't doing anything."

They couldn't see through the crowd what the man was doing at his trailer. But when he weaved through the crowd to get back to the steps, he had a crowbar in his hand.

He was going to force the door open.

Mae shoved Guy's shoulder. "Call him. Hurry."

Guy ripped out his phone and fumbled with it.

The man with the crowbar moved out of their view past the dining room window, headed for the front door. Mae heard the first, hard *thunk* of the pry bar being jammed into the edge of the door.

And Guy finally managed to dial the number.

Outside the window, Ansnorveldt's head snapped down to look at his phone. And his hand went up to tell the crowbar man to stop.

"Ansnorveldt, hi!" Guy said into the phone. She was amazed at how apologetic he managed to sound.

She could see Ansnorveldt outside talking into his phone, but couldn't hear what he said.

"Yeah, sorry," Guy said, "I'm running late. But I'm on my way. I'll have you inside in no time. No need to break the doors down. Ha ha."

Mae jabbed him in the back with her elbow for being so obvious.

Outside, Ansnorveldt said something else, and she was pretty sure his face was red.

"I know, I know," Guy said into the phone. "And I'm really sorry. Just sit tight. A few minutes! An hour at most!" And he hung up.

Mae didn't think Ansnorveldt would wait that long. "What do we do in an hour?" she whispered.

"I don't know," Guy replied. "I call again and tell him I had car trouble. Or traffic. Something. I figure I can buy us another hour. After that, we'll have to let them know we're in here and we're not going anywhere."

"They won't be happy."

"Yeah, but how crazy are they? We just keep everything locked up tight—"

Thunk.

The hard, sharp sound came from the entryway. And at first, Mae thought the rolled-up-sleeves cultist was trying his crowbar again. But she could see him outside at the bottom of the porch steps, nowhere near the door. She looked at Guy, and he was giving her the same questioning look. What was that?

They both crept past the dining room and into the entryway. Mae scanned the room quickly, and couldn't see anything different. There was no furniture, so nothing that might have moved and made the sound.

She turned back to Guy, expecting him to be as puzzled as she was. But he was waving to get her attention, and when he saw her looking, he pointed emphatically at the front door. It took her a moment to spot what he was gesturing at.

When she finally saw it, she almost shrieked out loud.

The door had unlocked itself.

Chapter 26

G uy looked out the dining room window. Ansnorveldt wasn't looking at the door. He was pacing the porch, obviously angry but diligently trying to appear zen-like so his followers wouldn't lose faith. None of the other cultists were anywhere near the door. None of them had unlocked it. It had unlocked itself.

The hole, which seemed to have gone dormant since they had sold the house, was trying to let its new owners in.

Waving at Mae to stay back, Guy crept forward and took hold of the brass deadbolt thumb turn. It was cold. Much colder than the air. So cold that it almost felt hot under his fingertips, and he had to resist the urge to jerk his hand back. As quietly as he could, he twisted it from vertical to horizontal again and felt the deadbolt engage with a soft *click*.

He waited to see if anybody outside would hear the sound. But there were no shouts, no flurries of activity. So he took a step back. And another. And finally turned to creep back toward where Mae was watching from the hallway.

Thunk.

The door unlocked again. Loudly.

Guy spun back, dashed the two steps and twisted the dead-bolt back to the locked position. And he held it there despite the cold metal biting into his skin.

He looked back at Mae and pointed down the hall with his free hand. "Kitchen door," he mouthed. If it was happening to this door, it was probably happening to that one too.

She nodded and disappeared into the shadows of the hallway.

As Guy gripped the lock, its cold penetrating deep into his fingertips, the doorknob right below his hand rattled.

Somebody outside must have heard the click, and was testing the door. But it was exploratory only, and lasted just a second or two before they gave up, probably thinking it had been their imagination.

Guy's heart pounded. What could he do now? He couldn't take his hand off the lock. And Mae was probably in the same position at the back door, stuck holding that lock. Would they be trapped like this for the rest of the day?

Except... the cult had just tried the door twice and found it locked. It was unlikely anyone would try it again. As long as the lock didn't make any more unlocking noises, they'd probably leave it alone until somebody came along with a key.

It was a definite risk, but better than being stuck holding the lock. So he got ahead of the hole's plan and—gently, so it wouldn't make even the slightest *thunk*—unlocked the dead-bolt. And then released his grip on it, and took a step back.

Nobody burst through the door. Nobody had noticed.

He allowed himself to feel triumphant for a second. He had beaten the hole at its own game. It couldn't unlock an already-unlocked door. If it wanted the cultists to try the door again, it would have to get their attention another way.

He'd just finished that thought when the door, pulled by invisible hands, flew open.

It swung hard enough that it cracked against the wall and vibrated with the shock. And suddenly, Guy was looking straight outside at a dozen startled faces looking in at him.

For a frozen moment, he stared at them and they stared at him.

Then he sprinted ahead and shouldered the door closed, slammed his weight against it and twisted the deadbolt locked. He leaned his back against the door and cursed the hole, which had just moved their schedule up by at least an hour.

His phone buzzed in his pocket.

Ansnorveldt, of course. But this time, Guy answered.

"What are you doing, Guy?" Ansnorveldt said. His voice quaked with barely contained rage. "You're inside the house. You were lying to me. No judgment. You're wonderful." He raised his voice so his congregation could hear "You're all wonderful!"

"We follow after!" came their chanted reply, muted by the distance.

"We're staying one more day," Guy said with all the force he could put into it. "You can have the house tomorrow."

There was a long silence on the other end. Guy could feel Ansnorveldt's anger radiating through the phone. And when he spoke again, Ansnorveldt sounded like he was talking through gritted teeth. "We don't want the house tomorrow. We want the house today. As we agreed upon."

"Yeah, well, that doesn't work for us anymore."

"The house is ours," Ansnorveldt said. "You're trespassing. We'll call the police."

Guy almost grinned. He'd expected that. He knew from experience that even if Ansnorveldt called the police—which he doubted—the cops would not break in and drag him and Mae out. It didn't work that way. And he had a cool reply chambered and ready to fire.

"Be my guest," he said with his best Clint Eastwood growl. It wasn't nearly as cool as he'd thought it would be.

Ansnorveldt hesitated. Guy had called his bluff and now Ansnorveldt probably had no idea what to do. Guy knew because he'd been on the other side of this situation himself in Bridgeport and remembered clearly having no idea what to do.

For a moment, Guy could hear other, distant shouts over the phone. Somebody was yelling something at Ansnorveldt, but he didn't respond to them.

"What's happening?" Guy demanded.

"One of the community suggested that we throw a brick through the window," Ansnorveldt said. "Thank you, Steve. I'll keep that in mind. You're wonderful." He lowered his voice. "He's not wonderful. Between you and me, I always hoped to see his name on the top of the sign-up sheet. It's the only way he'll ever be useful. Anyway, don't worry, Guy. I don't intend to throw a brick through the window."

"I didn't think so."

"This is a glorious temple and it would be heartbreaking to do damage to something so wondrous and sacred. Also, I don't have a brick." Guy heard somebody else's voice—presumably Steve's—faintly in the distance. Then Ansnorveldt came back. "Oh, apparently we do have several. But that's not the true reason."

"What's the true reason?"

Ansnorveldt chuckled dryly. "Because I don't need to. Tell me... was it you who opened the front door a few moments ago?"

Guy didn't say the answer out loud because the answer was no. The door had opened itself.

Ansnorveldt sounded smug now. "It seems to me, the first and true owner of this house doesn't want you in there. He wants me. And I think very soon you'll find out just how unwelcome you are."

He disconnected.

Guy stood with his back against the door while a new uneasiness set in. The air around him, the shadows, the dark corners—he'd gotten used to all of it looking oddly dead. He'd mostly stopped paying attention to it. But now that he looked at it again, all of it had an air of menace, as if he was the stranger in the house now and every shadow hid something that wanted him gone.

He shook it off. It had to be his imagination. He'd been in the house this long and survived, so he could stay in it one more day. And even if the house didn't want them in it, then what could it possibly—

Clunk, thump, clunk, thump, clunk.

Mae's clogs came down the hall from the kitchen. She was walking deliberately, making no attempt to be quiet. And two things felt wrong. One was that he now finally had to admit that the laminate floor didn't sound anything like hardwood. The other was that only every second step Mae took had the hard *clunk* of a clog. The other steps were softer, maybe even barefoot. She was only wearing one shoe. Why would she do that?

Thump, clunk, thump, clunk.

She stopped just out of sight around the corner. He could hear her breathing. But she didn't round the corner.

Why was she just standing there?

"Mae?" he whispered. His unease had expanded into full-on dread.

She didn't answer. He could sense her like a shadow.

Breathing,

The temperature around him seemed to plunge.

"Mae?" he whispered again. Something was very wrong, but he couldn't take his back off the door to go find out what it was.

Silence for another few seconds. He heard her breathe. Once. Twice.

And then Mae exploded around the corner, charging straight at Guy with a murderous fire in her eyes. He'd seen it once before, in Brooke's eyes right before she nearly crushed her future fiance's skull. And she was wielding one clog over her head like a club ready to swing.

Mae's head teetered high on her body, and her body felt 50 feet tall. Or 1000. The world seemed distant, tiny, insignificant, like she could hold up her hand and block from her sight everything that had ever existed. But she was perfectly aware of what she was doing. Guy was a tiny, squirming human form in the mists far below her and she was clubbing him with her shoe like she was swatting a bug. Again and again. As hard as she could.

It felt good. For her, anyway. Probably not for him. But she was certain that it was the right thing to do. She'd certainly considered it many times over the past few months. And just moments ago while she was standing in the kitchen holding the lock, something in the back of her mind had told her: yes, it's the right thing. You can do it now. And then the world had fallen out from below her and gone hazy, and she was a giant, towering thing. Everything below her was fogged and meaningless. She knew that what she was doing was right.

So every time she hit him, she said to herself, "Whammo! Whammo!" It was the right sound for what she was doing, and it made the attack all the more satisfying. Because it was good. She didn't know why it was good, but it was. And anything in her mind that told her to stop was just her head farting things up. Those thoughts were not to be listened to. She was a giant and she was making the tiny world better by beating Guy with a shoe.

Guy tried to block her blows with his arms, and she couldn't blame him. But she thought this would all be a lot easier if he'd just lie still and let her clobber him unconscious. He didn't do that, though. Instead, he scrambled past her and fled into the hall, and she was forced to chase him, her infinitely long legs sweeping through miles with every step, the whole world shifting around her as she strode.

As good as she felt about the shoe-clobbering, she was less clear about the words she was saying. She didn't even feel like she was saying them, although she could hear them coming out of her mouth. They didn't sound like words. They had syllables and syntax—she was aware of that. But the sounds that formed the syllables were guttural, almost primate noises. She didn't know what they meant, or how she knew how to do that. It didn't even sound like her. She was surprised that she could make noises like that, but only a *little* surprised. She had other things to focus on. Like hitting Guy until he stopped moving. That's what she was supposed to be doing.

Whammo. Whammo.

She caught up to him in the hall and tackled him, then stood on his chest with the one clog she was still wearing and resumed smashing him with the other. She slammed his shoulders and head, ignoring all his shouts of protest because she couldn't hear him over the noises she was making. She wished she had something better to hit him with, but all the furniture was gone, and she'd already checked for knives in the kitchen. The heel of her shoe would have to do. Unless, maybe, she could break some glass and use that. That would draw blood.

So she smashed the hallway mirror with the heel of her shoe until big shards of it came loose. And she picked one of them up like a dagger. There. That would do better.

A puff of moving air brushed past her ear.

She'd felt that before, but never when her head was miles off the floor and so deeply saturated in fog. She knew what it meant. But she didn't want to stop hurting Guy. Hurting him was good for some reason.

"Mae," a voice spoke into her ear. "Stop." It was clear this time. Unambiguous. No missed words, no muffled syllables, no uncertainty.

A gap appeared in the fog of her vision. And a hundred miles below her, straight through that clear gap, she saw Guy's face. It looked bruised, battered, and terrified. He was trying to shield it with both hands, and the terror in his eyes, she understood, was because of her.

But it had felt so good. It was right, wasn't it? Beating Guy to a pulp would help someone. It would feed starving orphans and plant oxygen-producing trees around their orphanage with tree houses pre-built in them. Or something.

"Stop," the voice said again. It was insistent enough to push through all the haze of her mind and arrive at the center.

And she was suddenly mortified. What was she doing? There was no universe where this could be good.

She dropped the shoe, dropped the shard of glass, and lifted her foot off Guy's chest.

She forced out a word. "Guy?" It came out as a squeak.

She could feel the fog clearing, swept away by the winds of her conscience. And she felt herself shrinking, the ground rising up at her and her head descending as if on an escalator, until she was her usual height off the ground. And she wondered who she'd been for the past few minutes, because it certainly hadn't been her.

She covered her mouth with both hands in the horror of what she'd done. "Guy, I'm sorry!"

He raised a hand toward her and she grabbed his forearm and gripped it, helping him get to his feet. He looked furious, and he had every right to.

"Didn't see that coming," he said.

She threw her arms around him and hugged him with her eyes closed. Partly to check if she'd broken any bones but also because she wanted to.

"Didn't see that coming either," he said.

And she felt the anger go out of him as he hugged her back.

And then someone, presumably Steve, threw a brick through the window.

Chapter 27

T he brick made a surprising sound. Guy would have expected a glassy, cinematic *crash* followed by the *tinkling* of shards scattering across the floor and the heavy *thud-crack* of the brick striking the hardwood and crushing a few scraps of glass beneath it. Instead, it made a *thwack* sound like somebody hitting a tree with a baseball bat. The brick came through cleanly, taking out only as much glass as it needed to. It hit the floor on its short end and tumbled end-over-end right between Guy and Mae's feet until it came to rest against the wall.

The window was still there. But now it had a hole in it. Even in his stunned, bludgeoned surprise, Guy was mildly disappointed that the hole was not cartoonishly brick-shaped.

He stared at the window. Then at the brick. Then at Mae. Her eyes were locked on the brick, and she had the stunned look of someone who, having never had a brick thrown at her before, suddenly had a brick thrown at her.

They were stupefied long enough for the second brick to hit. This one was more committed to success than the first. It struck with determination a foot to the left of the original hole, fully exploited the weakening of glass that the original had created, and shattered the entire pane. Shards exploded inward, shoved with such force by the brick that some of them made it to Guy's legs and showered across his boots.

Cheers erupted from the cult outside. They had their way in. They would be right behind that brick. The door was unlocked again so they could just come in that way, but they didn't care. The window was the way.

Mae looked angry now. Guy worried that she might try picking up the brick and throwing it back. But that would take things in a direction that couldn't possibly go well. A mob would be coming through that window any second, and just by sheer fervor and numbers they were a formidable yellow-smocked force. A brick in somebody's face would only make them more dangerous.

So Guy said, "We gotta go." And he tried to push Mae toward the hall.

She resisted at first. Until they both looked out the window at the same time and saw the screaming wall of yellow coming at them across the yard and swarming onto the porch like smock-clad insects who'd spotted a picnic.

She stopped resisting, and he pushed her past the staircase and the basement door. He kicked it closed on his way past and dead-bolted it. It wouldn't stop the cult going from down there, but anything he could do to impede them even for a second was better than nothing.

"Where are we going?" Mae demanded.

They could hear the mob in the dining room behind them now. Some had made it through the window and were calling to the ones outside, offering to help them in, telling them to hurry. The whole cult would be inside soon.

"Kitchen," Guy said.

If they were lucky, the cult would be happy with their one entry point and wouldn't try to make another one at the back. Guy and

Mae would be able to get out the kitchen entrance and run across the back field. The cult would have no reason to follow them.

But the mob was already at the back of the house too. As soon as Guy made it to the kitchen he could hear shouts from outside and the heavy thud of somebody slamming their shoulder into the door. And then the heavier thud of someone else helping them do it. The door shuddered and the hinges snapped almost free. Guy wondered how much longer the good, expensive hinges would have lasted against the onslaught, because the cheap ones gave up almost right away.

They were trapped. Guy wondered what the freaks would do if they caught them. Throw them both down the hole as bonus sacrifices? Earn a few more murder points with their murder god?

Guy's mind raced through his mental map of the house. Both exits on the ground floor were blocked. The carriage house was padlocked from the outside. There was no way out.

They had to go up.

"Stairs," he said.

He spun around and tried to pull Mae back into the hall, but she was already scrambling that way, yanking on cabinet handles to slingshot herself forward.

She hit the hall first and he sprinted around the corner behind her. The hall was already filled with yellow smocks. They were disoriented, meandering, not sure of the geography. But as soon as they spotted Mae, they locked on and came straight at her, a shrieking yellow storm surge.

She didn't hesitate. She plunged up the stairs four at a time, so fast that Guy struggled to keep up.

"All the way up!" she yelled back at him as she circled the second-floor landing and kept climbing.

He forced himself upward, sweating now. His heart strained to fuel his muscles as much as he needed, and his lungs gave up altogether. But he could feel the thunder of the mob's feet on the stairs below him. He dug into a previously untapped fuel reserve somewhere in his intestinal tract and kept pushing upward.

Mae cut a hard right at the top of the stairs, straight into the little kitchenette. And Guy clued in to where she was going.

The turret. The little balcony at the top of the tower, accessible only by a concealed door in the kitchenette.

The roar of the cultists was still below them when she reached it. Guy guessed that they hadn't made it beyond the second-floor landing yet. There might be time.

Mae heaved the kitchenette cabinet until the hidden door swung open and she dove through, landing in a seated position with her back against the tongue-and-groove paneled balustrade wall. She kept low beneath the railing so the wall would hide her from anyone on the ground, and frantically waved Guy through. He dove after her and rolled until his back was against the wall beside her.

She crawled forward, yanked the door closed, and slid back against the wall with him.

They sat there, breathing fast in the shade of the turret roof, hoping desperately that the turret door was as concealed as they thought it was. Hoping the cultists would not see it, and would give up the chase.

For a few seconds they heard the thumps of footfalls beyond the door, and he thought he saw the curtain move in the only window he could see from where he was crouched. They held their breath and waited for the frenzied zealots to crash through the turret door.

But the mob never came. And after a few minutes, they heard a *thud-scrape* from beyond the door.

Mae looked at Guy and mouthed the words, "What was that?" And Guy shrugged in response.

Mae shuffled back to the door and pushed it. Gently at first, then with all her strength. It refused to open.

Guy's heart sank. The cultists hadn't overlooked the door. They'd seen it and blocked it with something to trap Guy and Mae on the balcony.

Mae pounded on the door. "Hey! You can't do this!"

But the silence in reply emphatically said that they really, really could do it. Mae gave up at the futility of it and sat down hard with her back against the wall. And she fumed.

Guy shifted his legs under him and moved into a slightly more comfortable position with his back against the balustrade wall next to Mae.

"Do we call someone?" she asked.

Guy shook his head. Who could they call? They were still technically trespassing, so the police would drag the two of them away before any of the cultists. Anybody else they might call to come rescue them would only become a trespasser along with them. And Ansnorveldt would have no trouble convincing authorities that everything was fine and no dangerous human sacrifice ceremonies were about to happen.

As the sun descended and twilight fell over them, they sat in frustrated silence, listening to the cultists unloading their vehicles below and bringing all their things inside. Guy could imagine them claiming rooms, turning all the bedrooms into dormitories or bunkhouses or whatever cults called the rooms where they slept in big, culty human heaps. Or maybe they weren't concerned with moving in. Maybe they were entirely focused on the basement, and the hole. Or maybe they were all planning to hurl themselves down the hole. Knowing you'd be dead later in the day would certainly make the logistics of moving into a new place more manageable.

"You okay?" Guy finally asked Mae.

She nodded. It wasn't convincing.

"What do you think they're doing in there?" Guy asked with a nod toward the door.

"I haven't heard anybody come upstairs since we got here," she replied. "I bet they're all in the basement." She checked her phone. "We can't just sit here."

"I know."

"We have to stop them."

Guy had already mostly convinced himself that stopping them was impossible, but he wondered if she might have a plan. "How?"

She fell silent again. Except to say again, "We have to stop them." Then silence for real.

Guy shifted himself around to crouch under the railing. And he inched his head upward to look over the rail and down into the front yard.

The cultists were nowhere in sight. Their vehicles were still parked below except for the cargo van which had apparently been emptied and then driven off to be returned. The hitched trailer full of stuff wasn't full of stuff anymore. The dirt of the yard was a mess of footprints and tire tracks, but all the cultists themselves had gone inside. He guessed, as Mae had already suspected, that they were all in the basement. Probably chanting or orgy-ing or doing whatever it was that cults did before they sacrificed people.

He was about to sit down again when his eyes fell on something out in the yard past the vehicles. It was a hulking form that cast a long shadow in the light from the porch and for a moment he couldn't tell what it was. He had to squint to discern it, and wondered briefly if some supernatural monster had arrived in answer to the cult's call.

But it wasn't a monster. And when he realized what it was, an idea exploded into his mind. He couldn't believe how quickly it appeared, a fully formed plan, like somebody had jammed a blueprint into his mind and unrolled it.

He stared at the shape and its shadow for a long time.

And finally he said, without any certainty at all that it was true, "I know how we can cover the hole."

Chapter 28

G uy whispered into his phone: "Luther!" Mae could sense his rising exasperation. "Luther, shut up and listen to me." Luther apparently wasn't listening because Guy was forced to listen for a few seconds. Then he said, "Yes, I know it's after five. Yes, I'll pay double time. Whatever. Will you just listen?"

Mae stopped listening and focused instead on looking over the rail into the yard below. There had been no activity at all in front of the house since the cultists had stormed inside, and it was still remarkably quiet down there. She worried that it meant they were all congregated in the basement already. And she worried even more that it was too late and they'd already performed a sacrifice. Maybe several.

A movement caught her eye and she had to push her face painfully right up against the railing to see almost straight down.

There was somebody on the porch. She could see the front few inches of him draped in a yellow cult smock and sticking out from under the porch roof. He appeared to be leaning against the post at the top of the steps. And that's all he was doing. Just leaning.

So they'd left someone outside to guard the door. And she guessed that he wouldn't be the only one.

Guy finished his conversation with Luther. He tapped his phone off and squeezed it into his back pocket. "He'll be here in an hour," he said.

She checked her phone again. It was already 7:15. The cult's plan called for their underground friend to ascend at 8:47. Luther would be cutting it too close. "That doesn't leave much time."

"It's the best he can do. And he wants me to sign a waiver relieving him of liability or something. Whatever. He's coming. So let's just sit tight until he gets here." Guy put his head back against the balustrade wall and seemed content to have a nap for the moment.

Mae wasn't content with that. She had no idea if the cult needed to make their sacrifice exactly at 8:47 or if the sacrifice came long before that. Somebody could be teetering on the brink of the hole right now. She couldn't sit here while that was happening. But what could she do? Her mind ran through a hundred plans, all of them terrible. The worst ones ended with her dying, which seemed like a weird step for a plan to include.

While her mind sifted through those, part of it also became aware of a sound. A sound that froze her blood solid.

And Guy heard it too, because he opened his eyes and said, "Do you hear that?"

It was hard to believe that the sound carried this far. The cult was in the basement and they were 30 feet up in the tower. But it must have been channeled up through ducts or vibrated through the walls into a kind of echo chamber formed by the turret roof. Because she could hear it like they were in the middle of it.

Chanting.

Discordant, atonal, unsettling. It was not anything she would call "musical." Nor were the words in anything like a modern language. Even though she knew it came from a mob of ridiculous morons in yellow smocks, it sounded somehow primeval, like the fierce night cries of long-dead human precursors. It was a sound her primate ancestors might have heard echoing across the fields at night. A sound they would have shrunk deep into their caves to escape. It was an echo from a dark, cold time. And it affected her on a deep, DNA level.

Mae shivered.

The cult had started their ceremony. It was happening. And that meant somebody would soon be dead.

Whammo.

"We can't wait," Mae said.

She shuffled to the railing and poked her head up, looking down into the yard. The guard was still there at the porch steps. He seemed unaffected by the chanting. Maybe he couldn't hear it from there.

Guy hadn't moved. He shook his head. "Luther will be here soon."

"One of those people will be dead soon," Mae retorted.

She shifted back and forth across the turret, looking for an escape. On the right, it was a 25-foot drop interrupted only by the angled roof of the stairwell's leaded glass window bay. That wouldn't stop her fall; it would just hurt more. There was no escape to the right except by spinal injury.

They would have to go over the rail to the left, where there was a drop of maybe 15 feet onto the patio awning. If she clambered over the railing and dangled from it, she could reduce that plunge to about ten. Still not good. Plus, while dangling, her legs would be kicking against the window of one of the bedrooms. If anybody happened to be in there, she'd be hard to miss. She didn't expect that anyone would be, but it was a risk. Then she'd likely twist her ankles in the drop to the awning, roll off of it, and fall the remaining ten or twelve feet to the ground. So escape that way was by broken leg or ribs. Slightly less critical than the spinal injury to the right, but it would still hurt.

But there was another option. They could go up. The railing of the tower was roughly level with the gutter edge of the house's main roof. If they stood on the railing, they could shimmy around the side of the turret and onto the roof. Then, if they could make it all the way up the steep slope and down the other side, they could climb down a drain pipe or whatever other handholds they found. It didn't require injuring any parts of themselves, unless they were extremely unlucky.

Which, up until this point, they had been. Repeatedly.

But that was their way out of the turret. She made up her mind. She hoisted herself onto the railing.

"Mae?" Guy said with a note of warning. "What are you doing?"

"I'm going over the roof and down the back of the house. Then into the basement. You can come with me or you can stay here."

She didn't wait for his answer.

From here to the roof it was a jump. So she jumped it.

Her first thought was that the shingles were redder than they looked from the ground. When she'd chosen them, she specifically tried to get a hint of a dark, rusty color without spilling all the way over into actual red. And from the ground, she thought she'd achieved it. But maybe the oblique angle from down there shifted the hue, because up here with her face pressed against the roof, they were just red. Not rust, not red-adjacent. Red. She regretted her choice. She should have spent more time and looked at more samples.

Her second thought was that she was about to slide off the roof and die.

Now that she was past the point of no return, the roof seemed unclimbable. It would take an inhuman amount of traction to climb up it. The shingles weren't rough enough for her shoes to find any kind of purchase. And the angle felt far more vertical than she'd realized. Why did it need to be so steep? Rain didn't need that much gravity. It would roll just as well down a gentle grade.

She couldn't go up, and couldn't go back. She felt panic getting a more solid grip on her than her shoes ever could on the shingles. She clutched at every edge she could find, but couldn't get hold of any of them. Her heart raced and her hands turned slippery, which only made her situation more dire.

"You okay?" Guy shout-whispered from the turret.

She wasn't. But she didn't say that. Even if she wanted to admit it, she didn't feel like she could make a sound right now. Even opening her mouth to speak might disrupt her delicate balance and send her over the edge into a plummet.

But she wasn't currently sliding, so that was something. And she found that if she kept herself splayed flat against the shingles and slid her arms above her head and then down to her sides again, she could precariously inch her way upward. It would take a while, and it wouldn't look as elegant as the spider-climbing she had imagined herself doing. But it was better than falling.

So she did it. She climbed. And, inch by inch, the shingles passed under her nose.

She had no idea how long it took. And she was dimly aware of movement on the roof beneath her feet. She hoped it was Guy following her, but didn't dare lift her head to look.

Night fell around her while she climbed, and soon she had trouble seeing how far she had left to go. But after what felt like agonizing hours, she arrived at the peak, where she was finally able to get a grip and catch her breath. Her cheek felt burnt off from scraping against the shingles, and every muscle in her body wanted a nap. But she had done the hard part.

Then she looked down the back of the roof, and could see immediately that going up had been the easy part.

Don't think about it, she thought. If you think about it, you'll chicken out.

She spun herself around, imagined that her feet and hands were suction cups, and began shuffling down the agonizing slope. Gravity seemed more intense than she remembered, like she'd crossed onto a bigger planet without realizing it and now she weighed twice as much. And vertigo was a persistent vortex stirring up her mind. She wasn't sure her muscles were prepared for this kind of strain, or her mind for this kind of terror. But she pressed on, resisting the urge to just let go and try to slide the rest of the way.

To make matters worse, the chanting was somehow louder here. It might have been coming up one of the chimneys because it sounded amplified, a constant, echoing drone in her ears. It was tortuous, an underscore for her terror. She wanted to run and escape it, or even just to cover her ears. But she could do neither. She had to take it.

She had only gone a few feet when she began to sense something else. Something new.

She froze where she was, wondering if she'd imagined it. As much as she wanted to get down and get this intolerable climb over with, she pressed herself to the roof and stayed still, waiting.

And she felt it again. It was not her imagination. Her fear of falling mixed with a new kind of dread, and she thought her fingers might give out.

"Guy, did you feel that?" she whispered.

He had just reached the peak and was trying to figure out how to get himself over it. In spite of her growing sense of horror, she was pleased to see that it wasn't any easier for him. "Feel what?" he said.

She felt it again. It shook her to her core, and her feet almost lost their grip. She slid a few inches and only stopped herself by latching onto a slightly protruding nail with her fingertips.

"The house moved," she rasped. She couldn't believe she was saying it. "It moved. Twice."

"It's your imagination," he said.

But just as he levered one leg over the peak of the roof, it happened again.

It was not subtle. And this time, on top of feeling it, she saw it. It was like the whole house shifted upward a few inches and tilted a degree to one side. The shingles shifted to accommodate the new angle, sliding over each other like dragon scales. She could feel them grinding against her fingers as they fought for new positions. The house rose for a few seconds, then the whole structure of the house groaned and creaked as it descended back to its original foundation.

Mae craned her neck to look up at Guy. He'd felt it that time. He was clutching the peak and studying the roof with a look of horrified astonishment. "Stop it!" was all he said, and she didn't know what that meant.

As if in response, the chanting entered a new frenzy. Some of the voices turned to screams while others underscored with deep, guttural barks. It was the worst sound she'd ever heard, and she didn't want to hear it anymore.

And whatever the lunatics intended the chant to do, it was working.

Something had moved beneath the house. Something was coming up.

The impossibility of that was too much for her mind to process, so she put it aside and focused on the thing she could understand—that someone was going to be thrown down the hole.

But piled on top of all her other fears and terrors was a new one—that it might already be too late to stop it.

And then the ground heaved again, like a balloon had inflated under the house and forced it three inches higher and into a tilt of a few extra degrees. The structure of the house, never designed to be moved, groaned and snapped in protest. The slope of the roof, already steep, became near-vertical.

The shudder dislodged Mae's feet. She kicked frantically, hunting for purchase with her toes, as her entire body weight fell on her desperately clinging fingertips.

And then those, too, gave out, and she was holding onto nothing. As the house rocked back into place, she slid down the roof.

Out of control.

Chapter 29

When the house rocked the first time, Guy's mind—which he had only just managed to get back together—broke again. He'd rebuilt a lot of houses. Houses didn't move. He spent a lot of time and money specifically on making sure they couldn't do that.

This one had moved. But it didn't seem to like it. He could hear the joists under the roof groaning and snapping. He could feel the shingles shifting under his fingers, pulling at each other in ways they weren't designed to do. He could hear seals breaking, pipes bending, nails popping, and screws snapping. He'd paid for all of them, and they were all being ruined. Somehow that made him angrier than the other obvious thing going on, which was that something was rising from deep below the Earth, apparently to cause rampant death.

Was it possible that the cult wasn't crazy? That they were right?

He couldn't get his head around that, so he focused on the house coming apart. That, at least, he could be angry about within the context of a construction budget.

"Stop it!" he said, as if commanding the house not to move anymore would make it all stop. He put his full weight on the peak of the roof as if he could hold the house together just with his hands and sink it back into its unstable dirt foundation.

And then it moved again. It rose a few inches higher and tilted to the side, and if he'd been on the other side of the peak, he would surely have been shaken loose.

Like Mae was.

He was so focused on holding the house together with his bare hands that at first he didn't see her sliding. But he noticed that she was gone before he heard her call out to him in a panic, "Guy!"

Without even realizing what he was doing or why, he hurled himself over the peak and dove after her.

His one thought was that he could hook his toes onto the peak, grab her by the wrist, and stop them both from sliding down to the edge.

She reached for him, and he stretched as far as he could. His fingertips brushed against hers, but that was all the contact he could make. Her hand slipped past his, and she was out of reach.

At the same time, his toes missed hooking over the peak. One of his feet held on for a second. But as soon as the house juddered back into its resting place, that foot lost its grip too.

And then he was no longer saving Mae from falling.

He was falling with her.

He slid head-first, the dry shingles sandpapering his palms raw. Mae slid backward ahead of him so they were looking straight into each other's faces as they slid the first few feet. He saw nothing but terror on her face. At least she wasn't mad at him.

But his hands were furious with him. He felt the flesh scraping off them. Then the friction from the shingles took hold of his shirt, and his belt caught on the protruding edge of one, and he was pivoted sideways. And suddenly he wasn't sliding anymore—he was rolling. It relieved him of the burn on his hands, but also meant that he was moving even faster toward the edge.

He collided with Mae and she made an attempt to stop him with one arm. But that just made her lose her traction as well, and then they were both rolling, both flailing their limbs, looking for a way to stop, both trying to grab each other so at least they'd fall together.

Mae went over the edge first. Though he was rolling, Guy was facing her at the moment she rolled off. He could only see the back of her head, and her arms making a last, panicked grab. She let out a short, explosive shriek. One second, she was there. The next, she was gone.

He had only a second or two to be horrified by that. And then he, too, hit the edge.

He was facing down when he reached it, and his vision was suddenly filled with gutter. He snapped out his right arm, dropped his fingers into the gutter and hooked them around the rim.

Then his body went over and all his weight was on those fingers. His arm snapped backward and his whole body jerked to a stop. His shoulder wrenched, and pain blasted all the way across both shoulders and down his spine.

But his fingers held, and he was hanging by the gutter. His feet swung below him and kicked against the siding. His mind had prepared itself for falling and hadn't yet adjusted to not doing that. He was dazed, everything else forgotten.

Except for one thing.

Somehow, hanging 30 feet above the ground by three fingers with Mae probably dead somewhere beneath him, his mind swept back in time and replayed in intricate detail a conversation he'd had last fall with Luther.

They stood in the mud at the back of the house, looking up at the edge of the roof. It was late afternoon, and fall, so the sun was already low and both of their shadows stretched over the muck and several feet up the back wall of the house. Guy could see their conversation playing out in shadows. Luther's Yankees cap made a silhouette like a duck.

"You have three choices," Luther said. "A stainless steel gutter is durable and attractive, and will coordinate with the existing exterior fixtures. That's $20 per linear foot."

"Uh huh," Guy said, waiting for the better idea that he knew was coming.

"An aluminum gutter, on the other hand, is more practical and popular but also prone to rust, and bending. That's a risk you'll have to consider. It's $9 per linear foot."

"Okay," Guy said. He still felt like Luther had a trick up his sleeve. It would be coming any second now.

"Or..." Luther said.

Guy nodded. Here it was. "Or?"

"Or," Luther said again. "There's vinyl sectional gutter. It gets brittle in the cold, and it's prone to clogging. And when it clogs, it sags. It will likely overflow more frequently. And because it's sectional, it can separate and leak through the cracks."

"And it's...?"

"Three bucks a foot. I might even have some intact re-use sections from a tear-down you can take for free."

Luther's duck-shadow twisted toward Guy, waiting for his answer. It didn't have to wait long.

An entire two-foot section of the re-use vinyl sectional gutter snapped off, and Guy fell with it clutched in his hand.

He braced himself for hitting the ground, and wondered in a flash how much of him would be broken by a 30-foot fall. Bones? Organs? Head?

The impact came much sooner than he expected. He felt like he'd only been falling for half a second, and was surprised by how much less painful it was than he'd expected. He landed on his shoulder and hip, and didn't hear anything break. It knocked the wind out of him, but his organs seemed to stay basically where they belonged.

He lay on his side, stunned, wrestling air back into his lungs, forcing them to work.

"Guy?" Mae whispered from next to him. And he was surprised by that too.

He finally clued in. He wasn't on the ground at all.

He was on the painters' scaffold.

He'd landed on the top level right next to Mae, who had only barely rolled out of his way. They'd fallen about three feet.

He had a flash of overwhelming relief. And, to pile one more surprise on top of all the others, he was surprised how little of his relief was at his own survival and how much of it was at seeing Mae still alive. That was something he'd have to explore later.

But not right now, because she still looked frightened and he didn't know why. Shouldn't she be as relieved as he was?

She motioned with her head toward the house. Her eyes were wide and she raised a finger to her lips.

With what strength and oxygen he could summon, he propped himself up on his elbow to see past her.

They had landed outside the window of one of the third-floor bedrooms. The lights were off inside the room, as they seemed to be everywhere except on the main floor. So at first Guy couldn't see what Mae was trying to warn him about. It was only when he shifted a little for a better view that moonlit reflections in the glass moved out of the way and he became aware.

There was a face just inside the window looking out at them.

Chapter 30

M ae didn't dare move. And the face in the window didn't react. There were no shouts, no alerts. The person didn't move at all. Maybe, somehow, they hadn't spotted Guy and Mae in the darkness. They were just looking out at the night, oblivious to the two people who had just plummeted onto the scaffold outside the window.

Mae gripped Guy's arm to make him stay still. They couldn't run. It was impossible for them to climb down the scaffold before the cultist inside could alert the others and send the whole mob swarming around the bottom of the house to the back. So Mae and Guy lay still and waited to be seen, waited for the shouts to come.

After half a minute or more, still nothing had happened. All Mae could hear was the chant rippling up from below, dissonant and baleful, voices from a dead age.

She risked another look.

The face was still there in the window. They hadn't moved at all.

Mae squinted, trying to see detail. And her breath caught in her throat.

What she'd thought was a human form wasn't a cultist at all. It wasn't even a whole person.

It was a woman's face, and little else. Translucent, thin, nearly impossible to focus on, like a faint and hazy reflection on the glass. Beneath the face, its torso faded to shimmering nothing. There was no body. Just the face.

And it stared straight into Mae with pleading eyes.

She knew right away who it was. "Gretchen?" she whispered.

The eyes shifted slightly, focusing on the sound of Mae's voice.

And then the face drew back from the window and dissolved into the darkness. It mingled with the shadows and vanished.

They both lay on the scaffold staring at the window, wondering if the vision would come back. But the darkness inside remained faceless.

"Did I just see that?" Guy asked, incredulous.

"I was about to ask you the same thing," she replied.

Mae wondered if, after all he'd seen, he would ever be the same.

And then the ground moved again.

It was the most violent push so far. The house rose a foot and rocked backward away from them, and the scaffold rocked in the opposite direction, nearly spilling Mae completely off the platform. Guy blocked her and held onto the rail with one hand while supporting her with the other, and they clung to the top as the scaffold swayed away from the house.

For a sickening moment, Mae thought it was going to topple. But as the great heave from below settled once again, the house came rocking back toward her and the scaffold swung forward and slammed against it, cracking a window with one of its corners.

And it wasn't the only thing that broke. The bricks on the outside of the house had finally gotten tired of all the moving around, and the mortar between them was spilling out in chunky mortar dust waterfalls. The house was coming apart. She could imagine that Guy's heart was breaking just as much as the walls.

"Let's go," Guy said urgently, and waved her toward the ladder.

He was right. It wasn't safe up here. She wasn't sure there was anywhere safe at the moment, but up here certainly wasn't.

She crawled to the ladder and clambered down it to the level below, then jogged across the platform to the next ladder on the opposite side. The lower they got on the scaffold, the louder the chanting became. Every instinct told her to get further away from that sound, not closer. But she forced herself on until she slid down the last few rungs to the ground.

Guy slid down right after her and they both pressed their backs to the outside wall of the house. Some of the bricks, loosened by all the subterranean heaving, shifted or crumbled behind their backs. Even in the dark, Mae could see the despair on Guy's face.

"I'm sorry about the house," she whispered.

"Don't worry about it," he replied sharply, wanting her to think he didn't care when he transparently did. But at least he wasn't openly complaining. That was progress. She thought there might be hope for this guy after all.

From here the chanting seemed to emanate from right below their feet, and it reached a fresh and agonizing crescendo. Quavering voices covered all the octaves, each singing a different note so none of it harmonized. It was becoming too much to take. Mae clamped her hands over her ears. It didn't seem to help much. The sound pierced right through them like they weren't there.

"I know," Guy said. "It's the worst. Is it supposed to sound like that?"

She had to hand it to Ansnorveldt. She wouldn't have believed those yahoos could even sing "Row Row Row Your Boat" in a round, and he had them very effectively reciting an atonal chant from before the beginnings of the Earth.

Unless it wasn't supposed to sound like that. In which case, they were just terrible.

Mae tried to ignore the sound, reminding herself that sacrifices were happening. She checked her phone, and her stomach squeezed into a fresh kind of knot it had just invented.

It was almost 8:30. They had barely more than 15 minutes.

"I have to get down to the basement," she said. "Now. Right now. Now."

Guy was at the corner of the house, peering around it toward the road, which was invisible in the darkness through the trees. He shook his head. "We can take care of this from out here as soon as Luther gets here."

"I can't wait," she said. She meant it literally. She could not wait. Every nerve ending in her body was electrified and she felt like if she didn't get down there and stop this right now then she might explode like an overloaded transformer. "They could be making the sacrifice right now. If I can stop it…"

Guy pointed toward the road. "There!" For a second a set of red tail lights glowed through the trees and then vanished behind another copse. "It's Luther! Come on, we can do this."

Guy had his plan, and it gave her some hope. But not enough. She shook her head. "You do that. I'm going downstairs." And she raced past him toward the porch.

Countless cautions raced through her mind: there's a guard on the porch; there will be more inside; the basement door will be locked—

But Guy grabbed her elbow to stop her and a flash of anger bolted through her. Didn't he know that she *had* to do this? She spun toward him, ready to rip into him. But the look of concern on his face softened her. He wasn't demanding that she do things his way; he was worried about her. It was still annoying, but not as much.

He grimaced and clamped his eyes closed, fighting some internal battle. She didn't know who the combatants were. But one of them eventually won out.

"You'll never get in that way," he said. He pulled a key off his key chain and pointed it down the slope at the side of the house. "Go in through the carriage house. This is for the padlock. They probably don't even know the back passage is there."

It was brilliant, and she chided herself for not thinking of it. The carriage house was lower than the basement at the bottom of the hill. There wouldn't be guards there. And the underground stairs from it went up to a big door at the back of the basement. She could get all the way to the hole without being spotted.

He released her elbow but kept his hand on her arm. Not holding her back anymore, but comforting her. "Luther will be here in a minute. Clear the basement if you can."

"If I'm not out by 8:45," she said, "don't wait for me. Just do it."

He winced at the thought. "Just please clear out before then."

She patted his hand. Several options for things to say went through her mind, but they all sounded like cheesy lines from movies she wouldn't watch. So she said, "Okay." And she immediately wished she'd gone with one of the cheesy options. Too late.

She ran down the hill toward the carriage house with the ever-intensifying eons-old chant somehow growing louder as she ran.

When she was halfway down the hill, the earth beneath the house moved again. She couldn't tell if it was a bigger heave than the previous ones, or if it just felt more intense because she was on the ground. But she was astonished at the magnitude of it. From here she could see that it wasn't just the ground directly under the house that moved. It was a circle around it, 50 feet in all directions. The whole circle bulged upward, and she felt the house rise and lean behind her, balanced on the peak of the bubble. Trees snapped and fell at the edges of the property, and huge patches of earth crumbled and broke apart. And this time, maybe because she was on the ground, she felt tremors rocking through the soil beneath her, and heard a rumble that might have been layers of rock shifting.

Or it might have been the roar of something gigantic and enraged. She didn't want to consider that. But she considered it.

The slope under her feet lurched and she fell, tumbling over shifting rocks and crumbling dried mud, until she fell hard onto the hard, flat dirt in front of the carriage house door. She wasn't sure that she'd stopped rolling because the ground kept moving under her for a few more seconds until, finally, gravity took over and the huge circle of earth fell back into place.

Mae shook off the disorientation and forced herself not to think about what was happening deep below ground. She had enough stuff to worry about up here.

She scrambled up the rough drive to the carriage house door. The huge padlock in the bottom corner gave way easily to her key. She tugged on the handle and the tilt-up canopy door swung upward with little resistance beyond the rust on its rails and the wobble in its wheels. It did, however, make a metallic shriek that reverberated into the space beyond, and Mae cringed. Was the underground passage up to the basement long and winding enough that the cult wouldn't have heard that noise? Surely their chant would drown it out? She waited a few seconds with her hand on the door handle, peering into the dark to see if any yellow smocks came swarming out of the passage.

She didn't dare raise the door the rest of the way, but just left it half-open and ducked under it. And then she was in the dark of the carriage house, squeezing around Guy's truck. She'd only been down here a couple of times since she'd bought her half of the house, and couldn't remember where the light switch was. She wondered if there was anything like a flashlight or lantern in any of the piles of junk stacked in the corners. There was a literal kitchen sink, so finding just about anything else wasn't impossible.

The chant was unbearable here. It came down the curving steps from the basement, amplified somehow by the smooth walls. It was difficult to focus on any of her thoughts; they were overwhelmed by the cacophonous, volcanic chant. From here, so close to the source, she could hear layers to the sound that hadn't been clear before. She wasn't sure how many cultists were participating, but it sounded like every one of them had a distinct role in the sound, each of them designed specifically to not harmonize with the rest. It wasn't dozens of voices singing in a chorus; it was dozens of voices clashing against each other. It was chaos in sound.

She pressed forward to the back corner on the right where she knew the stairs into the passage would be. And she used the light from her phone display to make sure she wouldn't trip on the way up.

The stairs were chillingly subterranean. Even going upward she couldn't help feeling like there was an enormous weight of cold stone over her head. The air was heavy and wet, like the passage had been recently submerged. It was narrow enough that she could slide both hands along the cold, smooth walls without even fully stretching her arms out. But she didn't want to touch the walls. They looked wet even when they weren't, and the stone had been cracked in places by the movements of the earth. Halfway up, she had to step around debris from above and she started to fear that the passage might be in danger of collapsing on her if there was another tremor.

Near the top, the passage curved to the right. And she started to hear voices shouting above the chant. She could make out Ansnorveldt's voice in particular, and although she couldn't hear what he was saying, there was anger in his tone. Something was wrong.

But had they made the sacrifice yet? Was she too late? She didn't know.

A faint square of light melted into her view above, and she shut her phone off. Ten more stairs up, she could see the heavy wooden door with the little barred window that separated the basement from the passage, and a few traces of light from the dangling basement bulbs squeezed through it and cast a dim yellow haze on the top few steps. She had arrived. She was in the basement. And she finally allowed the thought into her mind that she'd been fighting off this whole time.

The thought that she had no idea what to do when she got there.

Chapter 31

G uy ran away to the side of the house first so the darkness would hide him from the guard at the front door. Once he was far enough from the house, he cut hard to the right and ran toward the road. He hoped he could get to the end of the drive fast enough to intercept Luther and make sure he came up stealthily and not with high beams on and the radio blasting. Not that Luther ever would.

Guy considered that he might jump into the passenger seat with Luther, drive very fast away from this house, and never come back. He was pretty sure Luther would be on board with that.

But he couldn't leave the wackos in the basement to finish whatever cataclysmic nightmare they'd started. And he certainly couldn't leave Mae to face this alone. He knew staying could potentially get him killed, but he still wanted to do it. He didn't understand himself anymore.

With a noise like the collapse of a mountain, the ground heaved upward beneath him with such force that he was thrown a foot into the air. He landed and fell to one knee for balance, and was astonished to see an underground bubble rise beneath him, lifting trees and rocks and the entire house, then dropping them back into place. He remembered old videos he'd seen of underground nuclear explosions collapsing mile-wide circles of land. It looked very much like that, except with a cheaply renovated old Victorian mansion in the middle of it.

Whatever was coming up beneath the house was moving vast quantities of earth and rock to get out. And probably breaking all of the house's expensively repaired pipes and power lines. The thought of them all being destroyed caused him physical pain.

When it seemed like the ground had finished lurching, he started running again. He veered onto the driveway and followed it at a sprint, grateful that it was marginally smoother than the surrounding land.

Halfway down the driveway, Whitemarsh Road came dimly into view, and he could see Luther's vehicle turning onto the drive. He had wisely decided to leave his headlights off, and Guy silently thanked him for that. But it also meant that he couldn't see what Luther was driving. It was a shadow. A *massive* shadow. Much bigger than he had expected. What Guy had asked Luther to bring shouldn't be that big, so what was Luther driving?

Guy ran at it, waving his arms above his head and hoping Luther would see him in the dark. The monstrous vehicle slowed. Its air brakes popped and hissed, and its momentum carried it into a rolling freight-train stop.

And then Guy finally saw what it was. And his heart plummeted off a cliff and screamed on the way down. No, no, no, this wouldn't work at all.

Guy ran up alongside it and met Luther coming down from the cab. He barely even noticed that Luther was wearing flannel pajamas and a bathrobe, yet still had his cap with his pride-and-joy tape measure clipped to the visor. The man goes to bed early, Guy thought, and he measures stuff in his dreams.

Guy surveyed the massive vehicle. "Luther! What is this?!"

Luther stood with his back against it and spread his arms wide. "This is a two-axle telescoping mobile crane with a load capacity of 35 tons and a maximum hoist height of 144 feet—"

"Don't care," Guy said. He was in no state of mind for Luther's technical specs fetish. All he cared about was whether it could do the job. Which it couldn't. It was a huge, beefy vehicle somewhere between a semi tractor trailer and a fire truck, with a bit of tank-crushing military monstrosity mixed in. The telescoping crane on the back looked like the arm of a colossus, with a separate glass operator's cab mounted on the side. Sometime when saving the world wasn't so urgent, he hoped Luther might let him play with it. But at the moment, it was not at all what he wanted. "Where did you get this?"

"It's my brother-in-law's," Luther said. "He calls it Frasier. If you damage it in any way—"

"This is not what I asked for!"

"You requested something that can lift three to four tons and move it into the basement."

Guy was aware that he was flailing like an orangutan but he let himself do it because it helped emphasize the point. "How are you going to move this into the basement? It's bigger than the house!"

"I'm curious. What did you think I was going to bring?"

"Not this! Something small, but with a big shovel! So maybe we could roll it up from the carriage house!"

Luther sighed, took off his cap, and dabbed at his forehead. Which Guy knew meant that Luther was about to give him a dose of reality. He didn't want reality right now. He wanted a fantasy where everything worked out great and he won prizes.

"Guy," Luther said. And the fact that he had used Guy's first name only added weight to what he was about to say. "There is only one way to move that size load into the basement." He stuck his index finger in the air, then inverted it. "Straight down from the top. I presumed that you understood that."

Guy stared at him, agog. What Luther was suggesting would almost certainly destroy the house. All his months of effort, all the money and sweat he'd put into—all of it would be crushed beneath a 3-ton weight. It meant the cult could sue him. It meant they could take away the millions they'd given him, and win millions more from him in court. It even meant he could go to jail. It almost certainly meant losing literally everything he had.

"We can't do that," he said quietly, shaking his head. "No. No way. No."

"Very well," Luther said with practiced indifference. "I'll return Frasier to the yard, but the rental and this meeting are still on the books at double—"

And then the ground heaved again.

This time, a low rumble and a tremor came before the movement. For a second it felt like a volcano was about to erupt. And then the ground thrust upward. Guy and Luther were far enough down the drive that they weren't on top of it, so they could stand from an objective distance and watch a hill form under the house and lift it five feet. It was the most powerful movement yet, and too much for the ground to take. In a wide circle around the house, the dirt cracked and broke open, crumbling like a burnt pie crust. Mini geysers of soil burst into the air, and stones burst out of the ground, forced to the surface from below. Then it all fell again. Gravity took hold and the wide circle of earth plunged back into place. The house rocked for a moment like its foundations had broken off completely, and the big tower shuddered as the house settled into place. The sounds of timber and brick rearranging went on for several seconds after the movement had stopped.

It was too much for the little yellow figure of the guard at the front door to take. He stumbled away from the house, and even from this distance, Guy could hear him whimpering as he fled into the darkness, probably never to return.

Guy had seen these lurches happen several times already, but never as huge as that one. He watched Luther for a reaction. The rearranging of Luther's facial geography was nearly as astonishing as the rearranging happening to the ground. His face had finally formed into something that resembled an emotional response. He looked astounded. Stunned. His understanding of the world had just been altered forever, and his face reflected that. An actual facial expression on Luther was unfamiliar and disconcerting, like seeing Michelangelo's David suddenly crack a smile.

Guy's mind circled a decision that he didn't want to make. Something unfathomably powerful was coming up beneath the house. He didn't know what it would do when it got here. But unfathomably powerful subterranean gods probably didn't just come up for coffee. And he had the power to stop it.

He sighed, and silently whispered to himself, "Whammo."

"I'm sorry?" Luther said. He still hadn't taken his eyes off where he'd just witnessed the earth moving.

Guy slapped the side of the crane. And he couldn't believe he was saying it, but he said, "Bring it up. We're doing this."

Chapter 32

T he basement floor trembled constantly now. Mae could feel it transmitting up through her feet to her knees, and could hear the steady rumble from below as though an endless train was passing under her.

She pushed the big oak door open, fearing that it would squeak. But if it did, she couldn't hear it over the chanting and the shouts. The chant was deafening now, a violent assault of voices that filled the basement, as dense as liquid. It was almost unbearable.

And now she could see the source. The cultists were 20 feet away, ahead and to her left, all of them packed in a tight circle around the edge of the hole. They were little more than shadows under the stabbing light from the bare bulb overhead. And most of them were entirely consumed with their chanting. Some of them kneeled as if in reverence, others stood and waved their arms in the air, while still others had their heads bowed and seemed to be in a trance, lulled to semi-consciousness by the hypnotic noise.

But despite the commitment his followers were showing to the ceremony, Ansnorveldt did not seem happy. He pointed insistent-ly at a squat, balding man on the other side of the hole. "Glen!

Now is your moment! One leap and you will become immortal!"
He waved his finger down at the hole.

But Glen shook his head like a child who didn't want to take his
medicine and took a step back from the edge. "I'm... not worthy?"
he tried. It was unconvincing. He went straight back into chanting
with renewed enthusiasm, hoping that would make up for his
failure.

Relief washed over Mae. They hadn't made the sacrifice yet.
Now that the chips were down, Ansnorveldt was having trouble
finding anyone to make the leap. Certainly not Glen, who was
trying to hide behind a few of the others, who were at the same
time trying to hide behind him.

Ansnorveldt scowled at him, annoyed. "You've wanted this your
whole life, Glen!"

"I just joined on Thursday!" Glen protested.

"Your whole life since Thursday, Glen! Are you really going to
let all that be for nothing?"

The basement shuddered. Parts of the ceiling structure cracked
and rained wood splinters over the cultists and into the hole. And
it produced screams of terror from some members of the cult. The
ones closest to the hole backed away for fear of one of the tremors
toppling them in.

That was the opposite of what Ansnorveldt wanted. He turned
his fury on a tall 20-something woman who had a disappointed
look like she'd thought very wrongly that this event would include
cake. "Patricia!" Ansnorveldt raged. "He ascends! We're running
out of time! Just close your eyes and..." He made a diving motion
over the hole with his hand.

Patricia shook her head and clung to the wall, and tried the same
chanting-louder thing that Glen had attempted to confirm how
good of a cultist she was.

Ansnorveldt made an exasperated noise and threw up his hands.
"Useless! This never happened to Jim Jones! If I was him, the
punch bowl would still be full and I'd be the only one dead!"

"You do it!" somebody yelled from the corner. Mae didn't see who it was.

And neither did Ansnorveldt, which was fortunate for whoever had yelled because the cult leader's eyes flashed with anger. "It's not a sacrifice if I do it! It would be selfish to keep all that glory for myself! A sacrifice has to be self*less*! That's why I am selflessly sacrificing one of *you*!"

Mae was starting to think she'd come here for nothing. There wouldn't be a sacrifice at all and, without a sacrifice, that thing coming up the hole would have to go back down, probably disappointed in the commitment level of modern acolytes. She stayed where she was at the passageway door and hoped that Guy was close to finishing his part of the plan.

The earth jolted yet again.

This time it produced a new crack that traveled all the way across the basement floor, almost exactly bisecting the hole. A large chunk of the foundation wall broke off and fell, the concrete shattering on the floor like a collapsing ice shelf. The wooden beams overhead groaned in protest and two of them snapped into ragged, splintered ends like breaking bones.

Mae thought the house might be coming down on top of them. And the cultists must have thought it too, because the chant broke for the first time. Half the cultists forgot that they were supposed to be chanting and backed away, looking for a way out.

It inflamed Ansnorveldt even more. "Don't stop!" he raged at them. "Back to the edge where he can hear you!"

A few of them tried to shuffle forward again, and to resume their chanting. But it didn't have the same zealotry as before. Most of them were distracted with fear that the house might fall on them at any moment. Ansnorveldt had seemingly not warned them things might get supernatural.

So when the earth did its most violent shift yet, it threw them into a panic.

All thoughts of worshipful sacrifice were abandoned, and the chant turned to frantic screams that were both louder than the chant and more musical. A few of the cultists sprang to their feet and fled for the stairs, shrieking and babbling. And the others quickly decided that those were the smart ones and raced after them as a mob.

Ansnorveldt hurled himself into their path, blocking the bottom of the stairs. "Stop!" he bellowed. He'd gone from benevolent vessel of bliss all the way to frothing-at-the-mouth lunatic. And Mae started to worry that he might do something drastic, even psychopathic.

As the cultists demanded that Ansnorveldt get out of the way, she crept forward, ready to intervene but not knowing how.

Some of the cultists tried to shove past Ansnorveldt onto the stairs, but he blocked them and even shoved one of them back with some force. "Nobody leaves until this is done!" he roared. "I've sealed the door! Somebody jump down that hole or we're all staying here until the house falls on us!"

Cries of fear burst from some of the cultists.

Mae saw an opportunity. Guy had told her to clear the basement, so that's what she'd do.

She made her move.

She charged into the light next to the hole. Nobody noticed her until she shouted, "There's another way out!" And she waved her arms back at the passageway she'd just come up.

The cultists nearest to her spun and looked at her. But they seemed uncertain. She could read all the questions on their panicked faces. Who was this shrieking woman? Was she helping? Should they throw her into the hole?

Two more overhead beams split at once with a thunderous *crack* and half the basement floor heaved to the right while the other half heaved to the left, creating a fault line that bisected the hole. Some of the cultists lost their balance and toppled while sawdust and insulation showered from above and filled the air with noxious debris.

It no longer mattered to the cultists who this shrieking woman was. They liked what she was shrieking.

They swarmed toward her and she jumped aside and ushered them through the big door with waves of her arm. "Straight down!" she yelled above the constant rumbling and din of panic. "Get out and get clear of the house!"

She lost track of Ansnorveldt in all the chaos, but assumed that he wanted very badly to murder her. She hoped that, instead, he had given up on his ceremony and fled up the stairs.

One of the older cultists stumbled at the door and Mae crouched to help her up by the arm. Back on her feet, the woman didn't have time for gratitude. She barreled down the stairs after the others and would no doubt fall again before she got to the bottom.

"Be careful!" Mae called after her. Then she spun back to the basement to see if she'd gotten everyone out.

And Ansnorveldt was there.

He stood a foot away from the edge of the hole. His hair was powdered with sawdust and ragged bits of particle board, and he must have stumbled against something because there was a bleeding gash on his forehead. His face quivered with rage.

And he held Ruby in front of him.

He clutched her hard by both arms and held her firmly at the edge of the hole. She looked down into it with an expression of mortal terror. She didn't dare struggle because Ansnorveldt's grip was the only thing keeping her from falling.

"Please don't. Who will bring pastries to the meetings?" she protested in a trembling voice. It was weak, but it was something.

"Ansnorveldt!" Mae screamed, and sprinted across the basement. And again, she didn't know what she'd do when she got there.

It didn't matter. Because she was too late.

"I hope you know what a sacrifice this is for me!" Ansnorveldt said into Ruby's ear.

And then he pushed her into the hole.

Chapter 33

L uther fastened a lattice of vinyl netting to the massive iron hook dangling from the crane, and Guy struggled to get the netting around its target. The stuff wasn't designed to encompass something so big, and after a few attempts it started to feel like installing a fitted sheet onto a much-too-large and lumpy mattress. And ugly. This mattress was also ugly.

The bane of his existence, the rock that wouldn't leave, Big Ugly Rock was going to save the big ugly world. If everything went as planned.

Which it almost certainly wouldn't.

Guy tried again, yanking the netting down on one side of the rock, then running around the rock and yanking that side down as well. As soon as one side of the net slid down, the other side sprang up. Every time. This wasn't going to work.

"We need a bigger one of these nets!"

"That's the biggest one I have. It's a shark net," Luther said, his normal flat tone sounding much calmer than any situation involving shark nets demanded.

Guy hauled down on one side of the net with all his weight and felt the netting on the opposite side of the boulder break free again. He cursed under his breath. "Why do you have a shark net?!"

"As I've told you numerous times, I have many interests about which you know nothing."

The ground lurched, and Guy lost his grip on the net and fell on his back. The crane's arm bounced above him, violently shaken by the movement beneath the ground.

And as Guy struggled back to his feet, he caught some other movement out of the corner of his eye. Something yellow was coming at him from behind the house. And something else yellow. And then several other yellow somethings.

Cultists. A dozen or more, coming around the house at him.

They'd been spotted.

He shouted a warning "Luther!"

But by then it was too late. The yellow smocks swarmed up to him—

—and right past him.

They didn't seem to care that he was there, or that the crane was there. They ignored him, except for one who paused to yell at him, "You gotta get out of here!" And they all piled into their vehicles, started their engines, and skidded away down the drive.

So, Guy thought, things in the basement aren't going well for Ansnorveldt. He wondered if Mae was okay down there, and considered running down to the carriage house and going to find her. But he reminded himself that she had her job to do and he had his. He needed to focus.

He jumped up, tore the net off the rock, spun it in his hands like dough until it was less of a net and more of a very thick, twisted rope, and threw it around the boulder at the equator. With some fast manhandling, he was able to tie it off in a way that might—*might*—provide enough grip.

"That's it!" He stepped back to check how it looked. It looked not good at all, and he knew it. "Once we get it up there, how do we drop it?"

"You're sure that you definitely want to do that?"

"That's the plan."

"Because when we drop this thing, the house is done. You understand that."

Guy closed his eyes. All these months of renovation. All the tens of thousands spent. He was about to literally drop a big rock through the middle of it.

"I understand that," he said. "Just tell me how we do it."

"The hook releases by remote. It's an efficient system. Watch." Luther clambered into the operator's cab in one gravity-defying leap like a round lemur in a Yankees cap. Guy couldn't see what he was doing, but after a moment's pause he poked his head out of the cab. "See?"

Guy hadn't seen anything because nothing had happened. The hook remained hooked. "It's still hooked, Luther."

"That's impossible," Luther said. He ducked back into the cab for a second, then poked out again. "Now?"

As before, nothing had happened. The hook hadn't moved. Guy shook his head.

"That's interesting," Luther said. "It worked yesterday."

Guy fought back panic, frustration, and anger all at once. "So how do we release it?"

"There's a manual release at the top of the hook. But that's for removing the load when it's on the ground. You'd need to be *on* the crane to release it."

"Fine," Guy said. Even he was surprised by how little he hesitated.

He tore off his jacket. He was going for a ride.

Chapter 34

Mae stood in place, paralyzed by incoherent terror. Ruby hadn't even screamed. Ansnorveldt had just nudged her forward, and she'd silently disappeared into the black.

Now Ansnorveldt seemed as eager to get out of the basement as all the other cultists. He'd finally done his sacrifice and wanted his ancient god to ascend, but he apparently also wanted to watch it from outside where nothing could fall on him. He dashed away from the hole and up the basement stairs. Mae wasn't even sure he'd known she was there.

She stumbled to the edge of the hole in desperate fear. She was horrified for Ruby. She was mortified that the hole had received its final sacrifice. She was terrified to look into the hole and see what was coming up. But she had to look.

She fell to her knees at the edge. She could feel the familiar temperature drop and the push of cold air from the deep. The floor quaked beneath her. The ceiling crumbled above. The house was coming apart at the seams, shaken to pieces by whatever was coming up the hole.

She didn't want to see it. But she had to. She had to see how close it was, and how much time they still had to seal the hole. If Guy could get that rock down here, maybe this could still be stopped. Maybe.

She crawled forward until her fingers bent over the lip of the hole. And she looked straight down.

Only darkness. The cold air from below rushed at her with a ferocity it had never had before, forced upward by something rising. But it smelled different. The damp, earthy smell was mixed with other things. Ash and rot. Compost and burnt flesh. The foul morning breath of something massive awakening after millennia of sleep.

Without a doubt, something was coming up. But it was still too deep and too dark to see. Maybe, if Guy's plan was working, there was still time.

Mae drew back from the hole. And she was about to get to her feet when she heard something mixed in with the rush of putrid air.

A gasp.

It was a human sound, not in her mind. An actual noise from a person. And it came from the hole.

Mae didn't want to put her face into the foul wind again, but she choked back her disgust, clicked on her phone's flashlight, aimed it into the hole, and crouched at the edge.

At first she saw nothing. Just the same hole she'd expected. But as her eyes adjusted, she could dimly see that the light from her phone was glinting off something partway down the hole. Something straight and metallic. She swept the light side to side and watched how it gleamed, and finally managed to discern the shape.

It was Luther's ladder, lodged across the width of the hole about 30 feet down like a chicken bone stuck in the throat of the Earth.

And Ruby was dangling from it.

She had been spectacularly lucky. Landing on the ladder from such a height could have easily broken her spine, her neck, or any other part of her. But she'd somehow managed to strike it at an oblique angle and roll off of it, so it had slowed her fall and allowed her to get a grip with both hands before the rest of her rolled off. Now she was hanging by both hands, her feet kicking over the vast empty space.

Only the space was not empty. Not anymore. It remained pitch dark far beneath Ruby's dangling feet, but Mae now thought the dark itself was moving, rising up the hole. An eruption of shadow.

Ruby was alive. The sacrifice hadn't happened yet. But something was coming up to take it.

"Ruby! Hold on!" Mae yelled down to her. Pointlessly, because Ruby was already doing that.

"No, it's fine!" Ruby called back, her voice frail and distant. "I'll just let go!"

"No!" Mae barked back at her. "Don't do that!" Had Ruby lost her mind?

"This is a great honor!" Ruby said. "I'm the chosen one. I never thought I was, but I guess I was wrong, because here I am!"

Yes, she had lost her mind. "Just hold on!" Mae commanded. "I'll get you out of there!"

She checked her phone. It was 8:36. She had no idea what the status of Guy's plan was, but if it was working, then he'd be dropping the rock in nine minutes.

She didn't want to go down the hole at the best of times. And now was not the best of times. All she really had to do was wait for the rock. It would seal the hole and end this. It would be unfortunate for Ruby, of course, but Mae could leave right now.

But then again... whammo.

"Hang on, Ruby! I'm coming down!" she said.

But she was thinking: how am I doing that? Because there wasn't any obvious way. Ruby was 30 feet down at least. If she only had a rope—

But she did. Guy had roped off where he planned to dig his basement trenches. He'd had miles of the stuff down here. And

Guy never put anything away, so all that rope was probably still in the basement. If this was the one time he'd been organized and cleaned up after his work, she thought she might kill him.

Mae searched the corners of the basement and found the ropes in a tangled heap beneath the stairs, a few metal tent pegs still looped into them. Mae snatched up the entire bundle and attempted to unravel it as she dashed back to the hole. The mess of rope resisted mightily but she brute-forced it until one long end started to dangle free.

"Ruby!" she called into the hole. "I'm throwing you a rope!"

"It's okay!" Ruby's faint voice drifted up from below. "I should just let go!"

"No! Don't do that! Why would you do that?"

"I was chosen! It is my sacred duty! I will be rewarded!"

"Do not do that, Ruby! I'm throwing you a rope!"

Mae had untangled six feet, and the length was increasing more easily now. She pulled in a rhythm, watching the end of the rope slip down further and further.

Fifteen feet.

Twenty.

Finally the end touched one of the ladder rungs and Mae tried to swing it further out to where Ruby's hands clung. "Can you grab that?"

"I don't think so! But it's okay! I don't want it! Soon I'll be fused with the great universal Earth! My reward awaits me in the Collective Heart!"

Not only did she seem to have an inexhaustible supply of cult babble, but she also wasn't going to make this easy.

Mae would have to go down the hole and get her.

Chapter 35

Guy stood on Big Ugly Rock, one foot on the top hem of the netting and the other barely perched by its toes in a cleft on the side of the boulder. He clutched the metal hook above him with both hands and tried to convince himself that he wasn't dangling 20 feet off the ground. Which he was.

The crane made a grinding hydraulic screech as its fully extended arm hoisted him higher and he thought he could hear the clanking of chains deep inside its metal frame. He knew it could hold many times this much weight but he still feared that it would snap and drop him.

The dangling boulder rocked beneath the hook and he had to shift his weight to stay balanced. His left foot slipped free and he almost lost his grip on the hook, but he shuffled his toes back into place just seconds before his right foot came loose. He focused on keeping most of his weight on the hook because it was clear his feet weren't going to carry him for long.

He risked opening an eye, caught a glimpse of the dark ground swinging around far beneath him, and quickly evaded vertigo by shifting his gaze toward the house. It was some distance away and it was hard to tell from this far off, but he thought he had passed the height of the second-floor windows and would soon be high enough to swing over the roof. Where, he reminded himself, he would be forced to destroy the house.

The clanking and grinding of the crane mechanism stopped, and the rock jolted and swung. Luther pivoted the crane back a few feet, trying to catch the load and stop the rock from swinging. Guy clung tighter to the hook and closed his eyes again. He hoped being lifted up was the hard part and actually swinging over to the roof would be easy. But none of this felt easy.

A different noise rattled up from below—the motors that controlled the crane's rotation, he guessed, and the whole crane pivoted toward the house. The boulder swung beneath him like a heavy bag being pummeled by a boxer, and the hook supporting its weight screeched horribly in its housing, threatening to break.

He felt a sudden drop and his stomach surged into his chest cavity. For a few seconds, he felt distinctly like he was descending. He opened his eyes.

Something was very wrong. Luther hadn't had time to set up the crane's outriggers to keep it stable, so all the weight was on its wheels. And now its front wheels had lifted off the ground and were rising slowly as the rock, and Guy, sank lower. Guy could do nothing to stop it. He tried to shift his hands up above the hook and hold onto the structure of the crane instead, hoping that maybe it would stop the swinging that was making him sickeningly dizzy.

The crane's motor shifted into high gear and the rotation shifted direction. He was swinging away from the house again.

What was Luther doing?

Luther's voice, flat-toned even when he was yelling, blasted up from below. Guy could barely hear it above the roar of the motor. "The boom angle is wrong for this load radius! Not enough counterweight! We need to adjust!"

Guy shook his head furiously. It was the only movement he dared make. "No time! Just swing it!"

"I guarantee it will tip!"

Guy tried to picture the whole process in his head. He knew nothing about cranes and very little about physics, but he knew he didn't want to wait while Luther put on a pair of nerd glasses and worked this out with a protractor. He was already losing his grip on the hook, and he feared what might be happening to Mae in the basement. There wasn't time for caution. They'd just have to swing and hope for the best.

"Swing it!" he bellowed.

He couldn't see the look on Luther's face. But he didn't need to because Luther always had the same look on his face. For sure, though, right now he would be making disapproving noises through his beard.

Luther gunned all the motors. They roared, the whole bulk of the crane pivoted toward the house, and the rock, along with Guy riding on it, swung fast toward the roof. Metal somewhere in the crane's construction made a protesting groan and the motors at work *clanked* raggedly like chainsaws cutting through steel fence posts. The crane pivoted past its axis and swung Guy out over the peak of the house. Guy opened an eye and for a moment had a thrill of excitement that this was working, and he was over the roof where he should be.

But then the weight of the rock took over.

The crane had swung it so fast that the rock's tremendous momentum hauled the crane arm well beyond where it was supposed to stop. The entire truck tilted on its side, two wheels lifting off the ground by a foot, then two. As Guy and the rock sank toward the roof, Guy was dimly aware of Luther in the operator's cab leaning far out the door, trying to counterbalance the tilt like a sailor hiking out the side of a catamaran.

Even with Luther's considerable mass, it wouldn't be enough. The crane was going to topple, and the rock would hit the roof well off-center. It would almost certainly be lodged in the roof, and the truck would irretrievably roll. This whole endeavor was about to fail.

Guy felt his hands slipping off the hook. He hoped maybe he'd fall ahead of the rock, and then it would land on him and put him out of his misery.

And then the ground heaved.

Once more it was like a massive balloon inflating beneath the surface with the house riding it several feet up. Guy could see the few trees still standing near the house lose their roots and topple. And he could see more bricks breaking free of the house, and hear windows cracking from the strain. But there was one blessing in the horror.

The bulge in the earth formed right under the crane. And tilted it away from the house.

The truck's wheels *thumped* back to the ground. The crane leveled out and swiveled the rock back over the peak of the house.

By the time the house fell back to its usual height, the rock was dangling over the peak. Right where it should be.

Guy thought he heard a sound that he'd never heard Luther man make before. It was a whoop of glee.

The rock was in place. This was it. Guy was about to destroy his house, his life, and his future all at once. On purpose.

He got ready to unhook the load, and drop the rock.

Chapter 36

Mae had just lowered herself over the edge of the hole when the ground jolted again.

From above her, she could hear the house breaking. Beams cracked, seams between floorboards popped, and somewhere a mirror or pane of glass fell and shattered. Dust and wood chips showered over her.

By some miracle she didn't completely let go of the rope, and by another miracle the beam it was tied to at the basement wall didn't break. But she slid a few feet down and the rope burned her hands before she managed to stop herself again. Both of her palms seared with pain. But she tried to ignore it and looked down.

She wished she hadn't. The ladder was still there, lodged as solidly as a beam, its grip unbroken by the movement of the earth. And Ruby somehow still clung to it. All of that was good.

But the hole, which had always appeared bottomless, somehow appeared even more so now that she was in it. She was keenly aware of the infinite depth beneath her, and had trouble focusing on anything else. If her grip failed her even slightly, she'd be done. And she'd have a long time to think about it on the way down.

And even worse than that, the darkness in the depths seemed closer than before. It was still far down, but coming up fast. She could hear it now, dislodging dirt and stone, forcing countless tons of earthen matter and frozen air up ahead of it.

Mae closed her eyes against the frigid gale from below, dug her feet in hard against the smooth side of the hole, and slid down the rope inches at a time, trying to ignore that it was tearing the flesh off her palms.

"You don't have to do this," Ruby called up from below her. "I'm really, completely fine with letting go!"

Mae thought if that was true, she'd have done it already. So there was obviously some small chunk of rational brain left in Ruby. Mae ignored her protests and looked down again, trying not to look past Ruby at the shadow thundering up the hole. "Grab my hand!" she said. And she planted her feet against the wall, swiveled her body sideways, and tried to reach down to where Ruby clung. But she'd badly misjudged the distance. She needed to get another two feet down at least.

The ground shook, and Mae tightened her grip on the rope as dislodged pebbles tumbled around her. The ladder beneath her rattled and bounced. And the powerful jolt was too much even for the hole itself to take. The wall in front of her cracked, and she watched in horror as the crack spread downward like a creeping snake that slithered right past where the ladder's feet were jammed against the wall.

The ladder moved. As part of the smooth wall of the hole fell away, suddenly the ladder wasn't wedged in so tightly. One of its feet slid a few inches down, and the whole ladder pivoted a few degrees around the other foot. Ruby held her grip. But with the new tilt of the ladder, she was a good six inches lower than before.

Instinctively, she looked down. And so did Mae.

The mass, still impossible to identify in the darkness, was a few hundred feet below them at most. And it was rising faster than before. Mae could feel a steady vibration that conducted down the rope into her hands, and through the wall of the hole into her feet.

"I'm coming down! Just hold on!"

Mae tried to do what spies did in the movies when they rappelled down the sides of skyscrapers to steal secret documents. She loosened her grip and slid down the rope. But it didn't work the way it always seemed to for Tom Cruise. She quickly lost control of her slide, and the slide became a plummet. She gripped hard and the rope tore deeper into her raw hands. It stung so much that she couldn't hold on anymore.

She fell.

She hit the ladder at the same end where Ruby was clinging. She landed with her knees on the rungs and it sent a jolt of pain surging up her back even before her shoulders struck. When the rest of her hit, it hammered the breath completely out of her and she gasped for air.

Her weight jammed the end of the ladder down a whole foot. But, miraculously, the jolt also wedged some of its feet deeper into the wall and kept it solidly in place. But one foot was looser than the others. And the ladder, initially level across the hole like a bridge, twisted crookedly and spilled Mae off.

She'd only just landed and suddenly she was falling again.

But despite the agony in her arms and the ragged burning in her hands, she wrapped her fingers around the nearest rung and held hard. Her body rolled off, her already strained arms jolted, and she wound up hanging by both hands next to Ruby.

Ruby looked over at her, inexplicably angry. "Don't let go!" she protested. "I was chosen, so I go first!"

Mae was in so much pain that she could barely comprehend words. All she could do was cling to the frozen aluminum. "Nobody's... going.... first," she choked out.

"This is it! I merge with the great Collective Heart!" Ruby said. And she let go.

Chapter 37

Every muscle from Guy's fingertips to his shoulders screamed obscenities so foul that he wondered where they'd learned them. He'd been hanging from the crane for too long and the rock wasn't providing any purchase for his feet. He was in agony.

"What time is it?!" he screamed down to Luther.

Luther didn't hear him over the noise of the crane. "Hold on!"

The crane swiveled in fits and starts, adjusting the rock six inches forward, three inches back, another two inches forward.

Guy had no idea where the hole was in relation to the roof. But Luther had an innate 3D map of the house burned into his brain, and he insisted that he could hit the spot precisely.

But Guy's fingers didn't understand that. They wanted to sleep. "Luther!" Guy screamed. He didn't mean to scream, but the agony in his arms forced him to.

The crane adjusted another inch and then stopped. The rock swayed and Guy almost lost his grip. "That's it!" Luther yelled back. "Right there!"

"Are you sure?!"

Guy strained his neck to look down the crane arm. Luther was on the ground with his thumb in the air, eyeballing some kind of measurement.

"I'm sure!" he said, nodding. "That's it! Straight onto the hole!"

The rock was still swaying from Luther's final adjustments. Guy had to wait for it to stop. It had to fall straight. *Everything* depended on it falling straight.

"Drop!" Luther called up from the operator's cab.

"What time is it?" Guy yelled back. He didn't know if his fingers or his shoulders would wait. He forced his fingertips further around the crane arm. Forced his feet deeper into the clefts on the rock.

More than anything, he hoped that Mae was away from the hole. Out of the basement. Out of the house.

But what if she wasn't?

"It's 8:44!" Luther yelled up again.

The rock had stopped swinging. Guy could see the peak of the roof beneath him. He could visualize the path the rock would take. Luther's aim seemed right. But it had to be *exactly* right.

And what if Mae was still down there?

"Guy?" Luther called up. Anxiety turned his voice into a bellow.

It was now, or it was never.

Guy forced his screaming muscles to swing his legs off the rock and hook them over the crane arm, taking the weight off his hands. Then he peeled his right hand off the crane and gripped the release latch on the hook. His fingers, all the strength drained out of them, quivered on the latch.

He silently apologized to Mae in case she was still in the basement.

And he pulled the latch.

Chapter 38

With a *snap-twang*, the hook broke free of the crane, and the rock fell.

Relieved of its weight, the crane arm slingshotted three feet into the air, and Guy was nearly catapulted off of it. His legs shook free and he was once again hanging only by his fingers and trying not to slide down the crane arm.

He heard the *crash* beneath him, and almost didn't look because he didn't want to see all his months of work being crushed beneath Big Ugly Rock. But his need to make sure the plan had worked won out, and he looked.

The rock hit the roof dead center. The roof offered little resistance, the huge boulder plunging cleanly through it in a shattering of shingles and a snapping of beams.

But it didn't just punch a hole through. Guy had never finished digging the trenches in the basement. The roof had no support from the sleeper walls. It could not withstand the impact. So the roof came down. Nearly all of it.

But not just the roof.

As the rock heaved trusses down into the house, the bell-cast conical tower lost most of its support and toppled, its pointed roof collapsing sideways and shattering in the yard, narrowly missing the crane's cab and Luther inside it. Guy could almost see the entirely neutral expression on Luther's face as he was very nearly crushed to death.

Guy tried not to think about the destruction. He focused only on Big Ugly Rock as it plunged into the third-floor hallway and instantly shattered much of the laminate, punching through it like paper and hurling an explosion of shattered floor tiles into the air.

But then the rock stopped. It smashed through most of the way, but enough of the floor structure stayed intact to grip outcroppings in the rock and hold it there.

It was stopped dead. And hadn't even made it a third of the way down.

———

Without thinking, Mae let go of the ladder with one hand and lashed it out at Ruby's closest arm. Just as Ruby let go, Mae got her hand around Ruby's wrist and gripped hard.

Ruby's weight jolted her already-burning shoulder, and her fingers slid off the rung so she was holding only by the topmost knuckle of her fingers. She couldn't stay that way for long.

Then she heard the rock hit above. It was a hard *thump* and a cacophony of debris far above, followed by another hard *thump* that rippled a quake through the whole house.

She hadn't expected Guy to send the rock that way, but by this point, nothing could surprise her.

The rock was coming. And she couldn't move without letting Ruby go.

But she couldn't let Ruby go. She wouldn't be able to live with herself. Even if Ruby wanted her to, which she really seemed to.

"Let me go!" Ruby wailed in protest. She tried to twist her arm out of Mae's grasp.

But Mae held as hard as she could while every muscle in both her arms stretched to the breaking point.

Guy waited a few seconds, hoping the weight of the rock would eventually defeat the floor and keep it falling. The floor groaned under the weight, but didn't seem about to break. The rock was stuck.

In spite of all his agony, Guy sighed. He knew exactly what he had to do. It was dangerous, it was going to hurt, and, more than anything, it annoyed him.

He let go of the crane.

The plummet happened quicker than he'd expected, and he tried to keep his feet aimed downward and strike the rock with as much force as physics allowed.

The ragged edge of the roof's remains swished past him, and he landed hard on top of Big Ugly Rock. Pain jolted up his spine, his ankles twisted, and his knees buckled beneath him. He toppled sideways off the rock, down a sloping heap of roof debris, and onto an intact part of the floor.

The force from his fall was enough. The rock broke through.

Joists snapped, laminate floor cracked, and the boulder plunged down to the second floor. It took out most of the corridor wall as it passed, and the resistance from that threatened to send the rock into a roll and push it off course. But its sheer mass won out, and it hit the second-floor hallway right where it was supposed to. It punched a ragged hole and immediately destroyed several beams beneath it.

And stopped again.

Guy had lots of pain in lots of places, and he could have screamed about any of those. But he screamed at the rock instead. All it needed to do was obey gravity and fall. Rocks were good at that. Obeying gravity was pretty much all they did. But this one, besides being big and ugly, was refusing to do that.

He struggled to his feet, totally convinced that at least one of his ankles was broken, and limped to the edge of the hole where he could look down at the rock. It sat trapped in broken floor beams, looking like it intended to stay there and have a rest.

And despite how much he knew it was going to hurt, he jumped again.

Mae heard more hard *thumps* overhead, louder and closer. She closed her eyes, expecting to see the rock plunging through the ceiling any second. But the *thumps* stopped, and she started to fear that it wasn't going to make it all the way down. At the moment, she couldn't decide if that would be good or bad.

At the same time, the great *rumble* sounded very close beneath her. She didn't dare look down, but it felt inches away, like she'd be consumed any second. Death from above or death from below—which was worse?

Ruby, though, didn't have the good sense not to look down. She looked down.

And when she looked back at Mae, there was horror in her eyes. "What is that?!" she shrieked.

"I don't know!" Mae said.

"It's scary!" Ruby wailed. "I didn't know it would be scary!" For the first time, she gripped Mae's arm.

"What did you think it would be?!"

"Ansnorveldt said it was pure love! I don't think pure love smells like that!"

Mae's fingers on the ladder slipped far enough that the pinky lost its grip entirely. She was down to three fingers. But at least now Ruby was ready to stop being dead weight and help. "I'll swing you to the rope!" Mae called down. The rope seemed hopelessly out of reach over against the side of the hole, swinging free in the rushing wind from below. But what else could she do?

She squirmed her fingers tighter around the ladder, barely managing to get the pinky back on. And then, despite all that her muscles were telling her was impossible, she shifted her weight and started to swing Ruby, aiming her for the end of the rope.

She was just starting to get a bit of momentum in the swing when somebody appeared at the edge of the hole, peering down at her.

It was Ansnorveldt.

***

Guy landed hard on the rock, and felt more parts of his legs snap and twist. He rolled off and landed on his side in a pile of shattered laminate.

And, again, it worked. The rock started to move. Beams gave out and collapsed. Floorboards clattered from the second story onto the first. And then a great wrenching and snapping of wood as the rock plummeted. The floor beneath Guy almost went with it, and he had to scramble backward to stop from falling through himself.

The rock tore a long gash through the wall of the first-floor hallway, tumbled, and hit the floor again. A long section of the hallway sank under its weight—

—but didn't break. The rock was stopped again.

Guy wasn't even surprised this time. He would have been shocked if any part of this plan had worked as he'd intended.

But this time, it looked more like a delay than a full stop. He could hear the creaking of timbers as the floor sank under the rock's weight, inch by inch. It was still descending, but slowly. Given time, gravity would do the job for him and he wouldn't have to break any more ligaments.

He was about to back off, nurse his injuries, and let gravity do its thing when he heard shouts from below. From right below the rock. In the basement.

———

Mae tried to ignore Ansnorveldt and keep swinging Ruby. With each swing, Ruby's outstretched hand got a little closer to the rope. But she still hadn't managed to grasp it.

Ansnorveldt refused to be ignored. "What's taking so long?!" he demanded. "There's supposed to be a new and glorious dawn happening right now! I want my new and glorious dawn!"

Mae thought about asking him to pull them up, but it seemed clear that he wouldn't do it.

And he didn't appear to have noticed that the beams over his head were sinking toward him, inch by inch, gradually splintering. The rock was coming. There wasn't much time.

Mae put every ounce of her strength into swinging Ruby, and very nearly swung her own grip off the ladder. She wouldn't be able to do another one like that. This swing had to be it—

"Got it!" Ruby exclaimed.

And all her weight lifted off of Mae. Mae had hardly enough strength to lift her now-free arm and grab the ladder with it to give her other hand some relief.

But Ansnorveldt saw what was happening. And he grabbed hold of the rope and tried to shake Ruby off of it. "Let go! There is no new dawn without sacrifice!"

Ruby raged back at him. "You said the One Who Was Here First would protect us in his warm and loving embrace! I'm not hugging that thing! It smells like the Earth's ass!"

One of the beams over Ansnorveldt's head cracked sharply, and the whole ceiling sank another few inches. Mae was about to pass out, but even with her dimmed vision, thought she could see some of the rock poking through.

Ansnorveldt shook the rope harder. "Let go! Before it's too late!"

And then, suddenly, Ansnorveldt was gone.

Mae's vision was too dimmed to see what happened. But one second Ansnorveldt was there, and the next, he wasn't. Dimly over the roar of the wind, she heard sounds of a scuffle. And then clouds flooded over her vision from both sides, and—

"Grab my hand!" Ruby said.

The voice chased the clouds off, and Mae snapped violently awake. Ruby had her feet planted on the side of the hole, one hand gripping the rope and the other stretched out toward Mae.

The sides of the hole cracked and crumbled. No longer smooth and featureless, it was a maze of cracks and sharp, crumbled edges. And huge pieces of it were breaking off as the great mass below them surged higher. She could feel its cold breath on her feet. The roar of it was like the Earth coming apart.

With the last vestiges of her consciousness and strength, she grabbed Ruby's hand.

And then, to her horror, Ansnorveldt reappeared at the top of the hole.

"Hold on!" he yelled down. "I'll pull you up!"

Mae blinked, trying to clear her vision.

No, it wasn't Ansnorveldt. It was Guy.

She let go of the ladder, and Ruby swung her over to the rope. The rough vinyl burned against her hands, but she held on.

And above them, somehow, Guy managed to pull. There was somebody else with him—Luther, she now realized. They were pulling together. And slowly, Mae and Ruby slid up the side of the hole.

It seemed interminable, but also seemed to take no time at all. She didn't have enough conscious thought left to understand time. But finally, she hauled herself over the edge of the hole onto her belly, rolled over immediately, and helped Ruby get clear.

The wood splintered over their heads as dust rained over them. The last of the beams was giving away. The rock was coming through.

Somebody—Guy, Luther, or both—grabbed her and pulled her back.

They rolled to the side together, all the way to the wall, as the basement ceiling groaned and beams split, and for a moment it looked like the rock wouldn't make it all the way through.

Ruby was suddenly shouting. "Ansnorveldt, don't!"

Mae spotted him dragging himself across the basement toward the hole. His nose was bloodied—presumably from Guy knocking him out. And he moved unsteadily, shambling and stumbling like a zombie.

"You made me do this..." he wheezed.

He stumbled at the edge of the hole and fell to his knees.

The laminate tiles and subflooring overhead finally gave out, and most of the ground floor collapsed into the basement with the giant boulder dragging a stormy chaos of wood, plaster, sawdust, and insulation behind it.

Ansnorveldt saw it coming. And at the last second, he dropped to his belly and squirmed over the edge of the hole.

And as the rock came down, he disappeared into the dark.

The rock hit the hole slightly off-center. It crushed into the compacted earth around it and stopped dead while most of the construction of the house poured through the hole and piled on top of it.

But even in the chaos, Mae could see that the rock had missed the hole slightly. Part of the hole was still open, and even the whole house coming down on top of it would not be enough to seal it.

For a moment, she thought about kicking the rock to shift it just those few inches to the side. She knew it would be futile. Her feet wouldn't budge it an inch.

But then the cast-iron tub from the third-floor bathroom toppled in from above and *clanged* on the peak of the rock.

It was enough. The rock shifted.

It tilted all the way over until its massive bulk finally settled into the space with a thunderous *thud*—

—completely sealing the hole.

Barely a second later, something slammed into the rock from below. It made a resonant *thump* as it hit, like a heavy shoulder against a stone door. Whatever it was, it hit hard enough to shift the rock. The whole massive bulk rocked a few degrees to the side, and for a moment, Mae thought it was going to topple and leave the hole once again open to the air.

But the opposite happened. The shift twisted the rock in a way that let it settle deeper into the hole, wedging itself even tighter than before.

When something hit it from below again, the floor shook. But the rock didn't move. It would never move again.

Whatever was in the hole tried once more, and the rock still didn't move at all.

And then, for the first time in hours... silence.

Chapter 39

The good news was, the house wasn't completely destroyed. Four of the eight bedrooms could still be lived in, the kitchen and two of the bathrooms hadn't been damaged at all, and the tower had collapsed safely into the yard so there was no suspense about when it might come down. Structurally, the house was holding up better than Guy would have expected. It just had a gaping hole in it, as if they'd extended the hole in the basement up through all three floors and out what was left of the roof. It would let rain and birds in, but those were preferable to whatever had tried to come up from below. So, in a sense, the damage was a net gain.

That sense was stupid, though. Because in every *real* sense, it was devastating. The house was unsellable, irreparable without a serious outlay of cash, and unlivable.

And yet Guy had woken up in a pretty decent mood. Because it wasn't his house anymore. And the guy whose house it was—who would have had every right to sue him for dropping a rock through his brand-new house—was gone. Guy knew that he shouldn't be so giddy about a man dying from a fall down a bottomless pit and/or being devoured by a subterranean monster god. But Ansnorveldt had been pure evil, had done it to himself, and had displayed a sick affinity for yellow smocks. So it was hard to get too upset about it. Guy didn't know what would happen now from a legal perspective; this was, after all, a fairly uncommon real estate law situation. But he had a good feeling that he might come out on top.

So while Luther did a damage inspection in the first light of the morning, Guy was content to recline on the hood of his truck with his back against the windshield and marvel at how different the house looked now that the sun could reach it. The pool of shadow that the house had floated in was gone. Even with all the catastrophic damage, it was an improvement.

"It looks different, doesn't it?" Mae said from behind him. "I mean, besides being wrecked."

The last time he'd seen her, she'd been asleep in the driver's seat of her car, and Ruby behind her in the back seat. After all they'd been through, he'd expected them to sleep until noon. Both both she and Ruby must have been woken by the sun.

"I was just thinking that," he said. "I could almost live here. I mean, not that I need to anymore." He put his head back on his hands and let out an emphatically contented sigh. "Hey, I was thinking," he said because he had been. At some point through the night, he'd decided that Mae deserved a bigger share than what he had offered her. And also that maybe if he was nicer to her, she wouldn't disappear from his life quite so quickly. But he didn't say that part. "You should take an even $200,000. You earned it."

Her eyes went to the ground and he caught an odd look from Ruby like he was making both of them uncomfortable. And suddenly he was concerned. The sun chose that moment to go behind a small cloud, which only highlighted that something wasn't right.

He sat up and tried to read Ruby's face. It occurred to him that he still had no idea if she was closer to 16 or 70. He didn't know if that was something the cult had done to her or if that was just how she looked. But whatever it was, it also meant that he couldn't figure out what she was thinking.

"Have you checked with your bank?" Ruby asked.

He didn't like that she'd used the word "bank" while she had that look on her face. "Why would I need to check with my bank? About what?"

"You should check with your bank."

He slid off the hood of his truck and tried to maintain his patience. "Okay, let's say I check with my bank. What do you think they'll say?"

Ruby looked at Mae for some kind of approval, and Mae nodded slightly. She was still looking at the ground.

"Probably that the sale never closed," Ruby said. "You never got the money, and the house is still yours."

Guy's stomach felt suddenly like it was filled with all of Luther's concrete that he'd paid for and never used. And yet, he didn't believe her. What she was saying was impossible. "No. No no no. The deal closed on Saturday," he said.

"Did you check it?"

He didn't want to say "no." But that was the answer. He hadn't. He'd been busy getting ready to be besieged by a death cult. He'd just assumed the banks would do their thing like they always, always did.

The concrete in his stomach solidified a little more.

"I'm not a financial expert," Ruby went on. "But Ansnorveldt has... had... a friend at the bank. He's a high-ranking member of the Community—a second-degree Ovate. And he makes sure the Community almost never pays for anything. He has ways of making it look like money has gone places when it's never gone anywhere. Always on weekends when nobody's paying attention, so you don't find out until Monday. And we only needed the house for Saturday night. By Monday you wouldn't care because civilization would be over and you'd be groveling in servitude to the One Who Was Here First. So Ansnorveldt was pretty sure he could get away with faking the deal."

Guy looked at Mae, and she looked back at him like he was an unexploded atomic bomb they'd just dug out of the yard. She seemed ready to run. "Did you know about this?" he asked weakly.

"She told me last night. I didn't want to wake you."

He shifted his gaze back to Ruby. "And this 'friend' at the bank does this a lot?"

"Oh yeah, he did it for years. For all the Community chapters across the country. We've never made a single payment on our New Haven Fellowship Hall. It used to be an Arby's."

"Arby's?" Mae said, faintly surprised. "I thought Burger King."

Ruby scoffed. "We wish."

Guy fidgeted with his phone in his pocket, wondering if there was some way he could look into this and find out for himself. But it was Sunday morning. All he could do was leave a message.

"So..." Guy felt like the concrete had migrated into his lungs, but he managed to get more words out around it. "The $2.5 million?"

"Oh, we never had that," Ruby said. "If we had that, we wouldn't be meeting in an ex-Arby's that we don't pay for, that's for sure."

The concrete in his gut fully solidified, and Guy felt like he couldn't move. He looked back at the house and decided that he'd been wrong before. Even with the shadows gone and the sun on its face, the house was the worst place on Earth and he wanted to see it burn.

Mae seemed to sense that he wanted to be alone with his thoughts, which were all about how to subsist for the rest of his life on cup-a-soup and store-brand cereals. She led Ruby toward the black minivan, which had survived the cataclysm with only a light dusting of rubble.

Guy climbed back onto the hood of his truck, sat in the sun and tried to remember why he'd been so willing to destroy his house with a rock. Last night, somehow, it had really, really seemed like he had a good reason. But at the moment, with *his* conical tower reduced to a pile of debris and the dust still settling from where *his* roof had fallen through three of *his* floors into *his* living room, he couldn't think what the reason had been. It couldn't possibly have made sense, because he'd ruined himself. What could justify that?

And then he watched Mae giving Ruby an encouraging hug and helping her into her van. And all at once, he remembered the reason.

Chapter 40

R uby seemed anxious to leave, so Mae exchanged contact information with her and helped her use the van's snow brush to clear plaster and rock dust off the windshield.

But there was a big question that had been lurking in the back of Mae's mind all night, and she wondered if Ruby might have an answer. So before Ruby started up the minivan, Mae leaned in the window and asked it.

"So... the one in the hole..."

Ruby nodded. "The One Who Was Here First? He who has dibs on the Earth? He who—"

The list seemed like it was going to take a while, so Mae interrupted. "Yeah, him. He needed one more sacrifice in order to come up, right?"

"That's right. One more sacrifice at the time of the Galactic Conjunction Or Something would complete the Great Ascension."

It was disconcerting how Ruby could say such cosmically absurd things as if she was describing how to make lentil soup. But Mae pressed on. "And... before the rock blocked the hole, that sacrifice happened. Ansnorveldt... fell in."

"I suppose that's true. But Ansnorveldt never intended for the sacrifice to be him. He didn't want to be selfish."

Mae tried to keep the skepticism out of her voice. Did Ruby actually believe that line from him? "Right. So... was plugging the hole with a rock enough? Did we stop the Great Ascension? Or could he still be... you know... Great Ascending?"

Ruby hesitated. She frowned and her eyes flicked side to side as she worked out some mental logic. Then she looked over at the house and frowned again. "I think if he was coming up, he would have done it by now. Wouldn't he?"

"Does he have other ways of coming up? Ansnorveldt said something about other people building other temples..."

Ruby again seemed to be struggling to work it out. "This was the Great Passageway. His one, true path to the surface. All the others were stupid and wrong. I don't think he could come up any other way."

It was hard for Mae to be completely convinced. But Ruby had been through enough, and these questions were causing her anxiety. So Mae waved them off. "You're right. We stopped him. Take care of yourself, okay? No more cults."

Ruby looked stricken. "None?"

"You're in another cult?"

Ruby nodded. "Two."

"Do you have a day job?"

"I work reception for a urologist."

"Okay, well, maybe stick to that for a while."

"He's also in a cult. That's how I got the job."

Mae gave up. She could tell this would be a long and winding road. "Take care, Ruby," she said, and backed away from the window, hoping it would serve as encouragement for Ruby to leave.

Ruby took the hint and drove out, navigating carefully around Guy's truck, where Guy still lay on the hood, staring at the sky.

It seemed like it would be best to leave him alone and let him work through his crisis, so Mae didn't go back to him. And anyway, she had something else she wanted to do.

For the rest of the morning, Mae sat by the side of the hole—or rather, by the side of the rock—and listened

She tried to stay quiet and keep her mind clear. But it was difficult with all the sounds of debris settling around her and the occasional sledgehammerings or crowbarrings from Luther above as he surveyed the damage. Inevitably, her mind wandered..

She was impressed with how well the rock fit into the hole. It wasn't perfect by any means—not as though the rock had been specifically cut to exactly the size needed to fill the hole. But it was close enough, and irregular in all the right ways so that a narrow part of it fit down into the hole like a stopper and a wider part of it sank into the edges and created a seal. She was certain that to move the rock now would take a military-scale effort, maybe with dynamite. And if that ever happened, she'd feel bad for the rock. It didn't deserve that after doing this job so well.

The basement was noticeably different now. It might have been because it was now open to the sky three stories above—that was a big change for any room. But there was more to it than just that. The deadness was gone. The heavy feeling was washed away. It felt like the first spring day every year when it was finally warm enough to go out without a jacket. She half-expected flowers to bloom in the clay and bunnies to hop around among them. So maybe Ruby was right. Maybe they had stopped him—or it, or whatever—from coming up..

And yet she felt a creeping uneasiness

Because what if they left the house and then someday, years from now, somebody else took possession? It had happened to this house many times in the past. That's how she and Guy had arrived at it. Somebody else could find it tomorrow, or in a year, or in 30 years. And it could be somebody like Ansnorveldt, or Arthur Desmond Hole, who knew what the hole was and that the final sacrifice had been made. The rock would be an impediment to them, but it didn't have to be a permanent one. Yes, it would probably take dynamite to clear the hole. But people could get dynamite. If they wanted to open the hole badly enough—

In the middle of her thought, cool air brushed against her temple.

She froze.

Gretchen.

Mae held her breath, and let her eyes drift closed.

She was accustomed to the feeling now. She had a kind of sense memory that let her focus on where the presence was, and she could feel it now almost as well as she could see. She felt it draw close behind her and she resisted the urge to turn around and look for it because she knew she wouldn't be able to see it in this light. But it was there.

"Gretchen?" she whispered.

The presence flowed past her back, and she felt the cool electricity of it as it leaned in over her shoulder.

There was a whisper, a sigh of quiet voice that barely moved the air. It resolved itself through a slurred syllable into a word.

"Stay."

Mae opened her eyes. Had there been a word before that one, or hadn't there? Had she heard a hint of a long "o" in there? And maybe a "t"?

"Wait," she said. "Was that 'stay', or 'don't stay'?"

The presence pulled back from her shoulder and faded into the air.

Mae spun around. The basement was empty except for half the remains of the house piled in a heap.

"Gretchen. Should I stay or should I not? Don't do this to me!"

The only response she got was the sound of boots coming down the miraculously intact stairs.

A few seconds later, Guy's face appeared at the bottom. "Are you talking to me?"

Mae shook her head and flopped down beside the rock again.

"Stay" made more sense, didn't it? Stay and keep the hole safe? Stay and make sure no more Ansnorveldts came along? Stay and tend to the hideous rock that had saved the world? It would mean completely rearranging her life, giving up so much. And yet...

Whammo.

Guy sat down in the clay next to her. She saw him wince—one of the many injuries he'd sustained last night had given him a little reminder that it existed.

"I brought you breakfast," he said. He held out a chocolate Swiss roll cake wrapped in clear plastic. "Not caramel, but you know what they say about beggars and choosers and all that."

She didn't want it but she smiled and accepted it anyway.

Her plan didn't need to involve Guy. He'd sacrificed so much already, and been willing to give up everything last night to get the hole closed. She couldn't ask any more of him

"I'll buy your half of the house," she said. Even saying it scared her. She didn't have the cash, and didn't know where she'd get it from. Maybe she'd get a loan, or borrow it from her mother. Something. "I can't give you $1.75 million, but I'll get you back the $70,000 you spent on your half. I know it doesn't make up for all the renovation costs, but it's something. And then you can go. It's not your problem anymore."

He blinked at her uncomprehendingly. "I can go? What about you?"

"I'm staying." She inclined her head toward the big rock. "Somebody has to."

He shook his head. "You can't stay here. Nobody can live in this house. Look at it." He pointed upward. They could see all the way up to where a warbler was perched on the edge of the roof, wondering if it had just found the perfect place to build its forever nest.

"I'll figure it out," she said. But she didn't know if figuring it out was even possible.

More heavy boot footsteps signaled that Luther was coming down. They both watched the bottom of the stairs until he appeared, carrying a clipboard with a thick wad of paper clipped to it.

"Mr. Gillis," he said. "I've completed my initial assessment of the damage and how much it will require to repair."

Guy stood and brushed off his jeans. "Luther, do you know that I once worked out that every word you say costs me an extra $173 in reno costs? How many words are you about to say?"

Luther flipped through the pages on his clipboard until he had lifted all of them in a big stack that was roughly epic-Russian-novel-sized. "For the first time in all the various properties we've renovated, I am forced to recommend..." He let the stack of papers flop onto the clipboard with a heavy *thump*. "Give it up. Walk away. It is not worth it. I would suggest selling the property and letting someone tear the place down, but I strongly believe that nobody would want this property. Even without a heap of debris on it, it's worthless, and the heap only makes it more so. So I strongly recommend cutting your considerable losses and departing. Immediately." He held the clipboard in both hands against his expansive belly and waited for Guy's answer.

Guy responded faster than Mae had expected him to.

"Fix it."

Though his face, as usual, betrayed nothing, Luther's eyes shifted from Guy to Mae and back again. "You understand that the cost—"

"Doesn't matter. At least fix the roof. Keep the rain out. Get a bunch of umbrellas and nail them up there if you have to. Don't even think about building codes. Just make this place good enough that it can be lived in. We'll worry about the rest later."

Luther couldn't keep his eyes from widening just a fraction of a fraction of an inch. "You want to live in it?"

Guy paused and took a deep breath. Then he looked straight at Mae. "The second floor is mine," he said to her.

This was not going anything like Mae had expected. But the way it was going felt good. It went well beyond whammo. "That's fine. I'll keep the third. I like the kitchenette."

Guy thumbed towards the front of the house. "The kitchenette is down in the driveway."

"Yeah," Mae said, "but I assume you're putting it back."

"No promises." Guy slapped the side of the rock with a kind of affection and turned back to Luther. "But the answer is yes, Luther. I guess we're going to live in it."

Book Two

The story continues in "Deeper Downs"

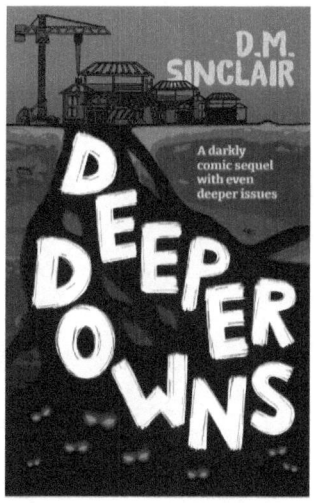

A darkly comic sequel with even deeper issues.
Now available on Kindle and paperback.

Acknowledgments

Even more thanks than last time to my wife, Nancy. I don't know that any of these books would exist without her support, feedback, and influence. And they certainly wouldn't be readable without her editing. This is the only page she didn't edit,, and its not good is

;

About the Author

D.M. Sinclair unintentionally grew up in the rural Ottawa Valley, and unwittingly studied Film and Video Production at York University. He then lived in Toronto and inadvertently began writing for television. He stumbled, bewildered, through writer and even head writer positions on numerous series that aired on Netflix, Nick Jr., Hulu, Network 10 Australia, and Universal Kids. He then wrote his first book "A Hundred Billion Ghosts" by randomly stirring a bowl of Alpha Bits with his finger. And the rest is history. He inexplicably lives in Ottawa again. Visit dmsinclair.com to grab a free short story!

You can connect with him at:

https://dmsinclair.com

https://www.facebook.com/dmsinclairauthor

Also By D.M. Sinclair

A Hundred Billion Ghosts

The ghosts of everyone who ever died suddenly become visible to the living. All hundred billion of them.

A Hundred Billion Ghosts Gone

It's been seven years since all the ghosts came back. In four days, they'll all be gone again. The clock is ticking.

Psychic Simon

Simon Grey is a bad psychic. But if he can solve this murder, he'll be the BEST bad psychic.